Fallen Willow

Also By Roxanne Tully

The Blue River Springs Series
1. *Wild Rose*
2. *Fallen Willow*
3. *Saddle Storm*

The Blades of Heart Series
1. *Becoming Mine*
2. *Hatefully Yours*
3. *Timelessly Ours*

The Hideaway Springs Series
1. *The Runaway*
2. *The Ruined*
3. *The Rogue*

Fallen Willow

ROXANNE TULLY

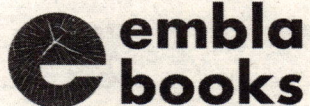

First published in the UK in 2026 by

An imprint of Bonnier Books UK
5th Floor, HYLO, 105 Bunhill Row,
London, EC1Y 8LZ

Copyright © Roxanne Tully, 2026

All rights reserved.
No part of this publication may be reproduced, stored or transmitted in any form or by any means, electronic, mechanical, photocopying or otherwise, without the prior written permission of the publisher.

The right of Roxanne Tully to be identified as Author of this work has been asserted by them in accordance with the Copyright, Designs and Patents Act, 1988.

This is a work of fiction. Names, places, events and incidents are either the products of the author's imagination or used fictitiously. Any resemblance to actual persons, living or dead, or actual events is purely coincidental.

A CIP catalogue record for this book is available from the British Library.

ISBN: 9781471420733

Also available as an ebook and an audiobook

1

Typeset by IDSUK (Data Connection) Ltd
Printed and bound by CPI (UK) LTD, Croydon CR0 4YY

The authorised representative in the EEA is Bonnier Books UK (Ireland) Limited.
Registered office address: Block B, The Crescent Building, Northwood, Santry, Dublin 9, D09 C6X8, Ireland
compliance@bonnierbooks.ie
www.bonnierbooks.co.uk

*To the ones who don't believe in second chances.
Until they're standing right in front of you.*

Playlist

Cowboy Casanova – Carrie Underwood
What I Want – Morgan Wallen, Tate McRae
I Can Do It With a Broken Heart – Taylor Swift
Leave Before You Love Me – Jonas Brothers
Just in Case – Morgan Wallen
Hurricane – Luke Combs
If You Love Her – Forest Blakk
Between The Raindrops – Lifehouse
Sunrise, Sunburn, Sunset – Luke Bryan
Forever After All – Luke Combs

Prologue

Dallas

5th April

I wonder how many other men have stood on a ridge like this—glaring at a patch of soil like it was the devil, but at the same time wanting to be swallowed by it.

No doubt Dad did when Mom was laid to rest. Torn between living and rotting in grief . . . and joining her in the quiet ground.

"Hey." My brother Wilder nudges me gently with his shoulder, snapping me out of my dark thoughts. I'm conscious again—but just barely—still staring at the dirt being smoothed over where Millie's casket rests.

I barely blink. Heck, I'm not even sure I'm breathing. Doesn't seem fair that I *get* to.

But I'll take a damn fucking breath if it means my brother will leave me alone. I inhale and release slowly, keeping my eyes on the roses tossed over the damn dirt.

"I'm good. You go on with the others."

Wilder glances back. "If by 'the others' you mean Dad, Silas, and Ginger, they're behind us."

Maybe if I stand here long enough, focus real hard— I'll wake up.

And my fiancé will still be alive.

"Come on," he presses, voice as tender as he can manage. "We're going to my house. Think it's best you stay with me for a few weeks."

Waking up . . . any minute now.

"Dallas. It's going to start coming down hard soon."

I'd say. Heavy, too. *Everything feels hard, heavy and . . . hollow.*

Thunder rolls in the distance and a moment later, I feel a hand on my shoulder from behind. It's a strong, familiar grip. "Son. It's time," Dad says, his voice rough with a hint of sorrow.

What is their *problem*?

They're not wrong. I've been standing here a while. But how do I walk away? I don't trust myself to move without my knees giving out under me.

"Go," I mutter. "If I'm going to fall, I'd rather there be no one here to see it."

After a beat, I hear one set of footsteps fade. And I've got a good idea which one remained. As if to confirm it, he squeezes my shoulder. Another pang of pain hits my chest. Dad knows how I feel. Probably felt it harder. He had nearly a lifetime with Mom.

"You're not going to fall. And if you are, we'll pick you up. Carry you, if need be. I know what you're feeling, son.

But I'll tell ya from experience, staring at a pile of dirt ain't bringing her back."

I roll my shoulders back, brush him off, and step to where I'd buried the woman I planned to spend my life with.

"Goodbye, Mil." I drop my rose and look up at the darkening clouds. "Rest in peace, my love."

It's a short drive back to the ranch, and I'm still dragging my feet as I follow Wilder into the main house.

"I don't need to stay with you," I lie to my brother. Because I probably should. The house by the river isn't even close to the finish line and there's no way I'm staying at Millie's cottage.

Wilder nods. "I know you don't. I want you to. I'm going to take care of things at the ranch. You take all the time you need."

"The house. I need to finish the house," I say, standing and pacing as if my toolbox is lying around here somewhere.

I should have finished it weeks ago, but the ranch had to come first. Keeping our stock healthy, the cabins full, and the grounds in good shape.

Millie always did joke that she wouldn't live to see the house finished. Seems unfair to focus on getting it done now.

Still—it's what she wanted.

"Not yet. Take a few days, weeks, maybe. You need to mourn."

"What good will that do?" I rasp.

Dad steps out of Wilder's kitchen with a beer. "Plenty. Take my word for it. You need time and you need family. Not work."

I look at my brother. Wilder's my business partner. Without me, he's alone in this. Our brother Silas plays pro hockey and doesn't have a cowboy bone in his body.

"I'll be all right," I mumble. "Busy season coming. People countin' on me." Even as I say it, the idea of doing anything but wondering how my life became a big black hole of emptiness, feels . . . paralyzing.

And that's not me. I'm always present. The one holding the reins. Wilder and I carry equal responsibility for the family brand, Blue River Ranch, but when push comes to shove, I'm the one who makes the hard calls. We both put in the same hours out there—endless hours. But this ranch needs someone who can feel when something's off. And that's always been me.

As if reading my mind, Wilder puts a hand on my shoulder. "Why do you think I want you to move in? Going to need you to talk me down when someone pisses me off out there."

I swallow hard. "Yeah, OK. Maybe just a few days."

Dad nods, letting me believe I had much of a say in the matter. "It's a good choice, son. I know it feels, er . . . *impossible* to breathe right now." He looks me in the eye. "But you will. Time will pass, it will heal, and you will move on."

Fallen Willow

If I had the energy, I'd throw something at him. It's been over ten years since Mom died, and he's still pretending he hasn't "moved on" with Ginger, their longtime friend and ranch manager. It makes sense that they're spending time together. She's been with the ranch practically since day one and there's nothing we want more than to see Dad happy again.

But I'll pass on asking how he thinks I can move on when even he still feels guilty for doing it. Because all I know is I'll never hear her voice again. Or see her bright smile.

I may be of sound enough mind to know Millie's never coming back. But asking me to move on from the person I planned to spend the rest of my life with? Seems like a betrayal to my own heart.

And I'm as loyal as they come.

1

Dallas

Six months later

"You'll be all right for a few days?" I crouch on my knees and wiggle the pink bunny in front of my seven-year-old daughter.

Daughter. *My* daughter.

Two words I've had to get used to saying together in the last few months, after Ellie's grandfather tracked me down at my ranch and told me about a *child* I had with an old fling.

It was the best and worst time for him to give me the news. I was three months into mourning Millie, still heavy in grief.

It's a miracle Cole and Maya Hartly entrusted me with their granddaughter—the only thing left of their daughter, Tammy. They've been taking care of Ellie since her mother passed away three years ago.

It's still hard to believe the sassy, sharp-tongued singer I met just outside of town—way before Millie—would leave me with a little girl who'll be in my heart forever, and yet never know her mother the way I should have.

She nods, her reddish-brown Shirley Temple curls bouncing as she does. "Why are you going again?"

My heart breaks a little. I never want her to feel she's being left behind. It's only for a few days but it's still not ideal when I'm trying to convince this girl I'm not going anywhere.

Like her mother.

Like her grandparents.

Not that they had any choice. Maya's diagnosis has had them traveling back and forth between New York and Florida for treatment. But lately, it's become too much for Maya, so they've made the decision to settle down south for good.

I remove my black cowboy hat, setting it down at my side, running a hand through my dark hair. "Well, kiddo, you know winter is coming soon."

"But it's not even Halloween yet," she whines.

"Yeah, but it'll be here soon enough. And Uncle Wilder and I need to get ready. You know how we feed the cows hay in the winter when the grass is all dead and covered in snow?"

She nods. Ellie's new to ranch life but catches on quickly.

"We have a supplier—someone who usually sells us a big ol' pile of hay. But this year, his field didn't grow enough of it. And we need a whole lot more than he's offering."

"Because you have a lot of horses," she says with a sharp nod, a bit of life sneaking into her small voice. Ellie loves our horses like family. If paternity tests didn't exist, that little fact would have convinced me just fine.

"Exactly. And your Grandpa Connor told us about a guy a few towns over who's got good hay and really good prices, but he won't hold them for long."

"Can I come?"

I give a little grin. "I'll be gone a few days. But Uncle Wilder and I can't leave Rose alone. That woman tends to get into trouble when unsupervised."

Ellie giggles.

"We need someone to keep an eye on her for us." I wink. I have no doubt this little one's going to tell on me but I've got a feeling Rose will get a kick out of it.

Ellie considers it for a moment. "Will you bring something back for me?"

I've known my daughter three months. She plays soccer, likes flowers, and is brave enough to give me a chance at being a dad. She's got exactly one stuffed animal—Buttons—a pink bunny with several loose threads and not a single button.

"How about a new stuffy?"

Her eyes drop for a moment like she remembers something. When she frowns, I'm instantly on alert, like I've said something wrong. Like I'm undermining her worth by offering a stuffed toy for abandoning her for a few days.

She looks up at me with hopeful eyes. "Maybe when you come back, we could go pick up Piggy."

I stare at her, wracking my brain to see if I can remember her mentioning a "Piggy" to me before.

"I left her on my bed to watch over all my things while I'm here."

My lips part. Because it's a reminder that we still don't have all her stuff yet. The custody transfer from the Hartlys to me is still in progress. It shouldn't take this long. Especially when both parties consent. But between the traveling for Maya's treatment and our social worker, Rachel, not wanting to push the matter on Cole, who's been busy fighting to keep his wife alive, it's taking longer.

Too long.

Because I'm not one who deals well with things floating in the air. No set dates. Nothing signed. Nothing but a damn test that says Ellie is mine.

"OK, but I'd hate to come back empty-handed. Is there anything you don't have at your grandparents' house that I can get you?"

Her expression turns mischievous and playful again, easing my tension.

I narrow my eyes at her. "What are you gettin' at, young lady?"

She shrugs innocently. "If you can't find something I'll like, how about a horseback ride?"

"I've taken you on a ride before."

"Where you stand beside me and walk the horse. I want to go faster and far."

My chest clutches. "Let's talk about it when I get back. But I'll still try and bring something back for you," I say, determined to stop somewhere on the way to grab a book or something she might like. "It's a promise."

She smiles with a seal-the-deal kind of nod.

"Now go grab your slippers, think I saw one under my bed and the other under yours." I perk a brow.

Ellie's an odd duck. All her socks somehow manage to match and pair perfectly, but her slippers can be found in the strangest of places, and rarely together.

She shrugs as if to say, *who knows how that even happened*? Then runs off.

I stand with a groan and look around the guest room of my brother's house. It's been six months since I moved in here after Millie's death. Three of those months I spent either locked up in my room, or getting into fights at the local bar.

I was a shell of the man I used to be. The one who put Blue River Ranch before anything else. Sunrise to sundown, and then some. Even long before Dad retired.

Wilder's a good partner, but there were times he'd had one foot out the door. He didn't live and breathe it like Dad and I did.

But he sure proved me wrong this summer when he held the fort on his own.

Technically, he had *some* help—from Rose. His best friend's sister from New York who agreed to lend a hand for the summer while working through personal demons of her own.

Didn't take those two long to fall head over boots for each other.

Another reason I should go and finish that house. Rose moved in with Wilder at the end of the summer. And now that Cole and Maya are staying in Florida until her next treatment, I've got Ellie living with me full-time.

She knows about the new house. I've taken her over there a few times. Mostly showing her the outside. The views, the new barn I built to house my horses. The upstairs wasn't quite ready for a child to walk around safely, but she got a good enough peek at the living space.

Now Ellie slides back into the room Jerry Maguire-style and I laugh, crouching down again to her height. "How 'bout I find you something nice for your new room at the house?"

She frowns and my world stops for a moment. The nagging fear she might be afraid to live alone with me—someone who's still a stranger in many ways—surfaces.

There's no "Rose" in our new house. A friendly, quirky female to be a buffer when I have no idea what I'm doing. To right my wrongs when Ellie's walking around talking all nasally and I don't think to get a tissue and make her blow.

She doesn't answer—in fact, disappointment settles into her features.

"You think you might be OK with that? Living in that big ol' house with me? We can still come have dinner with Aunt Rose and Uncle Wild some nights. Or . . . I can make some grilled cheeses, and it could just be you and me."

She considers it for a moment. "OK, but I don't want to wait that long. So if you get me something, I can just put it in my room here."

I don't know what's the bigger gut punch. My daughter being afraid to live with me in that house—or her losing faith that I'd ever finish it.

I smooth the hair on her head. "It's almost there, I promise."

She nods again, but even for a seven-year-old, there's doubt in her eyes.

I push a stray curl away from her face. "Want me to put this up for you?"

She pulls the scrunchie off her wrist, flings it to me and flips around. "Not too tight."

"OK." I straighten as I gather the loose curls before wrapping the bunch into a knot. "How's that?"

She flicks her eyes upward. "This won't survive monkeys on the bed."

I chuckle and pull her toward me again. "Well, if you get the urge, Rose is right downstairs to fix it for you."

"Thanks, Dallas."

I swallow hard. "You bet, kid."

"There they are," Wesley calls out as Ellie and I make our way down for breakfast.

A longtime friend of Wilder's and the ranch's head chef, Wes is practically part of the family. He's also

Rose's brother. The same one who twisted her arm into helping Wilder out this summer during my absence.

I can't help but wonder how much he regrets that decision now, seeing his best friend and kid sister in a romcom with no off button.

"What you got cookin'?" I ask, noticing Ellie still holding my hand like I'm a flight risk.

I want nothing more than to assure her I'm not going anywhere. Not for long anyway. But I'm pretty certain her mother and grandparents thought they'd never have to leave her either.

I squeeze her hand right back.

"Rose and I made pancakes the *Evans* way," he says, giving Ellie a wink and bumping hips with his sister.

Rose waves her spatula around. "Ellie, want to help me flip? Wes thinks a first-grader could do better than I can."

My girl rushes over and Wes lifts her up, carefully positioning her in front of the stove as Rose hands her a silicone spatula.

I ignore Wilder's watchful gaze and take the seat across from him at the kitchen table.

"She all right?" he asks quietly.

"Course she is." I force a grin. "She's got Rose with her for the next three nights."

My brother flips a worried gaze toward his girlfriend. "Maybe I should stay too."

"I heard that." Rose sets a plate of pancakes at the center of the table. Half the batch are a perfect full-moon shape, the other more like melting-cheese half-moons. And one long one, almost spoon shape.

"That's a giraffe," Ellie says as I lift her onto my lap.

"That's what we're missing here, giraffes." I reach around her for it and break it in half. "Shall we give it the taste test and prove Uncle Wesley's first-grader theory right?"

She nods eagerly and takes her half, shoving it in her mouth. "So good."

"Agreed."

She chews for moment and I see those blue eyes working as she looks out the window. "Are you going to make these for me when we move to the new house?"

Three sets of eyes glance in our direction—or rather, mine—but I ignore them and focus on my girl, leaning in close. "Better than these amateurs."

She giggles. "When you get back, can you take me to see it again?"

I avoid a glare from my brother and tuck a loose curl behind her ear. Ellie knows the house isn't ready—or even livable—but it's been a while since I last took her over there.

And I haven't made a ton of progress. Between wrapping up the summer season, planning for fall harvest, working on the custody transition, and just . . . getting used to being a father, the finishing touches have taken a backseat.

I'd initially promised we'd be moved in by fall. It's now mid-October and not one piece of furniture is unwrapped. No boxes unpacked. Hell, I think there's even a room or two upstairs that still needs flooring. The only room fully finished is mine, since I've spent the night a few times, working on the house when Ellie's with her grandparents.

If Ellie saw it now, she'd lose any faith she has in me.

"Of course we can."

Her eyes light up. "I can't wait." She presses herself into me and I welcome the embrace. It's taken a few weeks, but I've finally stopped tensing when she hugs me.

I love that she's a hugger.

I love feeling her trust in me grow each day.

But there's still doubt in those eyes. Or maybe it's just me. Maybe deep inside I don't trust myself. So it's not fair to expect her to.

Rose lifts her apron over her head with a sigh and tosses it at her brother, breaking my train of thought. "You're right, Wes, I'm just not cut out to make pancakes the Evans way. You might as well finish the rest."

Wes narrows his gaze. "Don't Huck Finn me. We split the mix and you're finishing your half."

"I think the phrase you're looking for is *Tom Sawyered*." Rose reaches for Ellie's hand. "And no, Ellie and I are going apple-picking in Luke's orchard."

"Any left this late in the season?" Wilder asks.

Rose gives Wilder a pointed look and mumbles, "Not much else I know to do with a seven-year-old."

The annoying power couple turn their gaze on me.

I sigh and subtly nod as I turn away.

I know, I know.

She needs a nanny—someone full-time. Someone good with children. Natural, happy, reliable. Someone like Ginger, maybe. Except, Ginger's past the age of retirement so maybe someone younger. But not as young as Rose, who might be chasing other dreams and then abandon my little girl the minute she gets attached. And probably not someone in between either. Someone with her own family. Or worse—someone without and looking to start one here.

That settles it.

No nanny.

If Ellie and I have anything in common, it's that we don't need someone coming and going.

We'll be fine.

I growl low and move to the counter for a cup of coffee, then step out to the back porch like I'm checking the weather.

A minute later, the screen door swings open and my brother steps out.

"Everything's fine," I say, taking a sip and keeping my eyes on the fields.

"I didn't say anything," Wilder insists, taking a seat on the bench behind me.

"Good."

A beat later, he steps beside me, gripping the fence and facing out. "House is done, isn't it?"

I swallow the caffeinated liquid. "Still smells like sawdust. There's a draft coming from somewhere. Haven't found it yet. Need to get the heater unit installed. Furniture's still wrapped in plastic."

He nods but doesn't say anything as I mutter out the laundry list.

"She's not ready," I rasp, finally.

"Ellie's not ready, or you're not ready?"

"I meant the house."

"Ah, that's right. The house is a *she*. Forgot about that."

I think of Millie. The house I started building for us—for *her*. Almost every detail is her, how she wanted it. A bedroom facing the river. A spiral staircase. Crown molding throughout the entire space. And even though there are details that won't be hers, she'd have loved it. Or what it will be when I'm done with it. As picky as she tended to be, I can't imagine her not loving it. Every brick, board, and nail was set with her in mind, her eyes lighting up the way they did with just the idea of it.

It's been a "she" since I started building. Now every time I step into that house, it's Ellie I consider. What she'll see through her eyes. What she'll feel, smell . . . love.

Part of me feels like it's always been meant for her. Every time I ride up to it, I have visions of her playing in the yard, or up in her window.

"You want us out of here?" I pivot.

"That's not what I'm saying. Just wondering what's holding you back. Busy season's over and you've got more than enough help."

"Just needs some finishing touches. I'll take care of it when we get back."

I have to.

"Good." He glances back at the house. "Because that girl knows this isn't her permanent home. It's about time you give her one."

His words hit my chest and I scoff to play it off. "Can I take Rose with me?"

Wilder's shoulders drop. "You can do everything she does."

"Even bathtime? And there's other things. I've heard Rose mutter something about Ellie feeling warmer than usual. How would I know the difference? What if there's something she's afraid to ask for, how will I know?"

Wilder shakes his head. "I don't know. But it's not like Rose has any experience. And between you and me, she loves Ellie . . . but she wasn't exactly planning on stepping into the role of mom whilst you find someone to hire."

I place my hat back over my head. "I'm not hiring anyone."

"Dallas, you can't—"

"I've got this. We're in a good place now—or gettin' there at least."

His jaw locks, like he can't hold back. "That why she calls you by your first name? You talk to her about that yet?"

"I'm not pressuring her to do anything," I snap quietly.

Wilder holds up his hands in defense. "I said *talk* to her, not *tell* her. She probably just needs to know it's OK to."

"Come on, let's hit the road. Sooner we go, sooner we get back." I push off the fence. "You start the car, I'll go say goodbye."

2

Willow

I adjust the elastic band of my ponytail and try not to stare too hard at my reflection in the mirrored wall running along the far side of the open space.

It's my fourth self-defense class in two weeks, and already I feel this quiet confidence that I can take on anything.

Maybe not any*one*—I'm still only five-foot-three—but the few skills I've picked up in my short time here are enough.

One decisive move is all I'll need.

In most cases.

I inhale sharply through my nose and focus on my instructor. Today, Travis is in a red padded suit standing at the front, watching us like he's about to pluck out the weakest link. He smiles too easily for someone whose job is to pretend to attack people and show us all the different ways we could die if we don't act fast enough.

"Remember," he continues, hands behind his back as he snakes around us, "if you can't get away, the only option you have is to survive. Hit first. Hit hard. It's all about impact. Hesitation will be your downfall."

Not in my case.

Falling in love is my downfall—*was* my downfall. *Trust* was my downfall.

And it's a mistake I won't make again. For a third time—it's a mistake I won't make a *third* time. Because Eric wasn't the first man to leave me with regrets.

But mark my words, he's my last.

From this day on, it's me against the world.

I feel my heart rate kick up a notch and my focus cloud. I blink, trying to mentally shake him out of my mind, but it only makes me dizzy.

I glance at the others, needing some kind of assurance I'm not the only one completely off balance here, but the women around me are not only focused, they're watching Travis like they're ready for war.

Panic rises in me as Travis turns his gaze on me.

Get a hold of yourself, woman. You're literally paying the man to do this.

"Red. Up front."

Red? Oh, he's referring to me—the only woman in here with auburn hair. I push back my annoyance and lift my chin as I march to the front.

I'm confident all right. Confident I'm not fooling anyone.

"Let's start simple," he begins, following behind me. "Palm strike. Step in, aim for the nose. You have under a second to disorient your attacker."

No pressure or anything.

Standing beside me, he demonstrates it into the air. Swift and poised. A few women mimic the motion, but I apparently missed my cue.

"Again," he huffs as he demonstrates a second time.

Is that . . . frustration in his tone?

Dammit, focus.

As if to make up for my delay, I mirror him the second time he does it and pound my palm upward as I step forward.

"Nice. Remember, power comes from the hips. Vocalize if you need to. A good grunt goes a long way."

I feel my cheeks flush and try again.

Step, palm, hip, strike. This time, I release a growl from the core of my chest. And even though I can't put my finger on it, there's something satisfying about it. Like the breath you release after finally breaking the seal of a tight-lid pickle jar.

"Now," Travis exclaims, moving in front of me with a sort of thrill like he finally has a real opponent. "Eyes on me, full speed, no hesitation."

My heart pounds, but with a curt nod, I square my stance.

He meets my eyes. "You've got one shot to show him he picked the wrong girl, Red."

He lunges.

My gasp gets stuck in my throat. The word "girl" still lingers in the air by the time I react. With a tightened jaw, my palm slices through the air before I can control the impact. One sharp thrust against the padded helmet and he reels back with a grunt.

Shoot—forgot to vocalize.

Applause breaks out behind me but I barely hear it. My hand stings. My pulse roars. And my fake attacker—looks as stunned as I feel.

I straighten, sucking in a steady breath. *No girl here.*

Travis removes his helmet, giving his head a little shake. "Remind me not to cut you off in traffic," he mutters with a grin.

I release a breath with a small smile. "How 'bout you just get my name right for now. It's Willow." I move back to my place in the third row.

When class is over, I grab my duffle bag and thank Travis before stepping out into the hall.

Leaning against the wall, I breathe. Really breathe like I haven't in days.

I can totally do this. I can take care of myself.

My moment of empowerment dies fast when I check my phone.

Eric.

My ex-boyfriend of nearly two years ruining a perfectly productive Tuesday afternoon. We broke up earlier this year when I realized he was stringing me along like cheap entertainment. Not a woman he'd cherish, love, and respect for the rest of our lives like I stupidly believed.

He's not even here and I tense everywhere. Holding my breath, I open his message.

> **Eric:** *You live like a pig.*

What? No.

I read the rest.

> **Eric:** *Found the ring by the way. Grabbed a few other items too. Gifts from your admirers?*

I must still be on an adrenaline rush, because I hit the dial button. He answers on the first ring.

"You *did not* break into my apartment. I told you I'd send back the ring."

"Hey, who's this pink pearl necklace from?" he asks casually.

"Put it down and get out."

"Probably not even real," he mutters and in the background I hear the tinkle of something being dropped, followed by what sounds like his slimy fingers lacing through my jewelry box.

I know it's with me—it's always with me—but I slip my hand into the side pocket of my duffle bag and scrabble frantically for it.

My grandmother's ring. The dark green, emerald-cut stone sitting over a gold diamond band. I sigh with relief.

Glancing down the hall, I whisper into the phone sharply. "Take that worthless piece of junk and don't touch anything that doesn't belong to you."

Eric would have had to propose for that diamond ring to mean anything to me. But he didn't. The ring was only meant to control me. To make me believe he was mine—when in reality, it was a marker. A way to stake his claim for when I was singing at the local lounges and bars downtown while we were together.

How could I have been so blind? I fell for his charm, his confidence. But underneath the polished law-school grad with big plans for our future . . . was someone who hated when I laughed too loud, dressed too revealing, or spent time with anyone who wasn't him.

He scoffs. "Didn't hear you say that when that guy at the bar had his hands on you."

I growl. "Eric, I swear—"

"Where are you? Come home, let's talk this out."

"We don't have *a home*. I'm finishing out the lease like we agreed. Now get out before I call my good friend Larry from down the hall—you know, the ex-MMA fighter? He'll haul your scrawny ass out of there before you can blink twice."

He waits a beat. That same tight silence that tells me he's waiting for me to stop rambling the way I do so he can be serious for a moment. "Something's come up. I need my security deposit back for this place. You, uhh . . . you're gonna need to move out."

"What? How much was the security?" I don't know why I ask. I know I can't give it to him just to hold off moving out until the end of the year.

"Double the rent."

I release a breath. "Fine. I've got a place lined up anyway," I lie. My plans to move in with Rose completely fell through when she decided to stay in Colorado—for school . . . and for the hot cowboy who wouldn't back down until she gave him another chance.

Heck, I don't blame her. She doesn't have to live by my self-imposed rule to never date again. She still believes in happily ever afters.

I've fallen in love enough times to know that's just not how the world works.

"I can help you pack," he says with a hopeful tone. Like I'd ever willingly let that man near me again.

"Don't make me get a restraining order against you, Eric. Get out of my apartment."

"Restraining order? Come on, Willow, it's not that serious."

I clench my teeth. Resisting the urge to confront him for manhandling me—and not in any fun, kinky way—at my job last month, when a friendly, albeit tipsy bar patron was giving me a tip.

Eric never got physical before, but once was enough to drive me to sign up for these classes. In a few years, I'll be able to support myself financially. And, thanks to Travis, I can now defend myself in any physical situation too.

"I was drunk."

"I don't care. I just want you out, Eric. Now."

He sighs and there's a quiet beat before he says, "You can stay until the end of the week."

"Four days? You need to give the building more notice than that," I argue. He's the lawyer. He should know.

"Did that a few weeks ago. That's what I came by the bar to tell you that night."

"So instead of telling me I need to move out, you decided to restrain and threaten me instead?" I seethe. If it were possible, I despise him even more.

His tone softens. "It was a misunderstanding. You know I don't like seeing you with other men."

"I could have been fucking him over that piano, and it wouldn't have been your concern, Eric," I hiss, feeling my blood pressure rising.

"I'll give you a day to cool off, but you're going to need help packing. I'll stop by tomorrow."

"Take the damn ring and go," I grit out before hanging up. My throat clogs as I suck in a deep breath, exhale and repeat.

When my eyes stop burning, I make another call.

She doesn't answer on the first ring. She never does.

When I'm about to give up, her voice comes on the line. "Hey, sweetie. Lovely hearing from you," she says with surprise in her tone.

"Hey, Mom. How's your tour?" My mother isn't a singer like me. She's a writer. A writer of historical romances, the kind with all the fancy ball gowns on the cover. She's almost always either on tour or at a writers' retreat, leaving her apartment in Manhattan empty for most of the year.

Which brings me to the reason for my call.

She sighs. "It's tiring, but it's the job. Lucas sent me comments on my first draft for *Lady in White* yesterday. I swear the man is deliberately trying to make me miss my deadline." I tune out for the rest, waiting for her to pause so I can ask the dreaded but desperate favor. When she goes on, I wonder if it's a sign that maybe I *shouldn't* ask. Maybe this is my chance to reconsider and find an alternative. Because it's going to come with a price.

She takes a breath. "So, to what do I owe the pleasure? Do you need money?"

As usual, the woman doesn't hold back.

"No. Well, not exactly. My apartment is being renovated—for a month. They want to start soon. Like tomorrow soon. Can I stay at your place for a bit?"

If Eric thinks I'm going to stay at the apartment and wait for him to show up, he's got another thing coming.

"Oh."

That's it. That's all she says. She's going to make me drag it out of her.

"Is it a bad time? Are . . . *you* renovating too?" I ask slowly.

"Well, no. Not exactly. I am heading back, but I'm having a photoshoot for my new book this weekend at the apartment. You know it's got that wonderful view of lower Manhattan and . . . well, I can't have extra . . . *things* around."

"OK, Mom. I get it." I sigh but don't end the call just yet.

"You know the Lennox Hotel is one of my favorites. Perhaps you can—"

"You know I can't afford that, Mom."

"Well, you would, if you took my advice for a change," she mutters.

"I'm not getting married just so I could afford a stay at the Lennox, Mom."

The woman is also the trustee of the inheritance my grandmother left me. Locked up until I'm twenty-eight—or married. It's not a fortune, but it would be enough to buy a modest home in the suburbs, a decent car, and high-end coffee for a year.

"There's nothing that says you have to *stay* married. Heaven knows, with or without that stupid clause, you'd be separated within a year."

Ouch.

"What's that supposed to mean?"

"All I'm saying is, with the chaos you call a love life, I'm not holding my breath for a happily ever after."

It shouldn't hurt. Because she's not telling me anything I don't already know. In fact, she's simply saying everything I've convinced myself of, so I should be glad she's given up on me.

After all, I have.

"It's only another four years. I'll wait."

"You'll wait. The Lakeview Estates won't," she mutters.

I roll my eyes at my mother's mention of the brand-new development in Long Island I had my heart set on.

One she made me apply to "just for fun" so I could get a taste of it.

It worked because I wanted it too. A big dream home in the suburbs isn't something many city girls aspire to in their mid-twenties. Especially not musicians. We dream of traveling, entertaining, living out our passion from anywhere—even tiny downtown apartments.

But not this musician. I don't want to travel or have a big audience in my future. I want enough high-paying gigs so I can afford my own equipment, a sound room to record an album or two. And since we're dreaming . . . a living room with a grand piano. A big, bright kitchen to brew coffee and burn pancakes because I'm busy humming the tune of my next hit.

The Lakeview Estates was perfect. Quiet town, big yard, amazing lake view surrounded by greenery. When I first heard about the project close to a year ago, Eric and I were still together. Still planning our life together—or at least *I* was.

When our relationship died, my dream of owning a home at the Estates didn't die with it. Access to my inheritance did.

At least for another few years.

Because I refuse to marry just to buy my dream house.

"Just think—" Mom continues. "In a year, you could have a clean divorce and five hundred thousand dollars."

"Goodbye, Mom. Good luck with the tour."

"Wait, where will you stay?"

"I'll figure something out." I decide a healthy dose of guilt and worry might do the woman some good.

"Hang on, hang on." She sighs. "How about you come Sunday night? Pack a few necessities for a few weeks and we'll have a ball."

I shiver. "You . . . don't have another tour?"

"Not until my next release in February."

Living with my mother was never a ball. In fact, it's a nightmare. She keeps her place looking like the cover of a magazine at all times. It's unlivable for someone like me. I'm no slob, but I've been known to leave the occasional milk carton out.

And there's no doubt in my mind that that woman is going to keep on pressing me to get hitched, just so I can cash out.

But I'm out of options. And it will only be a few weeks.

"Sounds great," I breathe with a forced smile. "I'll, uh . . . stay with a friend till then."

Three hours and a hefty suitcase later, I stop by the Lock Bar where I play piano four nights a week. Not exactly my dream job, but since Eric got me kicked out of all the fancier places I've played, it's all I have left. Thankfully, his outbursts have been useless here. Billy is immune to all things jealous boyfriends.

"Hey boss," I call over the ice Billy dumps into the sink behind the bar.

He glances at me, quickly scanning my non-work-appropriate attire. Usually, I'm in something low-cut, black, and sexy. Today, I'm in an oversized hoodie and a pair of skin-tight jeans. Then his eyes land on my suitcase.

Billy mutters a curse and sets down the bucket. "What'd you do?"

"What?"

"You skipping town? You in some kind of trouble?" He points a finger. "Is it that slimy ex of yours?"

I smile at him and set my apartment keys on the bar. "I need a favor. The biggest I'll ever ask."

He sighs. "Where's the body?"

I laugh bitterly and tell him about my call with Eric. When he's done cursing like a sailor, I take his hand and set the keys in his palm. "Sell everything in there and send me the cash?"

He tosses them lightly from hand to hand. "Thought he gave you till Friday."

"He'll be back. And I don't want to be there."

He looks around and nods. "Where you going?"

"I owe a friend a visit in Blue River Springs."

> **Willow:** Hey, I promise I haven't been avoiding you. Just been a little hectic here.

> **Rose:** Sorry, who's this?

> **Willow:** You did not delete my number already. It's your best friend.

> **Rose:** You must be confused. My best friend is right here.

I get a picture of Rose with a little girl with shiny auburn curls and bright blue eyes. They're sitting on a porch showing off their matching beaded bracelets.

> **Willow:** Well then, I'll just have to find another friend to visit for a few days. Bye.

My phone rings instantly and I smile as I swipe up.

"Shut up. Are you messing with me? Are you finally going to come visit?"

I laugh. "I'm not messing with you. I've missed you. Packed a bag but no place to go since my bestie replaced me."

"Beat it, squirt," I hear her say to someone who giggles in response. "Assuming this isn't some cruel joke, what's the occasion? Is it my birthday?" she gasps. "Is your mother in town?"

I attempt another lighthearted laugh. "No, no. The bar is closed temporarily for a C-rating so I've got a few days off."

It's not a complete lie. Billy's bar did have to close two weeks ago, but we remedied the issues and it wasn't shut down for too long. And since Rose used to work there with me, she buys it.

"Poor Billy. Well, I'd love to have you. When can you come? Wilder left this morning with his brother for a few days so it's just me and Ellie until Friday."

I breathe a sigh of relief that Rose is wide open for a visitor.

When I get there, I'll tell her the truth.

Probably.

I hate lying but I'm also too proud to help it sometimes.

3

Willow

The trouble with having a best friend who's a therapist—or in school to become one—is you can't hide anything. The moment I arrived with my bags—Rose knew something was up.

My flight landed after nine o'clock in the evening and Ellie was asleep, so Rose's brother, Wesley, picked me up from the airport.

He hung out for just enough time to show off his cooking skills with a three-course dinner, and to brag about how *he* was right and I was wrong about Rose moving to the Mountain West.

Out of the three of us, he did most of the talking, while I tried not to focus on how my best friend was studying me silently until he left.

"Tea?" Rose asks now, stepping out onto the back porch with two steaming mugs.

I'm sitting out here on the swing, under a thick plaid blanket, enjoying the crisp air.

"I've had a long day," I warn her, accepting a warm cup.

"I didn't say anything."

I roll my eyes and take a sip, then continue to stare off to a distant light over by the side of the river.

She follows my gaze. "Oh, that's Dallas's house over there."

I squint at the structure that looks too far away to still be on the ranch. "I thought he and his daughter live here."

"They do. The house isn't finished. On its way though, I think." She hums longingly. "You should see it, Will, it's stunning what he built. Twice the size of this place, spiral staircase, enormous kitchen. And the backyard—big enough for a small farm."

I try and picture it—the image she's painting as I stare at its surroundings, what it must look like in the daylight. "Must be a killer view."

She sips her tea. "It's not downtown Manhattan, that's for sure."

I cock my head at her, catching the wistfulness in her voice. "You like it here?"

"I love it here," she confirms, her tone serene, settled. *Belonging.*

My gaze drifts back to the distant light. "Well, that sounds promising—the house, I mean. Sounds like he wants to give her the world."

I don't know the man aside from a one-time encounter when he stopped by the Lock Bar while in New York visiting Ellie's grandparents. He never took his black cowboy hat off, was a little rough around the edges—like all of them. And was easily the best-looking man I've ever seen. I was also two margaritas in, so I'm hoping I imagined the part where I leaned in and sniffed him.

But this new detail about him—that there's a house he built with his bare hands for a little girl he never knew he had—tugs at heartstrings I didn't know I had left.

My father never took the time to do anything like this for me or my mother. He lived off her money and kept trying to find ways to get into my trust fund. The idea of my deadbeat father building anything other than bad credit is laughable.

"Yeah. If it were initially for her."

"It wasn't?"

Rose shakes her head, a sadness crossing her features. "The plans were designed for Millie."

She says the name like I'm supposed to know who that is. I think back, remembering where I heard it—in one of Rose's chatty catch-ups about all things Blue River Ranch and the Thorne men. "Oh. Right. His . . . fiancée, who . . . died, right?"

She nods, but it's ever so slight, like her mind is somewhere else already. "To be honest, I love having Ellie here. She's such a delight, but I'm in school a lot and Wilder and I never spend any time *alone* together. I feel terrible for saying it because it's so obvious that Dallas needs us, but I didn't exactly sign up to be a part-time babysitter."

I wince. And I'm not sure if it's from the idea of my best friend—who's barely twenty-three—caring for a child she didn't ask for, or for the little girl who undoubtedly deserves more than she's getting. "Is the kid that bad?"

"No, she's amazing. But I have homework, and when I don't, I don't exactly want to make friendship bracelets—at least not all the time. And it's getting boring having to be careful not to get caught in the kitchen with my skirt around my hips, Wilder's tongue down my throat, if she comes down for a snack."

I laugh. "Oh, you poor thing, you. How do you live like this?"

"It's not funny. I'm twenty-three and I feel like I became a mom overnight."

I scrunch my nose. "It does sound like a strange living situation you got here. Should've gotten the apartment with me." At that thought, my smile fades.

And Rose is quick to notice.

She sinks back into the cushions, watching me.

I wait a beat before starting. "Eric came to the apartment this morning."

She sighs. "What did that self-centered jealous asshole want?"

"The ring back. He took it. And then told me I need to vacate the apartment by Friday."

She curses under her breath. "He didn't try anything, did he?"

"I wasn't there. I was . . . in my self-defense class," I blurt out.

"You're taking self-defense? Did someone get handsy at the bar with you?"

"Sort of." I pause. "It was Eric."

"What?"

"Few weeks ago, I was playing at the bar and a guy was getting a little too close after I finished my set—drunk, obviously. Eric comes in out of nowhere, knocks the guy off his feet, and Billy sends us both into his office to work it out."

"Why would Billy do that?"

"He didn't want me stepping outside with him. Didn't trust him."

"Hmm . . . don't blame him. You've been broken up for almost six months, this is downright stalking. So what'd you do?"

"Threatened him with a restraining order once and for all. Told him I could take care of myself and he needs to stop showing up where I work like he's got a claim on me."

Rose waits for more.

Sighing, I tell her the rest. "He threw me up against the door and said, 'Show me how you can take care of yourself.' Tried to prove that I'd be helpless if a situation got . . . physical."

"Oh God, Willow. Did you call the police?"

"Eric isn't . . . harmful. He's just a jackass trying to make a point." I brush off.

"And he got to you," Rose points out—seeing right through me.

She's not wrong. As much as I hate to admit it, he got under my skin, burning into me like a brand. And the only way to get him out—is to prove him dead wrong.

"I don't want him to be right," I admit. "So I've been taking these classes and I'm *really* good. I just need a distraction. And . . . a place to stay a few days? Maybe through Sunday?"

Her eyes light up. "Of course. You're always welcome." She chews her lip. "But the guys are back on Friday and . . . it's a little tight here . . ."

"And it's not your place. I know. It's fine. I have some friends in the city I can stay with." It's a lie and Rose knows it. I cover it with the truth. "Then I'll be moving in with Mom temporarily. Hopefully no more than a few weeks, just until I can secure an apartment."

"Oh Lord." She thinks for a moment, until an idea sparks. "Wait, we have guest cabins." She snaps her fingers. "When Wilder gets back, I'll see if we have a vacant one. It's off-season now so I doubt they're all full, other than the fall harvest guests."

I release a breath with a hopeful groan. "That would be great."

"But I'm so glad you're here. I've missed you. Come on, you look exhausted. Tomorrow we'll catch up some more—like how on earth you think you'll survive living with your mother for a few weeks."

"Desperate times," I mutter.

"I'll get you settled in Dallas's bedroom."

My stomach flips. Not at the mention of Dallas Thorne again who, I won't lie, I've thought about more than a few times after our brief encounter at the bar. But at the idea of *sleeping in his bed* tonight. Will it smell like his black hoodie that's now tucked in my suitcase?

The one Rose gave me one night we were working late at the bar. Dallas lent it to her before she left town and I insisted on keeping it. If only to help her forget Wilder, and anything associated with him, of course.

It had this woodsy scent I thought was just from the town or built into the thread or something. But when I saw the mountain man it belonged to? I became deliriously addicted to the damn thing.

I'd never admit this to Rose, but I didn't wash it for weeks.

I remember skipping away after he tried to reclaim it—and felt his eyes on me the entire time I played piano.

He was—in a word—*smoldering*. The kind of cowboy you pull right out of a movie.

I shake my head. "Maybe I could take another room? The couch maybe?"

"Don't be ridiculous. I've already changed the sheets and there is no other room except where Ellie is sleeping."

"Right." His *daughter*.

Maybe I was wrong, maybe I mistook the smolder for *God, I hope my daughter doesn't grow up to play piano at a local bar and dress like that.*

It's what I imagine my father thinking if he ever bothered to check in on me.

"In that case, Dallas's room it is."

4

Willow

My eyes flutter open at the sound of heavy footsteps and whispers. I stifle a groan.

What time is it?

The light filtering in through the curtains suggests it's morning. *It can't be morning already.*

My head hurts.

My body hurts.

"But I think my slipper is in there," a small voice whisper-whines outside the door.

"I'll get you socks. Don't go in there. Willow is not a pretty morning person. You've been warned."

Oh. The kid. Right.

I twist out of my cocoon. It's been a while since I've been a guest anywhere. Is it polite to sleep in? I don't know, but it can't be polite to wake your guest either.

I huff and twist back under the covers.

"Put these on, then come downstairs. *Quietly*," Rose hisses.

Poor kid.

I'm a slipper girl myself. Can't imagine having restricted access to continuous warm hugs for my feet.

I sit up and look around for it. Sure enough, a single pink fluffy slipper is tucked under the private bathroom door. I must have been too exhausted to notice it last night. Slipping out of bed, I reluctantly tiptoe over and pick it up. Moving to the bedroom door, I stand behind it, twist and pull on the knob slightly, and drop the slipper just outside. It lands with a soft thump.

I hear a small gasp on the other side and quick quiet steps draw closer. "Thank you," she whispers, a smile in her voice.

I close the door without a word and smile back.

Thirty minutes later, I slip on my own blue-green hand-knitted booties and follow the coffee aroma downstairs.

"Morning, sunshine," Rose calls from the kitchen. "Coffee?"

The little girl's silky wild curls are the first thing I see when I step in. They frame her bright blue eyes and tiny knowing smirk, like we share a secret of some kind.

I give her one that matches. "Morning. You must be Ellie."

She nods from her seat at the table and lifts up her foot to show me the slippers. I lift mine right back.

"Why were you in Dallas's room?"

My brows shoot up. *"Dallas?"*

Rose gives me a pointed look as she sets my coffee down.

"Oh right, well. Your—Dallas, was kind enough to let me use it while I'm here."

She frowns. "But I heard him tell Uncle Wilder that he doesn't plan on bringing women to his room."

I laugh. "How old are you?"

"Seven. But I'm a young seven."

"Is there an *old* seven?"

"I turned seven last month."

"Well, happy belated, Ellie. My birthday is *next* month. So you could say I'm an old twenty-four."

She giggles. "Dallas says he's just old."

I laugh from the pit of my stomach. "He sounds funny." I stand and meet Rose at the stove and raise a brow.

"She hasn't started calling him . . . anything else yet," she whispers.

"I got that. Maybe someone should tell her what you call men who gave you life," I mumble.

She shushes me. "And what are you calling *your* 'man who gave you life' these days?"

"Not the point," I grit. I glance back at Ellie. "I'm no *therapist*, but in my opinion, the longer he lets this first-name basis go on, the longer she'll believe he's fine with it."

"He obviously isn't," Rose argues.

"Obvious to who?"

"OK, you need more coffee, lady. And food, sit down."

I huff and take a seat across from Ellie. "So what do you do for fun around here?"

"Rose and I went apple-picking yesterday. And Grandpa Connor takes me on pony rides after school sometimes. On weekends, Wesley takes me to the kitchen and we bake cookies."

I narrow my eyes but don't call out the obvious. Instead, I rest my chin in my hands, elbows propped on the table. "And what do *you* like to do?"

She shrugs. "I like soccer, unicorns and princesses, making bracelets, and I'm on book four of *The Magical Woods*. Oh, and I like to sing."

I sit up. "Now you're talkin' my language. I love to sing. I play piano too."

Ellie's eyes light up. "You do? My grandma plays too." Her smile fades at the thought of her grandmother, who I know from Rose's stories is ill. "She said she'd teach me one day." Her head drops. "I don't think she will."

Uh-oh.

I look for my best friend to step in with all her early-development education and help me out here.

But Rose is pre-occupied like she received terrible news on her phone.

"What is it?"

She blinks, setting her phone on the counter. "Oh, nothing. I, um, hey, Ellie, let's go grab your backpack and put your shoes on. I'll take you to school in the golf cart."

"OK." She jumps up.

I perk a brow. "Is this *the* golf cart?"

"The one and only. Wanna ride with us?"

"Sure." I grimace after another sip of the dreadful coffee. Pushing off my seat I dump the rest of the it in the sink. "You got a Starbucks around here?"

"Wilder's not big on coffee. That French press over there is Dallas's, but between him and me, we finished all the good stuff. We can grab a better brew at The Shack, that's the ranch bar and kitchen."

"Good enough for me. I'll just clean up and catch up with you two outside."

The second they're gone, I pick up Rose's phone. I wouldn't put it past my ex to start harassing my best friend, trying to get to me.

But it's not Eric that's got her upset. It's a text from Wilder.

> **Wilder:** Hey Blue, just checked in with Ginger and we're fully booked on guest cabins until next Friday, then closing for the season.

> **Rose:** Can we keep one open for her?

> **Wilder:** I would, but that would mean keeping staff on. How close is she with Wesley? Close enough to crash on his couch?

> **Rose:** No. Maybe I can get her a room at the Inn.

> **Wilder:** I'm sorry. I'll cover it if you can get her a room there.

My stomach sinks. First my mother agrees to take me in with pity, now I've become a burden to my best friend. Well, that's not going to work. I read on.

> **Wilder:** By the way, Dallas decided to stay through the weekend, but I'll be home Friday.

> **Rose:** Oh. Then she can stay in his room through the weekend.

> **Wilder:** Or you can book her a hotel, drop off Ellie with Ginger and *we* can finally have a night alone.

Rose didn't reply but I saw the conflict in her expression.

Maybe I can sleep in the airport for two nights. If Tom Hanks's character in *The Terminal* can get away with it, I sure can.

I meet them outside. "Hey, good news, my mother's photoshoot got canceled so I'm going to head back Friday."

Rose frowns. "Oh. Are you sure? We can find you something here."

I shake my head as I climb into the golf cart. I'm not a good liar, but I do need to up my game when it comes to Rose so I give her a playful brush-off and a wink. "Don't be silly. Besides, I'm not sure how long I can put up with all this peace and quiet."

Rose laughs. "Give it a few days, you might just fall in love with it all." She pulls on the lever and turns the wheel, pulling us out of the gravel driveway and down the hill, with the rich green land stretching ahead and the mountains just behind us.

Yeah, I wouldn't be surprised if I did.

5

Willow

This morning when my eyes blink open at the bright lights, I know where I am. The last few mornings have left me disoriented, though the days have been nice. Peaceful. I thought the kid might bother me but she's actually all right. I stretch and something moves beside me. I gasp and pull down the covers.

"Slippers!"

Ellie opens her eyes with a giggle. "You sleep funny."

"When did you get in here?" I grumble.

"When I woke up." She bounces.

"And when was that?"

She shrugs. "I don't know. But it's your last day here and I wanted to see if Rose was right."

"About what?"

"That you're not a pretty morning person."

I cock my head. "And?"

She smiles mischievously. "You should sleep a little more."

I reach for a pillow and whack her with it. She falls back laughing.

It's not until now that her words settle in. *Your last day.*

I've been so busy *breathing* these last two days that I forgot I was supposed to think about what I'm going to do. Look for a cheap rental in the city, maybe even get a second job—at least for the next four years. Then I can buy that house in the suburbs. The one they'll build just for me. Marry no one and record an album by thirty.

Rose comes into the room. "There you are. Come on, girl, we've got to get you dressed for school."

"Can't I stay home? It's Willow's last day here."

I scrunch my nose, pouting at Rose to help the kid out. But honestly, I wouldn't mind hanging out with her a few more hours. Not like I'm rushing to anything more appealing back home—apartment or not.

I nudge her with my shoulder and wink. "Your daddy wouldn't like that much. Come on."

She moves her big eyes to me, something sincere yet unreadable hidden there.

I flick a curl away from her face. "Besides, I'm not leaving till later tonight. I'll see you again."

"Actually," Rose corrects, "Ginger and Grandpa are going to pick you up from school today."

"Oh right," Ellie bounces beside me. "Ginger's making sloppy joes and cookies."

I pout—and I'm not sure how much of it is for Ellie's benefit this time. I stretch my arms out. "Looks like this is it, kid. Till next time."

She leans in and boy, does this kid know how to hug.

"I've got to get me one of these in the city," I tell Rose as she jerks the wheel, steering the golf cart off the road and onto the dirt trail.

"Second best thing I got out of this place. The cowboy being the first."

"Only *you* could steal something, vandalize it, and have the original owner gift it back to you."

She glances at me. "Says the woman who's wearing stolen property."

My eyes dip to my favorite hoodie—Dallas's hoodie.

"It's not stolen, you *gave* it to me."

She smirks and shrugs as she picks up speed. It's late afternoon now. Rose doesn't have classes on Fridays, so we've spent most of the day mooching around town, catching up without feeling the rush of city life behind us.

Now, as we race down a quiet and somewhat deserted path that runs along the edge of the ranch, my nose fills with an earthy scent that I kind of love. It almost, *almost* smells like the sweater I'm wearing when Rose first handed it to me months ago.

I jerk when she makes a sharp turn that seems to be away from Wilder's house.

"Slow down. Where are we going anyway?"

Fallen Willow

"I have to show you something before you go."

Frowning, I look ahead, my eyes gently stinging from the wind. The gravel crunches under the tires as we round a row of trees. Then I see it, rising out of the landscape like something out of a western movie.

The house sits just above a steep slope along the river. An empty wraparound porch stretching wide. Floor-to-ceiling windows reflecting the deep rose-gold sunset and faint shimmer from the river.

A silent breath is knocked out of me. *What is this place? Does someone live here?* It's positively . . . well, breathtaking.

I snap myself out of it with a few blinks, sucking air back into my lungs. "Let me guess," I start, trying to sound unimpressed. "Dallas's house?"

She nods and hops out. "Come on. It's empty and unlocked."

I jump out and follow her up the front steps. "Who would leave this place unlocked?"

I step behind her through the double wooden doors. There's no entryway. It opens up into a vast living space with high ceilings and exposed beams. A large fireplace runs along the far-right wall, an impressive staircase separating the living room from what looks like a sleek, modern kitchen. The living room is dark despite the big windows—probably due to the sun setting on the other side of the house. The kitchen, on the other hand, bleeds a warm glow from the overhead skylight. Like honey on glass, it stretches across the white tile floor and countertops.

I'm still spinning at the details of the unfinished beauty. "Needs some TLC, but you're right . . . this place is . . . something else," I whisper, words falling out in a hush as my eyes trail up the stairs, picturing the little girl looking for her slippers in the early morning. "Think Ellie will like it?"

When Rose doesn't respond, I turn to find her leaning against the stair rail, arms crossed, staring at me. "You don't have a flight back today, do you?"

"No," I admit with a sigh, hating that I had to lie to my friend. "I saw your messages with Wilder the other day."

She hooks a hand around the stair post and spins in a slow circle, all charm and glow, like she doesn't have a care in the world. My stomach flips with delight for her. "I figured. That's why I brought you here."

I narrow my eyes at her. "Here? I don't follow."

"Look, you're not staying at the Inn when this place is *completely* empty, and Dallas is gone through Sunday. Why let all this go to waste?"

My eyes dance around the space. "And where do you propose I sleep?"

"Don't worry about it. Dallas spends the night all the time when he's working on the house."

I bite my bottom lip. "And no one will mind?"

She rolls her eyes. "No one will *know*."

I shake my head at her. "You really are a wild one."

She gives me a mischievous grin. "Come on, it's still early. Let's grab some dinner in town and I'll bring you back here later."

6

Dallas

"Thanks," I rasp as Wilder drops me off in front of my house on Friday night. "And thanks for keeping it quiet for now. I don't want Ellie to know I'm here this weekend."

Wilder nods, looking at the house skeptically. "Think you can get a lot of it done this weekend?"

"Sure as hell going to try."

"Well, don't start tonight. It's late."

The drive back did take longer than planned. But we got everything we needed.

"Go on." I hop out of the truck. "Get home to your girl before she falls asleep waitin' up for you."

My brother checks his phone. "Might've missed my window. Hey, think you'll need any help this weekend? With Ellie at Ginger's I was thinking of taking a trip with Rose tomorrow. Just over to Hideaway Springs. Spend a weekend with some friends."

"Told you, I don't need help." I glance back at the house. "Think Ellie's mad I sent her to Ginger's for the weekend?"

Wilder scoffs. "How should I know? She's your kid. But it won't matter when they drop her off here on Sunday afternoon."

I nod as I make a mental list of the finishing touches the house still needs. Furniture to unwrap, curtain rods to put up, grocery store to clean out, rugs—shit, I know there was more . . .

"Sure you're ready?" Wilder snaps me out of my daze.

"I'm sure I don't want her doubting that I am." My hand tightens on the top of the door. "That and . . . I can't deliver the news without giving her this."

My brother releases a breath, nodding slowly. Then lightens the mood with a perked brow. "That's not a yes."

I flash him a cocky grin. "Get out of here before you miss that window."

"Night," he mutters and backs out of my driveway.

I move toward the house, gravel crunching under my boots as I go. The light on the porch flickers and I make a note to replace the bulb before sundown tomorrow.

Something's off when I walk in. Maybe it just feels cooler in here than last week.

Place needs heat. I've already arranged for heating installation on Monday. There's a space heater in the master bedroom that I'll move to Ellie's room for Sunday night.

Still too much to do there as well. Dresser to build. That damn canopy to hang over her bed. Rose found it in a catalog a few weeks ago and I didn't think twice. It looked simple enough to fasten over the bed, the decorative gold crown giving way to a sheer, pale pink veil that will fall around the headboard. According to Rose, it's "the perfect addition to any princess's bedroom."

I look around for anything else that feels off. The tarp has been removed from the grand piano. It was Ellie's grandmother's, but Cole said they hadn't used it in years and it might be a good addition to the house.

But I don't remember uncovering it. Shit. Hope those damn coyotes didn't find their way in.

I continue looking around for any signs of damage, but there's no light in here and I'm too damn tired to dig out a flashlight.

I leave my hat on the piano and head upstairs, following the humming noise from my room. Did I leave that heater running?

Stepping in, I pull my shirt over my head and drop it on the floor. The heat in the room hits me hard. *The hell?* I never have it up this high. I'm about to walk over to lower it when a wild shadow of limbs comes out of nowhere.

"*Ka-ya!*"

I dodge on instinct, but then an elbow clips my shoulder.

"What the—"

A foot misses my groin and hits my thigh, and I grab the flailing arms of the person attacking me in my bedroom.

I squint into the darkness, making out a petite woman with wild red hair, taking swings any which way she can. I grip her arms, and yank her around, pinning her to the wall. "Stop."

She sucks in a breath. "Let go of me or I'll scream. You're trespassing."

"*I'm* trespassing? This is my house."

In the moonlight, I see her eyes widen. "Dallas," she whispers. A soft, almost fucking *angelic* voice comes from the beast that just tried to knock me unconscious.

I let go like she's a disease I can't afford to catch and step back. "What the hell is going on here?"

She holds her hands up in defense. "Sorry, I'm sorry. I—I'm Willow. Rose's friend."

I release a breath, not entirely inclined to tell her I knew exactly who she was the moment she said my name. I'd never forget that voice. Those eyes.

I cross my arms with a glare.

Willow covers her face. "Oh my gosh, I knew this was a bad idea," she mutters, then sucks in a breath and tries again. "I wanted to give Wilder and Rose some time alone tonight and, well—you weren't even supposed to be here." Her eyes trail my bare chest, warm and lingering, landing somewhere along my mid-section.

I'm outraged. I swear I am. But who am I to interrupt a woman who likes what she—*fuck, what am I doing?*

I stretch out my arms. "I'm sorry—should I leave?"

She blinks, eyes snapping to mine. "No. No, of course not. I'll just—" She rushes past me to the bed, bare arms tossing sheets aside like she's looking for something, and that's when I notice the rest of her.

She's in the shortest pair of thin cotton shorts—either white or light blue, I can't tell. A matching short-sleeve shirt. Barefoot, she stands on her tiptoes as she reaches further into the bed for a thin cotton bathrobe and throws her arms through it.

"You'll just what?"

She swings around. "I'll just, um—well, uh . . ."

I tilt my head and walk toward her. "You'll spend the night here. We'll chat in the morning." Reaching around her, I grab the spare pillow and turn to walk out the door.

"I can take another room," she calls after me.

I look at the bed. "This one's already warm. I'll start the fire downstairs and settle down there."

"Dallas."

There she goes again with my name. Saying it like she knows more about me than she should. Maybe I'm mistaking the tenderness for something else. Maybe pity?

I stop and turn back. Can only imagine how much her friend has told her about me. About the grieving, the child I never knew about. The house no one thinks I'll finish before the winter.

"Look, Red—"

"Willow. Don't call me Red."

But I don't want to call her *that* either. The name is too goddamn pretty. I've heard it once or twice from Rose. And then that night at the bar when we met. Felt it roll off my tongue too easily. Like it had always lived there—longing to be said out loud.

Jaw tight, I shift my gaze, mentally stepping back as if I've crossed some invisible line. A creeping weight settles in my chest that can only be described as guilt.

It's a simple enough request—valid, in fact. But who the hell knows what else I'd do for this woman if only she asks in that sweet raspy voice again. That does it. She needs to go. "You're lucky I'm not calling you *an escort* out of my home."

Her expression shifts as she sets her hands on her hips, glaring at me. "It's not like I broke in. The door was practically wide open. And I wouldn't exactly call it your *home*. More like a work in progress."

My eyes blaze and as much as that comeback stings, the stir in my stomach to keep going with this gorgeous spitfire is stronger.

Which means I need to put this to rest. I'm clearly mentally drained for even considering bantering like two adults fighting their attraction.

I scoff. "You know, if I weren't lookin' to help my brother and his girl have some alone time myself, I'd be dropping you off at their door right now. So why don't you just say thank you and goodnight."

She blinks and jerks back. "Fine, thank you. I just get a little annoyed when people call me Red, OK? My self-defense instructor called me that and I whacked that guy in the nose. Sure he told me to, but you get the point."

I bite back a chuckle and point back to the door where she greeted me with her panicked assault. "*That* was self-defense? Our ranch manager Ginger would'a had more luck whacking a guy unconscious with her pocketbook."

That seems to hit a nerve and I don't take pleasure in it. Willow crosses her arms with a huff and tilts her head to the side. "Wasn't expecting anyone. And I'm kind of in the middle of nowhere."

"Well, neither was I. And it's not nowhere. It's my ranch."

"Wilder's house is on the ranch. This . . . is so far out, looks like it never quite made it *off* the ranch."

I swallow because she's right. The ranch is my home. Always came first. Till Millie became number one. But there were days she felt like she was competing.

This is where she wanted it, I almost say.

"Yeah, well then, why stay here? Alone?"

She shrugs. "How often does a city girl get to stay in a place like this?"

Her tone is almost wistful and it makes me wonder. I lean against the door frame. "Ghostly?"

"Stunning," she says without hesitation. "A bit larger than I imagine is necessary, but doesn't make what you built here any less remarkable."

I frown. "You like it?"

She breathes out a chuckle. "*Like it* is . . . an understatement."

I stare blankly at her, trying to figure out what it is about her admiration for the house that hits me differently. I shake my head and grip the door handle.

"Goodnight . . . Willow."

She blinks uncomfortably. "Goodnight."

An hour later, I'm staring into the fire. Its flames blurring as my thoughts sink deeper into the redheaded wonder upstairs.

The one that took me days to get out of my head after I left New York. Who I could still hear singing at that piano, wearing my sweatshirt like she wanted to live in it.

My chest squeezes again with a new ache. Betrayal. I pinch the bridge of my nose. I need sleep. Maybe then I could stop thinking with the wrong organ. Millie has my heart—that's not changing. Not six months after losing her. Not ever.

Ellie is the only exception. She needs to be all that exists. In my mind. In my heart. In this home I've built.

If I'm going to be up all night thinking about *anything*, it's going be how I plan to finish this house in two days. Enough to make it livable anyway.

There's a little piece of me that wonders whether I imagined it all. That what just happened upstairs was the result of pure exhaustion.

But I wasn't brave enough to go back up there to confirm it.

Instead, I built the small fire, laid out some blankets on the dusty wooden floor, tossed the pillow over it, and sat down. Replaying—and condemning—every *real* moment from upstairs.

She likes the house.

The woman takes self-defense classes for whatever reason. Which means she's thinking ahead . . . or something happened. Yet she still wanted to spend the night here—alone, ready to take on whatever might come.

She's either certifiably insane. Or brave as hell.

One thing's for damn sure.

First thing in the morning, this woman needs to go.

I slip out the front door just past dawn. The chill of the early morning shouldn't be as biting since I spent the night on a cold floor.

Hopping in my truck, I head down to the stables to check on Trouble. She's my feisty, stubborn horse. Her dark coal color reflects her temperament. But I like her. When we ride, there's nothing like it. She's proud, fast, and dependable.

And I'm pretty sure she feels the same.

"Hey, Trouble." I stroke her muzzle. "Want to do some rounds with me?" Grabbing a blanket and bridle, I mount up and take her out across the pasture.

After checking the fences and cattle, I ride up the ridge to Wilder's to have a little chat with my brother's girlfriend.

I loop Trouble's reins over the rail and step in through the back porch, into the kitchen.

Coffee's already brewing but there's no sign of Rose.

With a low grunt, I wash my hands and make myself a mug.

"Hey," a harsh whisper from my brother. "You're *supposed* to be in Scottsville through the weekend, which is what I told Rose, like you asked me to," he reminds me.

I hadn't wanted to risk Ellie finding out I'm back and leaving her with Ginger through the weekend while I finish the house.

I hold up a hand, but he doesn't stop.

"She sees you down here this early, we both have some explaining to do."

"She's just the person I need to see, so why don't you call her down here for me."

Wilder frowns then rolls his eyes. "Dear Lord, what'd she do now?"

I cross my arms just as Rose enters the kitchen, her eyes gleaming in that way they did on her first day at the ranch. The way I knew she was just what my brother needed. "Dallas, you're back. Did you drive all night?"

I grin. "Nope. Got in last night. With Wilder actually."

My brother pins me with a hard glare.

Rose looks confused. "But where did you—" Her eyes widen.

"My house. You know the one, by the river."

She glances at Wilder. Then over my shoulder like she's expecting to find someone. "Uh—are you alone?"

"Course I am."

She fidgets playfully. "Did you find, um . . . were there any . . . critters in the house?"

With one brow up, the corner of my mouth twitches. "Oh, just one. Pretty big one, actually. Feisty little creature, found it on my bed of all places."

Wilder jerks. "Holy shit. Did ya toss it back outside?"

I tear my eyes off Rose lazily to look at my brother. "Oh, I thought about it."

"But you didn't, right?" Rose stammers.

Wilder folds his arms, suspicion etched across his face as he leans back against the wall, watching us.

"No," I say flatly.

Rose releases a breath, then looks at Wilder with a tentative smile.

He pushes off the wall and rolls his eyes with a sigh. "Feel free to drop Willow off here later." Then he addresses Rose. "I'll go reschedule our weekend getaway."

7

Willow

I stuff the sheets into the washer and start the cycle, grateful the house is equipped with working machines. Washing his sheets won't clear my conscience for last night—it's just common courtesy. The comforter, on the other hand . . . No way I'm stuffing that California king into the washer after just one night. Not like I used it much, practically kicked it off in the middle of the night with that space heater cranked up so high.

And I . . . may have kicked off my panties in the process. But I will *not* be judged. Broody Dallas I met at the bar months ago was sexy enough. But shirtless Dallas? All rough-edged with a thread of tenderness? That was damn near criminal. How else is a girl to shake visions of broad chests and abs for days out of her system?

Hence the extra splash of fabric softener this morning.

I step back into the master bedroom for my things, squinting against the sunlight cutting through the uncovered windows. Dust catches in the rays as I pad across the cool floorboards looking for those damned panties.

I thought stripping the bed would help, but they're still missing.

I fling pillows aside again, frustrated. It couldn't have been a sock or scrunchie I lost. It *had* to be underwear.

Giving up for now, I grab the rest of my things and make my way down before Mountain Man returns and finds me snooping. Last thing I need is for him to "help me look" for them.

With any luck, a coyote will sneak in and sneak off with them. And that'll be the most action my panties have seen in over a year.

I inhale deep to clear my mind and find that peace I felt when I settled in last night. The place still faintly smells of fresh lumber and something muskier, earthier.

My gaze drifts over the wall as I make my way down the stairs. The wooden beams, the rustic wagon-wheel chandelier, the subtle, intentional way the still-wrapped furniture has been placed.

My heart breaks for him in a new way.

And a little bit for her. She'll never get to see what he's done here.

I reach the bottom step with a creak and nearly jump out of my skin with the sudden sound.

"*Jesus.*"

Shaking it off, I hurry to the kitchen, taking in the view of the riverbend and mountains through the open windows, remembering it with the sunset last night.

I place my oversized tote on the counter and begin searching for my charger in the black hole of a bag. A dead battery played a key part in my inability to call or text Rose last night. You know, just to let her know that if I'm arrested for trespassing, I'm taking her down with me as my accomplice.

I growl in frustration, giving up on my charger—well now, that's two things I've lost. But that also depends on where you start. This morning—two. Four days ago—my apartment, my mother's respect, assuming I once had it, and basically most of my belongings, since I have no doubt Billy will have sold them all by now.

Uh-oh. I check the time on the clock above the stove. Nine fifteen. Yep, it's after nine and I'm spinning out of control.

I need coffee.

My predator eyes start scanning the dusty white countertops looking for a clue that there's caffeine in this place.

It's not looking good. Not even a kettle.

My eyes lift to the cabinets—a beautiful navy blue with gold hardware—hanging above the white-tiled splashback. Three brass-finish pendants hang low over the island.

It's the perfect kitchen. In the perfect house. Built by an imperfect man who's either endlessly grieving with his hands or scared to finish something because of the new chapter it'll bring.

One with a new girl in his life.

I look around sadly. Give us a day and Rose and I could definitely do some damage here. All it needs is a woman's touch.

And maybe a working heater. I shiver from the chill as I move around the kitchen, pulling on a few under-counter cabinets to check for supplies.

I find a few clean rags under the sink and a spray bottle that smells citrusy. "Might as well make myself useful."

I aim at the dusty counters and shoot like a kid with a water gun. Hitting every target in sight. Then set it down and get to work, bringing out its natural shine.

I coat the island next and do the same, until a knock on the door makes me jump. My head snaps to the sliding doors.

Dallas is standing outside, eyes peering out toward the fields. He's holding a purple coffee mug and a paper bag.

Confused, I move toward the door and pull it open. "You knock?"

"Last time I didn't, I was attacked."

I inhale the morning air and scent of leather drifting off him and roll my eyes. "Hardly."

He steps in with a frown. "What's that smell?"

I close the door and sweep my gaze over him. "Was about to ask you the same thing."

"Still making a habit of sniffing people?"

I'm usually quick with my comebacks. But the fact that he remembers that little detail makes my brain go hazy.

"Here—" he starts, setting the mug and bag on the counter, then scowling at the remaining mist along the marble. "Rose warned me not to engage until you've had this. Then I'm taking you back over there."

"See you follow directions well," I mutter before lifting the mug and taking a sip of coffee.

He spreads his hands defensively. "What, it was the first thing I said."

"*No.* You knocked on your own door just so you can comment on being attacked last night, grunted about the *Refreshing Grapefruit* all-purpose cleaner I found under *your* sink, called me out on sniffing you—which I did *one* time. Then made me sound like some sort of addict who needs a fix."

He stares at me for a moment, and it feels a little too long. "Drink your coffee, darlin', I got work to do."

I release a breath and take another sip.

There's a small ache in my chest. Can't blame the man for wanting me out. Heck, I don't even blame my ex for wanting me out.

I'm no one to them.

I set the mug down, pulling at the greasy paper bag. "What's in here?"

"Pumpkin bread. Ginger made it."

I stick my nose in and inhale the fresh-baked goodness. "Hmm. Rose told me about Ginger."

I take a bite, chewing slowly, which only seems to irritate him more as he sighs heavily, looking around the place like he just wants to get to work.

"All right," I say, washing it down with the warm liquid. "I know when I'm not welcome. Let's go 'saddle your truck' or 'hit the hay' or 'wrrrangle the road'?"

A laugh breaks out of him. A genuine one that lights up his eyes as he looks at me like I'm crazy. "What the hell were those?"

"Oh, come on, one of 'em had to be right."

"Not even close. 'Hit the hay' means go to bed, wiseass."

"Least I got the 'go' part right," I mutter.

He folds his arms and cocks his head to the side. "You done?"

"Do you have a charger I can borrow?"

"For heaven's sake."

"What? My phone is dead. Since you're clearly on some warpath to work on the house—and want no one around—I was going to call Rose to pick me up." I lift my bag off the floor and onto my shoulder. "But if you're higher on getting me out of there, then let's—"

Dallas plucks the straps off my shoulder and tosses the bag back down. "What exactly did Rose tell you about me?"

"Nothing," I snap in defense of my friend. Then sigh. "Enough to know you built this for someone you lost."

He steps back, running his hand down his face. "Yeah well, pretty much everyone knows that." His jaw ticks.

I narrow my eyes at him. Surprised at how well I'm reading him. He's impatient. There's an urgency here. And I don't think it's just me. It's why he's here instead of with his daughter after being away for three days. Rose said he only spends the night when he's working on the house.

"You need to finish it," I guess.

His eyes snap to me. "Only thing I need right now is for you to stop talkin'."

I hold his gaze for a moment, wishing I knew how to back down, but I don't want to. "Why don't I help you?"

He scowls, glancing at the counters briefly. "And how on earth do you plan to do that? Talkin' a mile a minute sure as hell ain't movin' things along for me."

I fold my arms. "I mean over this weekend. I can help you. You don't have to do it all alone."

He stills and for a second it seems like I've cut through that thick layer he keeps around his heart. But then something flickers in his gaze. Raw and heated. Studying me like I'm the one under the microscope.

"Look, I get you either got no place to go, or you're runnin' from something." His voice turns ragged. "But I'm not your guy."

I swallow the stab against my chest. I'm not hurt by his comment—just offended. I don't need him as "my guy." I don't need this place as my temporary sanctuary. I was only trying to help.

Dumbstruck, my mouth drops before I speak. "I'm not running from anything," I breathe, wishing it didn't sound like I've been caught.

"No?" He cocks his head with a step forward. I take one back. "Why the hell you taking self-defense classes then?"

My pulse jumps but it's not because he intimidates me. It's the heat radiating off him. It sizzles. Before I realize, I've moved back enough to hit the back wall that separates the kitchen from the walk-in pantry. "So I could clobber assholes like you for getting in my face."

He huffs a laugh. "Well, you ain't gonna do it by clippin' them in the shoulder and thigh."

My eyes drop to his crotch. "I won't miss next time." I lift my knee but his hand snaps around it, catching me mid-kick.

I lean back against the wall, shoulders falling with a breath. Surprised at how easily I'm surrendering to him. As if realizing I don't find him threatening, his arms come up on either side of me, caging me in. "What'd he do?" he rasps, sharp and demanding, like he has a desperate need to know.

My breath hitches and my pulse spikes. His body is so solid. Radiating strength. The kind that promises protection.

Warmth spreads below my belly. And if anything is scaring me right now—it's my reaction to him. I shouldn't be curious. I shouldn't *want* to be pressed up against this wall as long as he's the one holding me. This is my cue to run.

But why does it feel like a test of everything I've convinced myself I never want again?

He leans in, exhaling just enough to make me shiver. His question still lingering between us.

"What'd who do?" I ask.

"Don't play dumb," he warns. "Tell me what he did and I'll *show* you how to protect yourself."

I blink, because my instincts were right.

And they're never right when it comes to the opposite sex.

I swallow. My body buzzing with something electric. A fire I can't seem to put out. But also something I don't want ruined with memories of my ex.

My jaw hardens because something tells me this is the way to do it. "He held me up against the wall just like this and told me I couldn't defend myself."

As suspected, he steps back, giving me space. "What'd this class teach you?"

I glance down, take a breath, and demonstrate. "Step in, palm out, hit up."

He grabs my wrist mid-thrust, then the other, and tosses them both over my head, holding tight. "Now what? And the right answer isn't 'scream *fire*.'"

I suppress a swallow. "Why not?"

"That only works in a public place. Where'd he attack you?"

"He didn't attack—"

"Where, Willow?"

"In an office," I shout in one breath. "My boss's office—when he came to the bar and saw a customer getting friendly after my set."

There's a beat before he continues—like he can picture it. "Headbutt right to the nose."

I meet his eyes. He can't be serious.

"No one's going to expect you to cause yourself pain. Might hurt like a bitch, but the second you do, you've bought yourself time to get away. Or as I've seen some cowgirls do at the local bar, dig your claws into his groin—then headbutt him. And now you've hurt more than just his pride."

My eyes stretch wide. "You teach a local class or something?"

He steps back with a heavy sigh. "Just stay out of trouble, and if you can't—remember: groin, nose." He picks my bag up off the floor. "Come on, let's 'saddle my truck.'" He chuckles to himself.

I don't move. "Do I have to claw you in the groin to let me stay and help?"

He throws his head back with a growl. "Willow, enough. I don't know if you've noticed, but this place needs more than all-purpose cleaner to get it ready for Ellie by tomorrow. I need to get moving, now, so grab your shit and let's go."

"Why tomorrow?" I demand.

"Because her grandmother died two days ago. I need to give her *something*."

I blink, trying to piece what one has to do with the other. "I'm sorry."

He shakes his head. "I'm sorry. She—she doesn't know. And before I tell her, I need to give her something permanent she can hold on to. Something to believe in the life I want to give her. That I'm ready for it and she should be too." He swallows. "It has to be tomorrow."

8

Dallas

The hell is wrong with me? How do I tell a stranger about Ellie's grandmother before I tell my daughter? Especially a stranger I need to get out of my head—and my house.

It's not like it's going to come as a surprise to Ellie. We knew it was coming, but that didn't make it an easier call to get. Deep in my heart, I'd hoped to spare my girl from the all too familiar pain of losing someone you love.

Maya's been in treatment, but last time I talked to Cole—Ellie's grandfather—they were planning on moving her to a facility. Doctors said they'd be surprised if she made it to Christmas.

I avoid Willow's glassy eyes. Evidence of her compassion. I don't need to know that side of her. "So if you'd please just go grab your stuff—"

Frowning, Willow turns on her heel, but she doesn't head for her bags. She marches to the living room and starts pulling on the cellophane and tarp-covered furniture. Starting with the loveseat.

"What are you doing?" I ask, my tone worn with fatigue and frustration.

"Unwrapping the furniture." She sniffles, and I'm relieved to find myself immune to it—too consumed by my annoyance.

"I can do that," I snap uncommittedly.

She spins. "And the floors? The heat? The lights? What about Ellie's clothes? You want her to live out of boxes? They need to be hung up and neatly stacked in that fancy dresser up there. You have less than two days. Let me help you." She swallows, eyes flicking around the room and voice dropping. "Like you said, I've got nowhere else to be."

My chest falls and I growl. "Walked into that one."

"It's fine." Her head snaps back to the piano like it keeps calling her. "And I'm sorry, but I can't do anything until I tune this for you." She pulls out the bench from under the piano and settles onto it.

Now you really do need to go.

A vision of Willow sitting at the piano in the bar in New York hits me all too aggressively. A vision that took days to get off my mind. Only for her to singe another one into my brain from my own home?

Over my dead body.

"I can't let you do that."

She runs her finger over the black top, it's a little dusty but she doesn't comment on it. She doesn't even look at me. A flash of excitement and determination is in her eyes as she lifts the fallboard. "I'm not asking."

Pushing up her sleeves, she wiggles her fingers and twists something gold and shiny on her ring finger. It looks a hell of a lot like an engagement ring. When she lets go, I get a better look at it. It's a fancy-sized emerald sitting atop a gold band.

Sure doesn't look like anything from this day and age. The back of my teeth clench as I berate myself for wanting to know. "You didn't tell me you were going to marry the guy."

Her eyes snap to mine. Then to her ring as she adjusts it again. "This was my grandmother's. I recently had my jewelry stolen but I always keep this one with me."

Anger coils in my chest before I can remind myself it's none of my business—and I'm certainly not about to make it my business. So I don't let myself linger on the relief that washes over me that she managed to save this piece—or the fact that it wasn't a ring *he* gave her.

"Why you here?"

She lifts her eyes to the ceiling as if to come up with something. "To watch the sunset. I hear they're incredible out here."

They're out of this world, actually. But I'm not about to give her a reason to stay. Especially when she's bullshitting me.

I push my hands in my pockets. "They're all right. Someone threatenin' you?"

She rolls her eyes. "Are all you cowboys looking for a damsel to save?"

"I don't think I've ever seen a damsel, but I sure as hell know you're not one." If the way she tackled me the other night gives any indication.

"Got that right," she mutters.

Stepping closer, I close the piano shut as she jerks her fingers back.

"I could have—"

"You're too quick for that. Now you want to help me? Fine. Whatever you see fit—dusting, tuning, maybe unpacking Ellie's boxes from her grandparents' old house—go nuts. But on one condition."

Her brows snap together. "I think the words you're looking for are 'thank you.'"

I clench my jaw and dip my head. "Tell me why you're here."

She hesitates as if measuring her options. Then gives in with a low sigh. "No one's threatening me. My ex. The man I thought was the love of my life—" she rolls her eyes like the idea of it is a joke now, "had a little bit of a jealous streak. Would make it a habit of stalking me at work. I thought it was sweet he was coming to see me play. But he'd just cause a scene when I got too much attention. Got me fired from some of the best gigs in the city."

"Guy sounds like an insecure ass."

She scoffs. "He was."

I rake my eyes over her as I reluctantly put together another piece of her puzzle. "Take it he's the one who put his hands on you?"

"Yeah," she says tightly, like she hates to admit it. "Anyway, he moved out months ago, even though it was technically his apartment. But . . . a few days ago—"

"He kicked you out."

She doesn't deny it and I curse under my breath.

"It was a blessing. The place had all kinds of building violations." She looks up at me and shrugs. "I've sort of got this last-resort place I can stay in the city until I find an apartment. But the woman's having a photoshoot of half-naked men there today, so I can't move in until Sunday."

There's a resentment in her voice that makes me ask. "This . . . 'last resort' is . . .?"

"My mother."

I give a small nod, then lift the piano lid. "Fine-tune away." A spark flickers across her face and I hold up a finger. "But *stay* out of my way."

There's a subtle nod as she holds my eyes—hers mixed with silent gratitude and embarrassment. But it's only a flash before she recovers quickly from both.

"Again," she nods humbly, like the favor is the other way around. "*You're welcome.*"

I sigh, muttering as I walk away. "I'm going to regret this."

About an hour later, Willow manages to find her charger—rolled up and stuffed in a side pocket of her suitcase. She made a big production of coming out here to the back porch to tell me exactly where she found it and how she "totally spaced" but that her coming out here was not to be mistaken for "getting in my way" but more of an "informative drop-by." Then she skipped on back into the house. I can't imagine she'd got very far inside while I've been out here, sanding and painting the porch rail and steps.

I hear her inside on the phone with Rose and sigh.

It shouldn't have taken me two hours on this part of the house. But it's hard to stay focused when it's quiet as an empty field out here and she's inside humming to some tune stuck in her head. Prancing around the kitchen and unloading boxes like there's some order to her madness.

I can still hear her in there—see her through the clear sliding doors. Right now she's multitasking with Rose in her ear and a dust wand in her hands.

My phone vibrates in my pocket and I sigh before pulling it out to check it.

Wilder: Letting her stay the weekend, huh?

Dallas: You're welcome.

I don't know why I let her stay. But it's safe to let my brother believe it was to give him and Rose the chance to get away like he planned.

Wilder: Never met her but she once held me hostage and grilled me on my intentions when I answered Rose's phone.

Dallas: Sounds right.

Wilder: Say the word, we'll come pick her up.

Say it? I should be screaming it. Instead, I shake my head like I'm doing him the favor here too and slip the phone back in my pocket. It vibrates again.

Wilder: Going once . . . Going twice.

Dallas: It's only a day and a half.

Wilder: And how's the last twelve hours work out so far?

Dallas: Go before I change my mind.

It's quiet when I return to the house from a few stops in town. It's almost sunset. Empty boxes are broken down by the back door. A whole *lot* of empty boxes.

I flip the switch in the kitchen. It only lights the pendants I've got hanging over the island. It'll do for now. Millie wanted the lights under the cabinets too. Something dim for when she makes her tea at night.

But this house isn't for her anymore.

I need to prioritize what *Ellie* needs.

Looking down, I notice the floors shine like they've never seen a speck of dust. I take my boots off before stepping inside.

It's quiet down here but I can hear faint shuffling above the kitchen—where Ellie's room is.

I set down the bags from the hardware store and the Thai restaurant on the counter, making a mental note to tackle the grocery store later tonight, before it closes. I plan on emptying a lot of shelves. Don't need the town folks watching me do it.

I've got a whole lot of cabinets to fill and not a clue what to fill them with.

What do seven-year-olds eat? Rose does most of the shopping and, sure, I notice the kids' cereals, yogurts, cheese crackers, and funny-shaped pastas, but we're not living in her uncle's house anymore. This'll be *her* house.

And I want there to be shelves stocked with everything she likes. With a healthy mix of wholesome and sugary snacks. Protein, vitamins, all that stuff a kid needs.

I make a mental note to ask Rose—if she's not too mad at me for ratting her out this morning. And maybe

Ginger too. Sure as hell not something I'll be asking Willow. The woman already moves about like she belongs. Like she knows what's best for Ellie better than I do.

She doesn't.

She's just *helping*.

After her story earlier, I damn near asked her to stay. Thought came out of nowhere. All I knew was I didn't want her anywhere near that asswipe who hurt her. Who got rough with her enough to make her feel she needs to protect herself.

Because she thinks no one else will.

She's not wrong to plan ahead. But the protective rush in me wants to knock the guy's teeth down his throat for messing with her.

My stomach bubbles.

This is exactly why she needs to go. I don't need another woman to protect. She's not mine. Millie was. And now I've only got her memory to protect. I should be more concerned with protecting Ellie from jerks like this in the future. Learning to be the kind of father she needs, so she knows a real man when she meets one. Build her a home fit for a princess so she learns to be treated like one.

Instead I'm picturing all the different ways I could deform this guy's face with a single hit.

With a sigh, I check the time as if there's merely hours before Willow is finally gone and I can forget my thoughts strayed for even a minute.

Heading upstairs, I find Ellie's bedroom door is open, so I pause in the doorway. Willow's on the top step of a short ladder, barely reaching the rod where she adjusts pink velvet drapes.

The setting sun pours in through the window, casting amber light across the room, where it dances off the empty walls—lighting up Willow's thick curls. Setting them ablaze in copper and gold, wrapping around her like she's the source of energy.

She freezes, and for a moment I think I've been discovered lurking and staring. But she doesn't turn. Her gaze drifts out, absorbing the colors.

I should peel my eyes off her and I swear I'm trying. I sure as hell shouldn't lower them to her perfect ass, but I do. And I can't find it in me to be sorry.

Blinking and cursing myself, I clear my throat. "We call it 'Sunset.'"

She turns her head and our gazes collide. Those warm brown eyes wide with innocence.

She's wearing jeans and a plain white tee. But I'd argue there's nothing plain about it. It's cropped just above her waist, lighting up that faded tan with a glow. Clinging to her in all the right places, giving those pert tits the spotlight they damn near deserve.

Shit.

This woman is hanging curtains in my daughter's room and I'm here comparing her to a sunset and ogling her like a perv.

And Willow's just the type to notice and call me out. But she doesn't. She steps down with a smile—wide and so fucking pretty.

"Sunset, huh? I like it."

I know she's playing along but I want to tell her that's not half as good as they get out here this time of year.

Especially from my bedroom window.

There I go again. I must be tired.

"Well, what do you think?" She sets her hands on her hips, raising that crop top just a hike more.

I blink. Am I supposed to know what she's referring to? By some grace of God, she gestures around the space and I snap out of it, looking around the room—because *of course* that's what she's talking about.

There's fewer boxes now and more . . . *room*. Most of them are now empty and broken down, lined up against the wall.

Ellie's bookshelf is stacked with colorful hardcovers, bookends, and pottery. The dresser is now topped with a few of her things. Her bed's made up with fresh linens. Come to think of it, the whole house smells like fabric softener and pine rather than sawdust and paint.

Willow even attached the veil to the canopy crown, which now rests neatly on the bed. She adjusts it evenly, flattening out a few creases.

"Just need a few screws and a drill, but I've already marked the center of the bed." She points to a few pencil marks on the wall.

"Thank you," I finally say, feeling like shit for making her feel like I was doing *her* the favor this morning.

She dusts her hands along her sides, concern lining her forehead. "It's a bit chilly here . . . especially after sundown."

"I know," I say on an exhale. "Heater's going in Monday, couldn't get anyone out here this weekend."

"Monday?"

"That's what I said. Come on. I got us some takeout. Hope you like Thai."

She frowns, narrowing her eyes at me. "What if I don't?"

"Well, it's what you're eatin'. Come on."

Willow's quiet on the way down but I can sense there's something brewing, something unspoken.

I get the feeling she's upset with me. Or maybe disappointed. But I don't pry. I don't *care*.

Instead, I unload cartons onto the counter while Willow grabs two glasses from a cabinet. "Got any filtered water here?" she asks dryly.

"I got beer."

She cocks her head at me like I'm joking. "No water, really? But you thought of beer."

"Calm your feathers. The kitchen tap water is filtered. I do *try* to think of everything, you know."

"Except how to keep a kid warm," she mutters.

"What do you want me to do, drag the guy over here on a Sunday?"

"No, I'm saying that maybe you think twice about rushin' her over here when the place is clearly not ready."

I give her an exhausted glare. "I'll make sure she's warm for the one night. There a chance you get feisty when you're hungry too? Or is it just a morning-coffee thing?"

She deadpans me. "Did ya get anything spicy?"

I point to a set of cartons. "These two."

Looking nearly satisfied, she smirks and settles onto a bar stool, pulling the two cartons toward her plate. "I'll be the judge of that." She tears open a pair of chopsticks and digs into the chicken dish first.

A small, breathy moan slips out as she chews. "There's a kick, but I've had better."

I perk a brow. "Is that right? Well, why don't you try the spicy tofu? It's a favorite of mine. Might need that glass of water though."

She narrows her eyes. "I wash down spicy food with a spicy margarita. But I'll be happy to pour *you* a glass."

I watch her with a smirk, pushing the carton over.

She dips her chopsticks in and grabs a cube of seasoned tofu drenched in the sticky red sauce.

There's a brief pause when it touches her tongue. She glances at me, then continues to chew slowly. Her eyes glisten but she holds herself steady, composed. I'm about to offer her water or a cucumber but her show is just too good to end.

Finally, she swallows. "This one's getting closer." Her eyes lift to mine. "Still had better."

I grin. "That why you turning red?"

"No." Her response is quick. "I'm red because you make me blush with your cowboy charm."

I laugh. "Wow. You'd rather pretend you got a crush than admit this is too hot for you."

"It's not *too* hot. It's just right. Really brings out—" She coughs. "All my senses."

I pull the carton over, still laughing as I take a bite.

"You're going to give yourself heartburn. Then who'll be laughing?"

I touch my chest. "You sure suck the fun out of eatin', Sunset." The nickname tumbles out before I can catch myself.

She blinks at me, one brow lifting like she's not sure if I'm insulting her or flirting. Hell, I'm not even sure myself, but it's all that comes to mind when I look at her now. Especially with the last bit of it coming in through the skylight above the kitchen, bringing out the natural glow in her hair—all too eagerly. Like it's trying to fuck with me.

"Well, you don't like Red. And just a few minutes ago, you said you liked sunsets."

"I was referring to the colors it brings out."

"So was I."

Her cheeks flush pink. "Think I'll take that water now."

I tear my eyes off her and fill the glass, then add some noodles to her plate.

"What's on the agenda tomorrow?" she asks.

Getting you out before Ellie gets here.

I glance at the living room. "I've got some early rounds to do in the field. And now that the floor's polished, we can unwrap the rest of the furniture."

She nods then points her fingers at me with a mouthful. "I think we should pick up some plants tomorrow too. And, you know, foods kids can eat without getting a stomach ulcer."

"I don't feed Ellie spicy food," I mutter, focusing on the food comment rather than telling her I'm not going to go plant and flower shopping with her. If I wanted any, I could pick them right off my field.

I glance around the space, reluctantly admitting to myself that the house could use some life.

I'm staring at the fire and it's past midnight again. Eyes shot, brain gone haywire.

That woman sure is a goddamn handful. One minute with her and you're halfway to losing your mind.

And here I am giving her a *fucking nickname*.

Not Gremlin or Cactus.

But *Sunset*.

And the way her cheeks heated at it . . .

I finally convinced her to sleep in my bedroom again tonight after she refused to mess up Ellie's bed.

I've got two other empty guest rooms up there with bed frames. But no mattresses. Those rooms weren't exactly priority.

And they don't need to be. Because Willow *is* leaving tomorrow.

I run a hand over my overgrown scruff. Hard to believe in a matter of twenty-four hours, I managed to pick more fights with this woman than Millie and I could possibly have in a season. Been more work than a broken fence in a blizzard.

She's beautiful, sure—but a stubborn spitfire more than anything. Thinks she's funny too. Willing to bet there's never a dull moment with Willow—hell, what's her last name?

It doesn't matter.

She'll be gone tomorrow night.

It's late, but sleep won't come, my mind on overdrive. I'm sitting leaning against the tarp-wrapped coffee table in just my sweatpants. I don't sleep in a shirt no matter how cold it might be.

I'm gazing at the crackling fire when I hear the steps creak and turn.

Willow's paused at the bottom step, her mouth dropping before she speaks. "Hi."

"Hey," I groan, sitting up.

She tears her eyes off my chest and I imagine she might be half asleep if her dreamy eyes are any indication.

"Something wake you?"

She blinks. "Just came down to make tea."

I nod and turn back to the fire. "I'd tell you to make yourself at home, but you did that yesterday." I grin.

She pushes her hair behind her ear. "Thanks."

A few minutes later, she switches off the light in the kitchen and steps out with a steaming mug of tea. That's when I notice what she's wearing. Or *not* wearing. She's in a familiar oversized black hoodie. Legs bare. A pair of thick blue knitted socks covering her feet.

I clear my throat, shifting my gaze to the blaze of the fire—still a reminder of what it took from me. How cold it left me and everyone who adored Millie. I hate that it's what's going to keep us warm for the next few days and the brutal winters. "Listen, if I don't get to tell you tomorrow, I appreciate your help today."

"You're welcome." She shivers and I hear a hint of chatter. My eyes snap back to her.

"You cold?"

She pulls the mug close to her chest and I imagine its warmth spreading through her. "The tea should help."

I tear my eyes off her chest and glance up. "You got the space heater on?"

She pulls her bottom lip. "I think I blew it. Turned it up too high or something."

"Oh." I feel like a fool with nothing else to offer her. "Um, fire's probably going to last most of the night if you prefer to stay down here."

Her eyes widen. "Alone?"

"No," I answer after a beat, since it's clear she's not keen on the idea of being ground level alone in the dark. Especially with the large glass windows and doors all around and no source of light for nearly a mile. "There's enough room here for the two of us." I point to the blankets I've got spread in front of the fireplace.

She glances at the fire, biting that bottom lip again. "Does feel warmer down here."

The hope in her tone has me shoving aside that growing, inexplicable guilt over straying from the woman I vowed to love till my dying day.

I toss one of the pillows to the other side of the makeshift bed, leaving room for her as she edges closer.

A gentleman.

That's all I'm being.

For a woman who's cold in *my* home. Making me responsible for her comfort.

That's all this is.

It occurs to me that we'd both benefit from me saying this out loud as Willow shamelessly takes in my bare chest and arms, firelight dancing in her eyes. Eyes I can just as easily get lost in. Until she breathes, "Think we can really do this?"

My lip twitches. "Sure. So long as you remember my eyes are up here."

Big, brown, mischievous eyes lift to mine with a hint of a smirk. "Yeah, well, you owed me one from earlier, cowboy."

The corner of my mouth tugs up. "Suppose I do. So we even then?"

She scans my torso once more. "Even."

I wait until she's settled in under the covers and sipping her tea before I settle next to her.

And I can almost hear what she's thinking.

The same thing I am.

This is a terrible idea.

9

Willow

His heat is the first thing I feel when I wake in the morning. It's far too . . . human and alive to be from the fire.

At some point in the night, he must have thrown on his shirt because my cheek is pressed against soft dark cotton. I resist the urge to stir against him, like a single breath might disturb the steady drum of his heartbeat.

He's so solid, it's unnatural. Everything about this man is unreal. The way he carries a love that death couldn't take away, the devotion to a daughter he never knew he had, the sheer sense of safety he exudes—I've never seen anything like it.

If he wasn't such a jackass sometimes, I'd say I dreamed him up right out of a western romance.

Because men like that don't exist. And it's only a matter of time before even a man like Dallas Thorne proves it.

A cold, sharp reality hits and I jerk back an inch. Like I'm in danger of getting caught up in yet another web. One that will take me months to crawl my way out of.

Dallas groans, low and throaty, stirring up a fizzy feeling in my stomach—and a little lower.

My face is no longer pressed against his chest as his eyelids rise, blinking slowly as he makes me out in his vision.

When his eyes lower, I freeze, heat filling my neck. It's a slow realization as I follow his gaze. Like in one of those dreams where you're walking down the school hallway and it takes everyone staring at you to realize you're in your underwear.

My bare leg is tucked between his thighs.

How did I not notice? How could I let that happen? Another low rumble in his chest as he rolls onto his back, releasing my leg, eyes now pinned to the ceiling instead of me.

I'm so mortified, I want to scream. Something to the effect of "Get over yourself, cowboy, we don't know who or how that happened."

But I'd be a hypocrite if I tried to point the finger at him. The leg-tucking is completely and one hundred percent my doing. It's probably why it felt so natural to me. Why I was so unaware of it when I woke up. It's my signature sleeping position when I share a bed with a man.

"Must've done that when the fire died out," I say out loud. *So don't make anything more of it than it was.*

That, I say to myself.

Because I don't do this anymore. Falling all over a man for his charm and promises. Promises we both know he'd break. Even if he won't mean to.

I'm not convinced that there's a forever out there for me. I'm even less convinced that I could ever be someone's.

But what I am sure of—is that if I were looking, I wouldn't find it in a man who's sworn his life to grief and grumpiness.

When I glance back, I catch him still staring at the ceiling, guilt and discomfort all over his features. My stomach squeezes and I wish I could do or say something to make it better.

"I know you offered to keep me warm, but that takes hospitality to a whole new level," I tease.

His mid-section jerks with a low chuckle as he meets my eyes. "We do take it seriously around here."

I push to my feet and clear my throat. "Thank you."

For last night. For keeping me warm and safe. And for letting an older version of Willow dream a little before the new one forced reality back in. "I'll go—make enough coffee to last all day." A gentle reminder as to why I'm here. "We're going to need it."

The faintest trace of woodsmoke and that familiar cedar scent clings to my clothes hours later. It's not just in my hoodie this time. It's in my hair, my skin. And I'm doing my damnedest to keep it from my thoughts. Reminders of being tucked up against Dallas all night are the last thing I need.

Men aren't on my roster anymore. At least for the next few years. And even then, it's going to take one hell of a Prince Charming to convince me to trust again. To fall again—into safer arms.

He took a quick shower after I disappeared into the kitchen—a totally normal thing to do when you've been sleeping on the floor by the fire. That's what the right side of my brain tells me. The left is filing her nails in the corner, cracking jokes that he couldn't wash me off his skin fast enough.

I tried to listen to the right. She's usually on point. Rational, logical, and unbiased. But every time we pass, his jaw tightens, eyes anywhere but on me. Like I'm a one-night stand he's pretending never happened.

It's ridiculous. But Lefty usually is. That's what Rose calls her when my insecurities start to surface. She also tells me a few ways to push her aside. Send Lefty back to her dark corner where I can no longer hear her. Eventually, she'll go away.

10

Dallas

"There's my girl," I rasp, pulling her close. Ellie wraps her little arms around me and I don't let go. "You smell like apple tarts. D'you save me any?"

Ellie bobs her head. "Ginger brought a basket of 'em."

I look up over her shoulder. Ginger and Dad are still unloading the truck with Ellie's things from Wilder's house. She still doesn't know that I've got all her things from her grandparents' house inside too. I tuck loose strands behind her ears. "You don't look too mad at me for leaving you a few extra days there."

She holds my eyes like she knows something good is coming. "I was, but then Uncle Wild and Rose said you had a surprise for me." She looks over my shoulder, impatiently. "Is it in the house?"

My smile is wide. Wondering if it'll always be this simple to please my girl. To win back her trust and her forgiveness when I screw up or break a promise. I tug her hands playfully. "It is the house, baby. It's all ready for you. For us." I gauge the look on her face. A response that seems too long for her to form. "If you're all right with that," I add, reminding her this is a choice.

When she looks at the house again, eyes flickering with hope and wonder, then back at me with a smile in her eyes, the tightness in my chest eases. She nods feverishly and I chuckle with relief, then push to my feet.

"Thanks again, Ginger." I ruffle Ellie's hair. "Hope she wasn't any trouble."

Ginger swipes at a tear from the corner of her eye. Then waves me off. "Oh, please. We had a blast. Right, sweetheart?"

"Yeah," Ellie giggles. "Especially when we made fun of Grandpa snoring like a bear on the couch."

My eyebrows lift just as Dad walks up from the truck, arms loaded with Ellie's bags. Clearing his throat and grumbling at the same time.

Freshly alarmed like I'd never seen her, Ginger starts to usher Ellie inside the house. "Let's get you all settled, sweets."

My gaze sharpens on Dad as he lingers behind, scratching the back of his neck. "Don't look at me like that, you heard the girl. It was the couch."

I narrow my eyes then realize something. I turn toward the porch steps. "Hold on. There's someone in there you should—"

"Willow," Ellie cries, racing up the steps. "I thought you left."

Time seems to freeze as we all watch this strange, beautiful redhead—who's still wearing my hoodie after sleeping in it all night beside me—embrace my girl, squeezing her like she knows her better than I do.

"I'm so happy I got to see you one last tiiime," Willow gasps, pulling back and holding her by the shoulders. "Wait. Are you moving in today?"

Ellie nods excitedly.

Dad stands beside me, eyes still on the duo at the top of the steps. Ginger, who is thankfully a lot more subtle—and friendly—than Dad, offers a hand almost immediately.

"Hello, Willow. Ellie was telling us all about you yesterday. I'm glad we got to meet you before you left."

All about her?

What's there to say? Exactly how much can she know about her in three days?

Despite myself, my gaze moves to Willow. I've seen the woman laugh at my expense. Smirk. Grin. But hell, that smile she's giving the two of them. It's a sucker punch to the gut.

She shouldn't have a smile like that.

She shouldn't have a voice like that.

Dad's eyes land on me with a raised brow. Same one I gave him a minute ago. I shake my head lightly. "Don't ask."

He nods once. "Fair enough."

I smirk. Dad never lets things go just like that. This is his way of saying, *I won't if you won't.*

And I'm perfectly OK with that.

Dad helps Ginger with the last step and introduces himself quietly. Willow gives him a soft smile. But it's not *polite*. It's warm, eyes glimmering with familiarity. Like they share the same interest.

Ellie jumps. "You want to come see my new room with me?"

Willow stretches her hand like a soldier. "Lead the way, Slippers."

Ellie grabs it like it's a nickname she's been responding to for years and drags her through the open doors.

I catch the tail end of Ellie's laughter—full-bellied and crinkle-eyed—and the lingering sight of *her* twisting playfully to follow, grinning like she belongs. Blending in to our closed circle all too easily.

The hell is happening here?

The tug in my chest is like a threat. And the only way to get rid of it is to gather up her things and make sure she doesn't miss her flight.

Dad hangs back, pretending to predict the weather as he squints out at the horizon. "Willow is Rose's friend, right?"

"That's right."

"Made quite an impression on your girl."

Well then, I must've met her alter ego.

"Ellie loves everybody," I lie. Ellie hates her new second-grade teacher—apparently she's tall and has a lot of rules; the woman at the library, because she stares into space and shushes everybody. And the social worker, Rachel, who thankfully she won't need to deal with much longer after the custody transfer is final.

"What about you?"

"What about me?"

"You hate everybody," Dad points out.

"I do not." My response comes quick and sharp, because I don't like words like that around Ellie. Especially when it's me he's talking about.

How could she ever learn to trust someone who doesn't like people?

Dad shrugs. "Well, unless they work on this ranch or are related to you. But I remember you bitchin' about all those times Millie hauled you out on the town—heaven forbid you have a social life outside this ranch."

I stuff my hands in my pockets. "Thought you weren't gonna ask." Dad's not one to talk in circles, but it's clear he can't help himself.

He holds up his hands. "You're right. I'll just . . . make my own assumptions." He starts to turn.

"She needed somewhere to stay. And I needed help here." I step up to the porch. "A . . . mutually beneficial *short-term* arrangement."

I glance past his shoulder, where I picture the coziness continuing between my daughter and the woman who's got no place here. The longer Willow stays, laughs, and fills the space that was never meant for her—the more my insides twist. An ache of guilt and anger. A woman I'm letting trespass on a life I planned for someone else. I shake myself from my thoughts, focusing again on Dad. "One that's on its final hour. Now let's get this little gathering over with so I can take her to the airport."

Dad follows me inside, shutting the door behind him—and locking it. He's always been protective of our property. Or maybe it's the people inside he's always been protective of.

He takes it all in—quiet, steady, measuring the work, every beam, every floorboard. "Those weatherproof?" he asks, nodding to the glass panels behind him.

And every window.

"Guess we'll find out during the next blizzard," I tease.

Dad shakes his head, not finding the humor.

"Place looks great, Dallas," Ginger comments, taking slow steps down the stairs. "Bit nippy up there, but I like it."

"Heater's going in Monday," I repeat for what feels like the seventh time this weekend.

Ginger wiggles a finger. "You be sure it does. That girl's going to catch a cold sleepin' up there."

I look at the fireplace. "I'll set us up down here for tonight. Supposed to drop to the forties."

Dad looks at me, one brow raised. "When you tellin' her?"

I know he's referring to the news about Ellie's grandmother. And I have *no* idea.

Willow returns and my heart stills for a moment. But she's alone. "Hey, Ellie's upstairs rearranging her stuffed animals in alphabetical order?" she frowns, like she's not sure how.

I smirk. "By name, I bet, not species."

"You used to rename the horses," Ginger says. "Your Dad had named them Silver, Snow, Rhino, and Larry. You remember what you called them?"

"Ginger," I warn.

"Oh, I want to know." Willow beams.

"Of course you do," I mutter, rolling my eyes.

Ginger smiles. "He named them Spout, Snout, Ricky, and Licky. Think he even used one of them names for his stuffy too. Snout, was it?"

"Spout," I correct like an idiot.

Dad chuckles.

Willow laughs and it's impossible not to watch as her head falls back, hair tumbling off her shoulders, and her hand pressing to her stomach like it hurts. "Oh man, that's good. How long did that go on?"

"Till he was twelve," Dad says with a grin.

Willow laughs harder, touching Ginger's arm like she's family. "Well, at least there's no proof. When I was twelve, I thought I could fly. So I stood at the top of our L-shape sofa, handed my sister a camera and said, 'Take a picture while I'm mid-air.'"

Ginger's eyes widen. "You did not."

Willow nods. "Got two pieces of evidence. A photo—and this scar on my bottom lip."

Ginger takes a closer look. "I don't see a scar."

I have to look away before my eyes become permanently glued to that bottom lip.

Also, I've already seen the scar. The night she attacked me. And a bit more clearly yesterday under the skylight of my kitchen when I caged her between my arms.

My stupidity started there. Faint as a whisper on her skin. Kind of liked it about her. Sure as hell didn't think *that* was how she got it. The corner of my lip twitches and I twist my neck—looking for that damn suitcase.

Dad grumbles. "Twelve, huh? Least you weren't wearing a cape."

Willow's brown eyes widen like she's insulted. "It was red with gold trim and I wore it proudly." She makes a Superman stance and then laughs to herself as she rolls her suitcase out from under the staircase. "Ready when you are, Spout."

Dad's eyes land on Willow's hand on the suitcase and his brows perk, but he doesn't say anything. Probably wondering where she spent the night.

"Oh, let me heat up a tart for you before you go." Ginger rushes to the kitchen. Willow follows, protesting that she doesn't need the calories.

I glance up the stairs. "I should go check on Ellie before I head out."

"What she do anyway? Willow. For work?"

I shake my head like it doesn't matter. "Plays piano at a bar in Manhattan, I think." I pause. "Sings too."

Dad nods slowly.

"What?"

He shrugs. "Don't look like that girl's in any rush to get back."

"You get all that in ten minutes?"

"I got all that from Ellie tellin' us Rose's friend surprised her with an impromptu visit *and* that she thought she left. Then she ends up here. Offering help. Don't take a rocket scientist, Dal."

"Did you have a point or can I go spend some time with my daughter now before I leave her yet again to drive to the airport?"

He looks me dead in the eye. "Thought about asking her to stay for a while?"

Is he serious? The hell for?

"Don't know what you mean by 'a while,' but no. I don't need anybody here. Not for Ellie. Not for me. Not for a week, not at all."

Dad looks at me like he understands my resistance all too well. And since he's the only one who does, I tell him. I lift my head to the darkening clouds, rubbing a hand over my jaw. "After Millie died, I didn't know how to get by. Hell, I didn't think I could or even wanted to. But then Ellie happened . . ." I sigh with an ease only she brings out of me. "And I figured it out. How to live, how to be there for someone who depends on me. She and I—we finally got our rhythm. A trust I'm building from scratch because I missed six *years* of her life. It's the one thing—the only thing helping me move past losing the love of my life." I swallow hard, my eyes darting to the expanse of my fields as I continue to accept life without her. "You were there. I don't need it. I barely crawled out of that hole once. I'm not about to go under again. Not when I've got a little girl depending on me. I'm all she's got. And she's getting all of me."

His eyes are warm but his jaw is tight as he takes in every word. "Son, I appreciate you don't want Ellie growing close to anyone, but . . . no one's talking forever. These are desperate times. You're going to need help. Especially with winter staffing around here being minimal. Early mornings, sometimes late nights—"

"Not her," I snap quietly.

Dad perks a brow. "Too pretty."

I shake my head. *Too fucking a lot of things.*

Willow's fierce but fragile, clever, witty. Beautiful as all hell, but her voice—if I hear her sing again, even hum, I'll lose my goddamn mind.

Before I have a chance to tell him to drop it—or see my girl for even a minute—through the window I catch sight of a familiar truck pulling up to the house. "It's Cole Hartly."

"Ellie's grandfather?"

I glance upstairs. "He must be here to tell her about Maya." I rub my jaw, panic creeping into my veins. "I haven't had a chance to call him to discuss when or how yet."

"Hell," Dad mumbles, then puts a hand on my shoulder. "Might as well get this over with. Want me and Ginger to go?"

Something twists in my stomach about Cole's visit. "No," I mutter. "Hold on a second. Keep Ellie upstairs, will ya?"

I'm in knots when I step outside. The man just lost his wife so I'm careful not to snap at him for showing up unannounced. Especially if he's here to break my girl's heart when it's supposed to be a happy day for her.

"Cole," I start, meeting him halfway—a good twenty feet from the front porch.

He nods and glances at the house.

"Ellie's just settling in. Listen, I'm sorry for your loss. I know you were hoping for more time—"

He nods again, eyes in the dirt between us. "Time, yeah. Never seems to be a fair thing, does it?"

"It can be."

"You know I'm nine years older than her. I shouldn't have outlived her."

His eyes are red, distant. And I feel his pain. There were many nights I thought the same thing. If anyone deserved to live longer, it was Millie. Woman knew how to live, how to make the most of life.

"Sure as hell shouldn't've outlived my daughter."

I swallow, knowing I couldn't bear to lose mine. But I also don't need to mention how many years I lost with her—important years—because he and his family kept quiet. "Tammy was special. But I do believe they're in a better place now."

"Just waitin' for me, I suppose."

"Listen, Cole, I understand why you're here, but I don't think it's a good time to tell Ellie—"

"I'm not here to tell her about Maya." He turns his gaze on me. Hard and decisive. "I don't think I'll be signing over custody of Ellie."

I stare at him. "What are you talking about?"

"It's nice that you've finally got a house for just the two of you, but what do you know about raising a little girl?"

I glance back to make sure Ellie's still inside. And see Dad stepping out. His eyes focused on Cole like he's a threat.

"With all due respect, Ellie's my daughter. There's a test proving it and I'm not so sure you've got much of a fight." I don't mean to attack. Not a kind, hurting man like Cole—but you come to my door threatening my family, and you won't see any of the Thorne men hold back.

"Ellie's all I have left," he rasps.

I step closer, my voice low. "No one's taking her away from you."

"Oh yeah? Then why isn't she out here?"

"I told you, I don't want her knowing about her grandmother yet."

His jaw tightens. Eyes dipping down to the ground again. "I've already spoken to Jenny. Told her I changed my mind."

"You did what?" Dad snaps from behind me.

I hold up a hand without glancing back, my eyes trained on Cole, my back teeth clenched. My emotions in check. "Cole. I know you're hurting, but taking Ellie away—"

"I'm not taking her away. I'm taking her *back*. I'm not abandoning her," he cries out and I blow into my fist to remind myself who I'm dealing with.

I place a hand over his shoulder. "Take a walk with me. There's no need to get loud."

He and Dad exchange a glare before I turn him away, leaning in close. "Look, I know there's still a few boxes we need to check, but I'm sure Jenny told you we can't turn back now."

Weakly, he pushes my hand off his shoulder. "You're wrong. Jenny suggested I get a lawyer and we can take it from there. I called Glenda. She said with your record, it shouldn't be an issue. She'll be calling Jenny to pause the process tomorrow."

"On what fucking grounds?"

"Everyone knows you're still grieving your fiancé. Saw it myself when I first met you."

I bite back a retort. One that calls him out for being guilty of the same damn thing. My voice is hoarse. "That's really not fair."

"That and the fact that you're a bachelor. I've got my sister ready to move in. Raised three daughters and an army of granddaughters."

I know Glenda Lost. The expensive town lawyer, PTA president, on the board of *everything*. She's a shark. Goes for the kill every time. But it's impossible to get her to take your case.

Unless . . . you tell her you're going after the biggest family in town.

I don't bother asking how he thinks he could afford Glenda. My money's on her taking the case for free.

When we started the custody transition, we didn't need lawyers. I only consulted mine over some logistics, but no one was put on retainer.

I turn back to look at Dad and I know he sees the anger in my face. The worry.

Cole and I watch as Dad walks back into the house. And I'm grateful for it. Dad isn't exactly friendly when it comes to threats to the family.

I'll handle this . . . man to man. From one grieving man to another.

"Cole, I think you need a few days. Why don't I come by with Ellie tomorrow? We'll both tell her about Maya and—"

"Forget it. You can't raise my girl here. In this house you built in the middle of nowhere, with nothing but you and your brothers. There's Ginger, I suppose. But Ellie needs—" He cuts off, eyes over my shoulder.

A hand touches my bicep and I still at the contact. "Hey," says Willow, and I hear the smile in her voice before I turn around. "Connor asked me to come out here and invite the nice gentleman in for some warm apple tarts."

He did what? "I don't think—"

As usual, the woman ignores me, stretching out her hand. "Hi there. I'm Willow."

Cole's lips part before he speaks. His tone changes. "Willow?"

"Like the tree. Or that Taylor Swift song—whatever your pleasure."

"Cole Hartly, I'm—"

"Ellie's *other* grandpa, yes, I'm slowly learning all the important people around here." She's still smiling brightly as she turns to me. "I helped Ellie unpack and your dad's starting the fire. See you inside soon?" She grips tighter onto my bicep and lifts up on her tiptoes, placing a feathery kiss to my cheek.

I still. Or maybe my heart stills. Soft lips. Warm breath.

I flex my arms, catching her waist on instinct to hold her steady. Our eyes are locked—hers giving nothing away.

They wouldn't.

But there's an unmistakable tremble beneath her hoodie as I set her down on her heels.

"OK then," she breathes, then tears her eyes off me, returning her gaze to Cole. "Well, it's nice to meet you."

"Er—thank you. And I'll pass on the tarts for tonight."

With one more glance my way, Willow turns back toward the house.

We wait in silence as the clouds seem to darken.

Cole turns a hard glare back at me. "I don't buy it and neither will Jenny, or Glenda, or the state of Colorado."

"Excuse me?"

Cole shakes his head. "That engagement ring looked like it belongs to Ginger. Not a twenty-something girl clearly not from round here." He stalks off with a grumble.

I scowl, following him to his truck. "Hang on a second. What does Willow have to do with Ellie?"

"I don't know where you found her. If she's a babysitter or a one-night stand—or both. I'm taking my granddaughter back."

"Will you—" I pause, blowing another hot breath into my fist. "I'm asking you not as Ellie's father, but as a friend. Take a few days to think about this before you call Jenny?"

"Too late. She'll be in touch this week." He hops back in his truck and fires up the engine. Wheels spinning in the other direction.

My vision is blurred. My jaw is clenched so tight it aches. I stare at the tire tracks of Cole's truck.

He's hurt. He's grieving.

But he was sober. No sober man comes to another man's house threatening to take their kid away and not mean it. But I *have* to believe this'll pass.

My hands fist at my sides and for the first time in months, I feel the need to scream.

The front door swings open behind me. I hear Dad's hard steps on the gravel a minute later.

"Why'd you send her out here?" I ask, not bothering to turn back.

"Who? Oh, you mean Willow. Well, tarts were gettin' cold."

I turn. "You noticed the ring on her finger."

"Hard not to."

I rub my hand along my jaw.

"Did it work?" he asks flat out.

"And you're still assuming she has nothing to go back to?"

"Son, when you've lived as long as I have you know a single woman when you see one."

I kick the dirt, not about to analyze that one. "Well, it didn't work. He didn't buy it."

His eyes trail the tire tracks. "He's not the one you need to convince."

"Convince of what?" I snap, but Dad keeps his tone cool, like some damn therapist.

"That Ellie is coming into a warm, secure, and loving family environment. Not one shrouded in grief."

I swallow down the fear. "Get real. No social worker is going to take that man seriously. He'll be fine by morning."

He won't be fine by morning. He won't be fine for a while. But it doesn't matter. He's just as alone as I am. If there's going to be a fight, it's going to be an equal one.

"Ask her to stay," Dad says firmly behind me.

I snap my head back like he's out of his mind.

But I don't focus on how serious he might be about Willow staying.

Because she's standing at the top of the porch steps.

With her suitcase.

11

Willow

"I just said goodbye to Ellie. Ginger is making her supper now, figured it's as good a time as any to get going," I say, hoping he doesn't catch the wavering in my voice because the last thing I want to do right now—is go.

The bag felt heavier when I dragged it out here moments ago. I've been in Blue River Springs less than a week, but it's the time I spent in this house, with this man and that little girl, that has my feet feeling fused not just to the pavement—but to the land itself.

That part doesn't scare me—driving away from the wide skies, clean air, and a home surrounded by nature's beauty. The part that does . . . is admitting that if you take away those two breathing souls from the equation, I'd be halfway to New York by now with nothing left to lose. Admitting that in the last two days, I've felt braver, steadier, and more alive than I have in years. I attacked a strange man in the dark of a home I thought was temporarily abandoned. Then stuck around and called him out on being a stubborn jackass. I helped transform this gem of a building into a home where he can raise a daughter he's been given a second chance with.

I'm not saying I belong here. But I'm supposed to just get on a plane and pretend I've got something better to go back to?

Connor gives Dallas a pointed look before coming up the stairs. "Thanks," he murmurs.

I wink back—hoping I didn't misread his cue earlier.

When Connor walked into the house after Cole arrived, I knew something was wrong. The man was simmering beneath the surface—and a little pale. Ginger noticed too and asked who was outside.

That's when Connor asked if I could step outside for a moment. Maybe invite Ellie's grandfather in for some warm tarts. His eyes landing on my ring finger again. The way they had when I grabbed my suitcase.

Connor may be an intimidating man, and I've known him less than an hour, but I trust him. The man was counting on my help for something, and I didn't think twice before giving a single nod and stepping out onto the front porch, where the glow of the setting sun caught my eye and a cool breeze brushed my skin. But nothing felt colder than the exchange between the two men a few feet from the house.

The rush I felt jumping to Dallas's defense hit me hard.

It's why I specifically touched his arm, letting my left hand linger in some poor effort of showing a united front.

The kiss wasn't planned.

It was instinct. A pull.

An emotionally charged slam against my chest, letting the man standing opposite us know that if he's here for Ellie—

He'll have to go through both of us.

Which is laughable since Dallas and I haven't been "united" about anything since the minute I arrived. Except when it comes to Ellie.

But when he put his hand on me, securing me against his side—everything in me tightened. Alarm bells going off at my body's reaction to him. I swore I had more control. I swore the romance door had been nailed shut since the last man who stomped all over my heart, but clearly the butterflies in my stomach think they've found an exception.

Whatever it was, I came back down to earth with lightning speed when I stepped inside—and saw my suitcase.

Connor drags his gaze from the New York bag tag dangling off the handle back to me. "It was nice meeting you, Willow. Appreciate the pest control." He glances at Dallas. "Even if it was temporary."

Harsh. I'm not sure I'd refer to a grieving man as a pest—as unwelcome as his visit might have been—but Connor is right. Because that man *is* coming back.

Dallas draws close to the porch steps, watching his father until he disappears inside the house.

I open my mouth—about to ask how I can help. Because I want to.

But the stubborn man cuts me off, jogging up the steps. I nearly jolt back from the proximity. That woodsy scent hitting me fast. A tease of what I'd be leaving behind.

If he lets me leave.

"That everything?" he rasps.

I blink. Then look down at my suitcase. "Yep."

He avoids my eyes, lifting my case and carrying it to his trunk, popping it open and tossing it in.

He pauses with a heavy breath, dropping his head and resting his palms on the edge of the trunk bed. Like he doesn't know what to do next.

My heart aches for him.

For Ellie too.

I worry that little girl's got a battle ahead. But I'm happy for her at the same time. Because she's got two men fighting to be the one to care for her. When I couldn't even get one to call me on my birthday.

I edge closer from behind.

"Get in," he barks, masking the tiny fact that he's falling apart right now.

"Well, all right." I nudge him aside with my hip and hop into the trunk of the SUV. Tapping my suitcase like I'm ready to hit the road.

He scowls. "I didn't mean back here."

"You don't want to talk about what just happened?"

"Not with you."

"Well, you won't talk to your dad. My guess is you're going to keep that scowl on till sunrise and avoid talkin' to anyone, hoping your little problem goes away."

"That's a good guess." He reaches up to lower the trunk door. "Last chance," he warns.

I cross my arms. "Not going anywhere until you talk to me."

"Oh, you're going somewhere." He lifts my legs and pushes them over to the side before lowering the door shut. Through the window I watch him stalk around to the driver's seat.

He buckles his seatbelt. "Best hold on to something."

I sit up on my knees, hands clutching the backseat headrest. "OK, fine. Don't talk to me. But ignoring this is not going to make it go away."

"I'm not ignoring anything. I'm just giving a grieving man time. He'll come around." He grips the steering wheel with one hand and starts the engine with the other.

I raise my voice over the humming. "Out of curiosity, what made *you* come around?"

He pauses, eyes meeting mine in the rearview mirror, like he fell for some trap.

Because I'm pretty sure I know the answer.

Ellie.

I hold his cold eyes. Softening mine enough for the both of us. "There has to be *something* you can do."

"There is." He pulls hard on the gear shift, throwing it into drive. "Getting you out of here."

Gravel kicks up from the tires and I jolt back with a yelp, sliding across the space, my arms flailing like they're trying to hold on to my dignity.

I manage to catch my breath when the road straightens but then he rounds the bend again—and sharply.

I roll like a duffle bag. "How many more curves are there on this damn ranch?" I howl.

He chuckles. "'Bout fifty."

I growl and use my suitcase for leverage as I grab hold of a coat hook and climb over to the backseat. From here, I whack him on the back of his head. He barely moves from the impact.

I grip his right shoulder, which he locks in place for me, as I climb into the front passenger seat.

He slows down until my butt hits the seat, but then swerves the second my seatbelt clicks.

"What's your problem? I just asked if you wanted to talk about it," I shout.

"Let's get something straight," he shouts right back. "*You're* the talker. Not me. I got nothing to say."

"Dallas," I breathe. "Someone might be *legitimately* threatening to take your girl away. You can't ignore that."

"I told you, I'm not."

"Then what are you doing?"

"Taking it as a goddamn sign," he mutters.

I blink. "A sign?"

His jaw tightens. "A sign. Message. 'Ever the hell you want to call it." He stares at the road as it grows dark. "Think it was coincidence that he shows up the same night Ellie moves in with me? The first night that kicks off fatherhood in every way, shape and form. Just the two of us." He waves an arm out. "Expectations. Things I should know, do, say." He gulps. "It's like someone tellin' me I'm not ready."

I stare at him wide-eyed. "I don't know what's more shocking. That you believe in fate or that you're considering this a way out."

He keeps his eyes on the road. "What the hell can I do for her that Cole's sister—who raised a tribe of women—can't?"

I shake my head like it's obvious. "She'd be with her *father*."

There's pure silence now and I turn to face the window.

"Kinda country do we live in that I got to have a wife to prove I can take care of a child?" he mutters.

If we're talking about signs . . . That's a damn good one that he doesn't want to give her up.

I turn in my seat. Since it's clear he's not going to ask what we both know Connor was suggesting. "Dallas. Let me help you. We've already planted the seed. Let's follow through and get you your kid."

His jaw tightens harder as he watches the road. "What time's your flight anyway?"

I avoid telling him I don't have one. That I was going to just grab the first one out as soon as I got there.

"I've got nothing but time, Dallas."

He pulls over in the middle of the highway. In the middle of nowhere. With nothing but dirt, trees, a dark sky, and stars around us.

He turns off the engine and faces me. "What time's your flight?"

"I don't have one."

He swallows, eyes dropping to my lips. Then pulls out his phone. I wait as he goes through a few steps on an app.

I sigh and settle into my seat.

"Window or aisle?" he grumbles.

I grin. "First class."

His lip perks. "Row thirty it is."

I shift to face him. "Why are you trying to get rid of me?"

"Because you're not staying here. I'm getting you on that plane so you can go sing, karate kick, and be a thorn in someone else's side."

I give a weak smile but my eyes are stinging. Not because he's asking me to leave.

But because everyone does.

Dallas's phone rings. The caller name pops up on the dashboard screen and he curses.

Noah Reeves.

"Who is that?" I ask.

He sighs. "Family friend—and lawyer." He pushes a button with a bit too much force. "Noah, I'll call you back."

"You're lucky I'm calling *you* off my normal hours."

"What's the emergency?" Dallas asks, practically with a yawn.

"Connor called me."

Another curse under his breath.

"I'm checking the status in the system right now. Jenny's already got the petition to stop the adoption process."

"How the—?"

I practically jump out of my seat at the holler.

"It only takes one party to have second thoughts for them to call pencils down on the custody transfer."

"Hell. The guy is out of his mind, Noah."

"Look, I'm not saying he'll win, because any court will see she belongs with her biological, *sane*, *sober*, and business-owning father. But until it's decided, it could take weeks or months of court dates. Till then . . ."

"Don't say it."

"She may have to go back to living with Hartly."

Dallas lifts his hands off the wheel like he's going to bang it but holds back. "How do I keep her, Noah?"

My heart thumps.

He's choosing to fight.

"Odds are in your favor—unless he gets dirty. I'll call you tomorrow when I know more." Noah hangs up.

Dallas's jaw ticks. "He already has got dirty," he mutters under his breath and runs a hand over his stubble.

But he's not putting the car back in drive.

The words are on the tip of my tongue. I can help him. I *should* help him. Lord knows no one's ever needed me quite like this little family does right now.

I should take a moment. Really consider what I'd be offering to do here. Would I really do this? Stay in this dust-covered, tight-knit town with this grumpy cowboy who one second goes from looking at me like I hung the moon. And the next like he's ready to toss me off it?

Heavens, I think I am.

I take a breath. "Look, I'm not saying we need to get married."

"Course not." He glances at my ring. "You're married to never getting married. You think I don't remember how fast you lied about having a boyfriend when you thought I was comin' on to you in that bar?"

I twist the band around my finger. I don't keep it on to repel men. But I have sworn off them for the foreseeable future. Or until I make my own future. Commit to making myself happy before anyone else.

And after Eric, I'm not exactly desperate for someone else to stake his claim, tell me what to do, where to sing, and who comes within three feet of me.

"Can we focus here and leave the digs aside for now?"

He grunts.

"You can't let that little girl get tossed around. I know that's no one's intention, but it's what will happen. If there's a chance that just my *presence* can help—" He sighs mid-sentence, and I need to raise my tone to be heard. "—then why won't you fucking take it, you giant bull-headed grump."

He twists his neck to look at me. Eyes stretched wide. He breathes out hard, the kind of exhale that says, *fine, you win*.

Without another word, he flips the car around.

It's a quiet ride for about five whole minutes until he asks, "You're not a fugitive or anything, are you?"

"If your first guess as to why I'm offering to stay and help is that I'm running from the law, you're in worse shape than I thought."

"Just sayin', it's not often a pretty redhead with a sharp tongue workin' toward a blackbelt drops her life to help a *giant bull-headed grump*."

I shift in my seat, muttering, "Especially one as appreciative as you."

"Now let's get somethin' straight—"

"Oh, this should be good."

"For all we know, Cole could swing by tomorrow sayin' he was high on whiskey and came to his senses. In which case, you'd be headin' back to Manhattan, Sunset."

"And if not?"

He waits a beat, twisting his neck like he's got no choice. "Then it's only right I pay you."

"Pay me? To act like your wife?"

"To take care of Ellie," he corrects, surprising me at how sincere he sounds. "Her eyes . . . lit up like I've never seen when she saw you step out onto the porch earlier."

I'm quiet as I remember it. But my silence seems to make him nervous.

"Unless . . . taking care of her is a dealbreaker."

"Ellie a dealbreaker? I'm doing this *for* her," I snap.

There's a shift in his gaze at my response. Soft with curiosity, tangled with caution. Something raw tugs at my heartstrings. The natural protectiveness at anyone taking interest in his girl. But with a flicker of hope for the very same thing.

I sigh, giving him more so he doesn't get stalker vibes. "And me." I roll my eyes. "Suppose a bit you, too."

"Oh yeah? That why you so attached to my hoodie?"

"While we're on that, if I could just get me one of those woodsy detergents you use, I'll happily be on my way."

His brows shoot up like I've insulted him. "OK, so not me. Then . . . why you? And spare me your wit. I want the truth."

My heart starts to beat loud against my chest. Because he's right, I would have used my wit to blow this one off—Rose would have seen right through it. And if the way Dallas is looking at me is any indication—he would too.

Truth.

"Well, I told you I'd be temporarily moving in with my mother until I find an apartment . . ."

"And you're far from excited about it?" he guesses.

My face twists and knowing my habit of rambling, I know better than to get into it. "I'll spare you the soap opera recap, but correct."

He nods slowly and I realize that wasn't a fair response to *the truth*.

I release a breath. "Maybe it's because I see myself in her—" I mutter. "Ellie, I mean. I was never in a custody battle." I scoff. "Not a conventional one anyway. I grew up with a parent who couldn't be bothered, while the other made me feel like she was stuck rather than blessed with me." I twist the ring on my finger, keeping my gaze on it. "When I was her age, no one fought for me the way you and Cole fought this evening." I jerk at the understatement of that admission, then meet his eyes with my truth. "I had to fight for that kind of attention."

His brows twitch as he watches the road, and I can barely see his eyes. Making it hard to tell if there's compassion in them . . . or pity.

"And if that's not honest enough, I don't *have* much to rush back to." I swallow the lump in my throat. "No one's . . . well, let's just say I'd be more of a nuisance back home. And while it's not lost on me I'd be just as much a nuisance to *you*—at least I can help you keep your baby girl."

After a beat, he huffs, glancing over at me for a brief second. It's enough to see the shift in his jaw, the warmth in his eyes. When he turns back, his chest lifts with a quiet inhale. But he still says nothing.

I sigh, easing the tension. "Plus, you know, my best friend is here. She's one of the few I have, so . . . may as well make it a habit of stalkin' her till I make a new one . . ." I chuckle, then pause when his eyes snap to me like I'm crazy. "What?"

"You don't have friends?"

I roll my eyes. "I know, big surprise there, right? Who'd want to hang out with me and manage to get a word in with all my rambling? I'll have you know I'm a fabulous listener. Not that you do a whole lot of talking—" I stop, eyes wide as I catch myself and sit back in my seat, watching the streetlights pass by as we head back up a familiar gravel road.

Dallas is quiet for a moment. "I just thought all you girls have . . ." He waves his hand around. ". . . friends, cliques, people you get all dressed up for on a Saturday night, ordering fireball shots."

"Rose doesn't do that. I sure as hell don't. Must be a cowgirl thing."

He scoffs, shaking his head. Leaving whatever's in his mind unspoken. Then, after a moment, he rubs the stubble along his jaw with a heavy sigh, as if that was a lot to take in. "On second thoughts, think your wit would've been just fine." He glances over at me and winks.

I gape at him just before smacking his forearm, then burst out laughing. "You're the worst." I shake my head. "But now I know for next time."

12

Dallas

I hoist Ellie up onto the kitchen counter. She's in her jammies, with that curly-girl bedhead, that'll stay like that until either Rose or I do something about it. Usually Rose.

But Ellie likes it bouncy in the morning for some odd reason. Never asked. Going to have to one of these days.

I push a few spirals from out of her face, then press my palms to the countertop on either side of her.

"All right, I got all your favorites. Pebbles, Sugar Flakes, box of pancake mix, the works—"

"Sugar Flakes?" Her eyes pop.

I hold up a finger. "But before breakfast, there's something really important I need to talk to you about. Two things."

Her face falls. "It's Grandma, isn't it?"

I blink. "Well—I mean, yes, but—"

Her eyes haze up like she's trying to remember the last time she saw her. "She got too sick?"

I nod. "Yeah, honey, she did."

Her pretty blue eyes water but she doesn't burst into tears. "I knew it."

I inhale, part proud of her strength, part worried about it. "Well, I'm glad you prepared yourself, but it's still very sad and it's OK to be upset."

"She gave me Pinky."

"Who?"

"The pink pig stuffy in my room. She told me her name was Piggy, but I thought she said Pinky."

The tears in her eyes never fall. If anything she looks confused. Looking up at me sincerely, she asks, "Do you think I should rename her Piggy? Like Grandma wanted?"

I blink.

How the hell do I answer that? Do I say *yes, you should, because she'd love that*. Would it make Ellie feel better that she's doing something to honor her grandmother?

Or do I say no, because we'd be making Piggy—or Pinky—a sad memory?

I step back, running a hand through my hair. "Why don't you keep callin' her Pinky. That way, we don't confuse Pinky."

She nods, relieved but still a little unsure.

Shit. Was that the wrong answer?

"I know what the second thing is," she says quietly, head dropping.

"You do?"

"I have to go live with Grandpa now? Because he's not taking care of Grandma anymore?"

"What? No. What gave you that idea?"

She shrugs, eyes still down. "I saw him here from the window yesterday."

"Oh. You didn't want to come and say hello?" Usually, she can't wait to see Cole when he comes to pick her up for visits.

She shakes her head and I don't blame her. I'm sure that man didn't look happy from *any* angle last night.

"Are you and Grandpa fighting?"

"No," I answer quickly. "No. Grandpa, well . . . he's just very sad right now. And . . . maybe a little lonely. Sometimes when you lose someone, you—" I'm about to tell her you go into a dark place and forget everything that matters—but I settle for something she might understand. "You forget who you are, the things that matter."

She furrows her brows. "I miss Grandma, too. Am I going to forget who *I* am?"

"No." I chuckle. "No, you're not going to forget who you are. You see, Grandpa and Grandma have been together for a long time. He doesn't know who he is without her. But the good news is that he'll come around." I straighten. "Until he does . . . I need to make sure you're safe with me."

She nods like she's slowly understanding. "If that's not the other thing, then what is?"

My eyes lift to the redhead standing in the archway of the kitchen. Her brown eyes pool—she shines in this light. Hell, I'm pretty sure she'd shine in any light.

I nod my head and Ellie turns, a knowing smile as her eyes meet Willow's. "Hi, Willow."

She's not . . . surprised?

I try to search for any other reaction. Anger? Disappointment? No. She just *knew* Willow was still here.

And seems to be all right with it.

When we got back last night, we briefed Dad and Ginger on Willow hanging out for a bit. That's how I put it. "*She's going to hang out for a bit.*" Because I didn't know what else to say. Everyone in the room knew why. And everyone agreed it was for the best she does.

Ellie was already asleep—safe and warm in her bed. Apparently Ginger sent Dad out last night to grab a couple of space heaters from the ranch office. They set one up in Ellie's room and one in mine. I felt awful for running out on her, missing tucking her in during my last effort to chase Willow out of town.

But Dad reassured me all that mattered was that I brought her back—and that Ellie is much safer for it.

Willow's knowing smirk right back to my little girl now has my head spinning.

"You two run into each other while I was asleep or something?" I ask.

Ellie shakes her head and wiggles a pink-covered foot toward Willow. "I knew you were here when I found my slippers next to my bed this morning."

Willow steps in, keeping her distance on the opposite side of the island. "Found one in the upstairs bathroom last night and went on a hunt for the other."

Ellie turns to me. "I like my slippers."

I know that. I almost say defensively.

Of course I know that. Ellie's always wearing something on her feet. Socks, booties Maya made her, and those pink fuzzy slippers that I keep seeing everywhere.

But I don't need another competition where my daughter's concerned, I remind myself. It's a good thing she likes Willow.

I think.

I perk a brow. "Take it that's where your nickname came from?"

Ellie's curls bounce as she bobs her head. "Willow was sleeping in your bedroom at Uncle Wilder's, and my slippers were in there. But Rose said not to go wake her friend because she's not pretty in the morning. But then Willow opened the door, stuck her hand out, and dropped them out in the hall for me," Ellie exclaims, like she's retelling the most incredible story. "She put them by my bed every day since—she says it's so I don't wake her again."

My brows rise. "Ah, so there was an agenda."

Ellie blinks. "I don't know, but Rose says she needs, like, a lot of coffee before we're allowed to talk to her."

"Don't I know it," I grumble. "Suppose we should hurry before she swipes those slippers off your feet." I step back and Ellie jumps off and beelines to Willow.

"Are you staying for a long time?"

Willow glances at me in a little panic. "That's a good question, uh . . . what's . . . well, what's a long time for someone your age?"

She thinks about it for all of two seconds. "Like *a lot* of sleeps."

Willow laughs. "Oh, you're in luck, kid. I do that a lot." She sits on a chair so she's more level with Ellie, while I try not to overpour sugar in my cup. "I was thinking, since . . ." She shrugs. ". . . I don't have much going on back home, and you and I had such a fun week together, that maybe I could stay and . . ." She stares at my girl like she doesn't know what to say. And now I'm the one panicking. "Hang out for bit, maybe teach you to play piano, take you to school, make you fun lunches?"

"Like a nanny?"

Willow winces and I try not to read into it too much. "Maybe. Would you like that?"

Ellie nods but there's something about it that doesn't sit right with me.

Willow nudges her. "Also, you give the best hugs."

Can't agree more with that. Ellie's a hugger and I love that about her.

She giggles and steps into Willow's arms. "*Now* can you tell me how long?"

Crap. Thought we dodged that one.

"I suppose till you get sick of me. Or my singing. Whichever comes first. The singing, most likely—I do that a lot."

Ellie raises her hand. "I have another question."

"Shoot."

Ellie crosses her arms. "If nannies are supposed to wake you up and get you ready for school, who's making your coffee?"

I clear my throat, stirring the caffeine in my mug. "I suppose I could leave you some in the morning before my rounds."

Willow tosses me a look, then crosses to me, her eyes fixed on my cup. She swipes it from my hands and takes a sip. Her lips cover where mine were seconds ago and I wonder—no, I *hope* it's intentional.

I watch her shoulders rise slightly as she inhales, and lower with a sigh as she tastes it. Her throat bobs as she swallows. Flicking her eyes to my chest she hands it back to me. "I'll make my own, thanks," she mutters.

She insulted my coffee. I know she's messing with me, but I can't think of a comeback. Because my stupid brain is trying to figure out how to flip this cup without making it obvious I want to taste her.

I suppress a growl. What is this woman doing to me? I shouldn't want to taste her—or have my lips seek out traces of hers like a desperate moron who's never been laid.

I set it down instead. My appetite shifting to something no level of caffeine can satisfy.

Willow raises a bored eyebrow and yawns. "So what's for breakfast, Slippers? Oatmeal?"

"Yuk."

Willow nods curtly but her head wobbles sleepily. "Powdered sugar it is." She turns toward the counter, blinking like she's lost. Then reaches for my mug again, this time gulping it all the way down.

"Not bad after all?"

"It's barely eight o'clock. It'll have to do if you want this kid fed and in a matching outfit for school," she mutters.

"Should I be worried?" I murmur back as Willow reaches for a box of my cornflakes. I know Ellie is not going to like them.

She pours them into a bowl and I peek over at my frowning seven-year-old.

A tiny level of satisfaction—or maybe validation—that I know my girl better than she does.

"It's day one, Spout, cut me a break. I'll be . . ." She yawns and damn, it's adorable. So adorable, I picture her doing it first thing in the morning . . . in my bed. "More on point tomorrow . . . probably."

I must be tired too because I'm fighting the urge to carry her back to bed. Props if I manage to get her to that guest room rather than mine.

I shake my head, snapping out of it just in time to find Willow wink back at Ellie as she sprinkles powdered sugar—as promised—into the dry cereal. I can tell it's not a lot—but Willow makes a whole show of it, like she's not leaving one flake unsprinkled.

Ellie brightens. "Yay."

"I've got to go," I rasp. "Rose'll be here to take Ellie to school before eight thirty. I'll pick her up."

"Why can't I pick her up?"

Too many reasons.

The minute a woman—who's not Rose or Ginger and looks like the human version of Jessica Rabbit—comes to pick up Ellie, the entire town will be talking. Especially with all the moms and teachers around during dismissal. Something I can't explain in front of Ellie.

"You don't have a car," I answer simply.

"Warm milk, please," Ellie asks.

"Warm milk? Who drinks warm milk?" Willow mumbles as she pulls the saucepan up off the hook and onto the stove. "Listen, lady. Big girls drink cold milk. You'd be the laughing stock of East Village Elementary if they find out you need it heated up first."

I slide over to her subtly. "You sure you going to be all right?"

She pours milk into the saucepan like it's a waste. Then meets my eyes. "Don't trust me?" she pouts.

Fuck . . . the pouting. And even though I know she's messing with me, why does she look so damn good pouting?

But right now? All I want to do is give that bottom lip a good, hard nip, leave it swollen, maybe a little bruised.

"I hope you don't plan on making that a habit—" I point to her mouth. "I don't like it."

I don't give her a chance to react. I leave her with those lips parted and move toward my daughter, giving her a quick kiss on her head before I walk out.

13

Willow

"I swear, if that man grunts at me or around me one more time—I'mma flip that silly hat right off his head," I mutter after Rose and I have dropped off Ellie at school.

I'm deflecting of course. Anything to keep my best friend from picking up the blush in my cheeks. The far-off look in my eyes. Because all I've been able to think about for the past hour is that heated blue-eyed gaze on my lips.

The bossiness.

It's all so . . . dangerously unraveling. Every move Dallas makes seems to be a deliberate challenge to the promises I made myself. Peeling off layer after layer of the pitiful protection I have over my heart. My sanity. My self-respect.

I'm done collecting scars.

And something tells me Dallas Thorne would leave the deepest one yet.

Because for a long moment there, *I liked it*. The low, gruff command that sent my pulse drumming wildly.

I liked it way more than I want to.

In my stomach, between my legs. Heck, I wanted to keep pouting just for that tone to throw me over its shoulder and teach me a lesson.

Oh, he'll teach you a lesson all right. That falling again is the fastest way to lose yourself again.

Rose smirks, turning her golf cart onto a local street. "I remember you saying cowboy hats are sexy."

"Yeah, well, the man under yours fell all over you. Mine is a grumpy, growly, and . . ." I clench my teeth, running a frustrated hand through my hair, "just a big ol' gorgeous waste of biceps."

Rose chokes out a laugh. "A what?"

"You heard me."

"Oh, I heard you call him and his gorgeous biceps *yours*."

I give her the side eye.

She gives me a grin. "Besides, I wouldn't call them a waste—he did build a pretty impressive house with those biceps."

"It's about the only thing impressive about him," I lie.

"Think you should cut him some slack. The man's been through some life-altering changes in the span of two seasons," Rose reminds me. "This dad thing is still growing on him and he's just taking it one day at a time."

Immediately, I sober up, feeling like a fool for letting my mind go places it shouldn't when all this man needs is my help. Not to trick me into falling all over him.

That's clearly a "me" problem. "Right. You're right. It's why I stayed," I remind myself out loud.

She squeezes my leg. "And I'm so happy you did. This is going to be great. Now you don't need to live with your mother—because we all know you'd rather sleep at the bar for a month than her apartment for one night. And you can save some money for a nice *elevator* building in the East Village."

"Hmm." I haven't given much thought to the "after," since no one really knows how long this case will go on. And I imagine I'm not going to up and leave once he gets legal custody of Ellie. It'll be too obvious.

"How much does a nanny gig pay around here anyway?" she asks subtly.

"Double what I was making at the bar, which I thought was pretty steep."

Rose smirks. "They do pay well. It's probably why Ginger hasn't retired. Then again, that woman lives and breathes this ranch just as much as the men do."

I frown. "I still think it's too much. Ellie's in school half the day. It feels wrong."

"The Thornes aren't hurting for money. They've got the land, the cattle, the guest cabins were full all summer too. They're not your typical big-city billionaires, but they've got money," she says reassuringly. "And don't sell yourself short. It's important, what you're doing for him."

"For *them*," I correct her. It's just as much for Ellie, if not more, as it is for Dallas.

Rose glances over, smiling at me politely. "Right." She presses a button and the ranch gates creak open, slow and wide.

I nod toward the button. "Boy, that thing sure would've come in handy that night you stole this vehicle."

Rose pushes through with a wistful grin. "Where would've been the fun in that?"

That's the difference between Rose and me. She had to overcome some serious struggles to trust men again. But it didn't stop her from falling hard for Wilder. For trusting him with her safety, and her heart.

A week ago, I would've said I wouldn't be caught dead falling for anyone's charm again.

Yet here I am . . . letting Dallas slip past every wall I've built.

"I'll drop you back at the house. I wish I didn't have to go to school today, I'd rather spend time with you," she whines. "But later, I'm teaching art for kids at the cottage if you want to swing by. Dallas is dropping Ellie off there."

"I still need to get myself settled and I need to organize those kitchen cabinets. This weekend, Dallas and I sort of shoved things any old place so we could concentrate on the rest of the house before Ellie arrived."

"Sounds exhausting. You tell your mom you're staying yet?"

"No."

"When is she expecting you?"

"Last night."

"Sounds like you've got a call to make when you get home."

I blink as she pulls up to the estate—the sprawling, endless property, interrupted only by the gentle stream of water that gives the ranch its name and the towering, breathtaking mountains that stand protectively on its periphery.

Home.

It's after three when I finally gather up the courage to call my mother. I'm slightly annoyed, but not surprised, that she didn't call to ask why I didn't arrive last night.

I move to the back porch, finding a little pathway of flowers to follow along the side of the river. It's chilly but clear out.

I press the phone to my ear, breathing in the quiet, earth-scented air, waiting for my mother's voice to ruin the peace.

The ringing stops and her voice comes on the line.

"Let me guess, you got your flight mixed up and are calling me to ask me to just drop everything and pick you up from the airport. Well, hop in an Uber, I'm not—"

"No, Mom. I'm still in . . . Colorado."

"Oh."

"I'm . . . going to . . ." I sigh, using Dallas's line again. "Hang here, for a bit," I say, calm as I can manage. "A job came up, kind of last-minute. Just . . . helping out."

"Did ya lose the one you had here?"

"No. But this one's a little more . . . well, it's important."

She gasps. "Did you get a gig at some fancy destination wedding? Luxury hotel resort?"

She almost sounds supportive. And I'm going to have to ruin it.

"I'm not singing or playing, Mom. I'm . . . helping this man. With his little girl." I give her the condensed version of my plan to stay and help "Rose's friend" so he can keep his daughter. As much as I don't like sharing someone's private business with my novel-writing mother—I had to share that part.

Silence stretches on the other end. Then finally, "Single dad? What's wrong with him?"

"He's having a rough year."

"Well, you've had a few rough years, who's going to help you?"

Actually, Dallas is helping me. In a strange way.

For the first time ever, I feel needed. If not wanted. I've been given a temporary power here. To save a little girl from being taken away from a father who's ready to give her the world.

My heart squeezes. It's almost like the universe is showing me what a real father looks like and giving me the chance to help him be one. Despite my personal doubts and scars.

And even though it's a far cry from belonging, I feel grounded here, fearless. Like I can breathe. The endless banter with Dallas has me not only defending myself, but confronting demons I've been hiding from. Without realizing it, he pushes me to face them.

And for the first time, I want to.

"Mom, please don't start."

"I don't like it, Willow. I don't like you living with some strange man in a strange town when you're supposed to be thinking about buying your—" She gasps. "Willow. Oh Willow, please tell me this was your plan all along."

"What?" I'm almost afraid to hear.

"Marry this man, Willow. But get yourself a prenup, because once you get your money—"

"Mom," I snap. "There are more important things than money—your one-track mind is exhausting, really. You haven't even asked how old she is or her name or anything like that."

She sighs. "How old is she? What's her name? Tell me all the things," she adds robotically.

"Forget it."

"Fine, fine, fill me in on all the boring stuff later, but please think about what I said."

"I will not. I told you, I'm waiting the four years for the money. I'm not going to ruin someone's life by tricking him into a—"

"Who said anything about tricking him? It would be an *understanding*. A marriage of *convenience*, darling."

"The only understanding here is your one-track mind, Mom."

"Well, my one-track mind got me a penthouse on Park Avenue, six number-one bestsellers, and my independence. Your big heart and open mind got you kicked out of *six* five-star venue gigs and a job as a nanny for a family you don't know."

You forgot to mention kicked out of my ex's apartment.

I blink away the sting in my eyes. Glancing back at the house built for someone else.

"They need me, Mom."

She sighs again, this time with a sliver of sympathy. "Everyone needs something, Willow. But when will you start taking care of your own needs?"

"Maybe I am," I mutter. But she doesn't miss it.

"Is this about the man?"

"No." How can it be about some brooding cowboy with a stone-set jaw and no-nonsense scowl?

Very easily—that's how. If my response to that throaty, domineering tone has anything to say about it.

"Good. Plenty of time to think about it later. You fall in love now, you lose everything."

"How's that?"

"Use your imagination, sweetheart. Look at what love got you so far."

I think about my self-defense class. My belongings gone. My pride and self-esteem with it. My heart sinks. The reminder to keep my guard up is like a slap in the face. "No one's falling in love here, Mom," I assure her half-heartedly.

"All right then. Love you lots. Take care. Call me when you're coming home."

Somehow, her *home* doesn't sound as welcoming as the one Rose referred to earlier.

It may not be mine, but there's a little family counting on me to make it theirs.

My lips curl into a smile. *So I'd better get to work.*

Roxanne Tully

I sweep the dust off the top of the piano mid-song. It's not often I get to play during the day. But the house is quiet. Clean. And now—dustless. And the view is unparalleled, pulling me under some Blue River spell. As if this town, and everything in it, is magical. My fingers keep moving across the piano keys—steady and sure. Grandma would be proud if she saw me now. She used to watch my eyes, making sure I only glanced down every so often, keeping my eyes on the pages of the song instead, or closed when it felt right with the song.

Something about this view makes me rethink a windowless in-home recording studio—one I've kept outlined in my head for the last two years. Windows or glass doors usually let in unwanted noise from outside, but if I had a view half as remarkable as this one, I'd figure out a way. Heck, if I could afford it, I'd keep a piano in the living room to write music and another one in the studio to record.

It makes my chest open up, the notes and words pouring out. Like I'm singing to more than just a roomful of patrons, or the sticky stain on top of the instrument from some thoughtless guest. It's almost a reminder to keep that big picture in mind. Not check the time for when my set is over.

I release a breath and let my fingers rest for a moment.

Other than a few texts from Dallas earlier, I haven't heard from him.

But I know he's been home. Because at some point—either while I was out with Rose in the morning or with Wes when he picked me up for lunch—several packages were brought into the house. Including the mattresses for the guest rooms.

I once again slept in Dallas's bed last night—brand-new space heater and all. And I did *not* spend the night debating if I should go down for a cup of tea.

The man is officially my employer. I shouldn't be thinking about his abs—or the V-shape lines that dip out of sight beneath his jeans.

I need to focus on the *point* of this whole thing. And it's not "to test my willpower."

It's to keep Ellie where she belongs.

With Dallas.

He's nervous about Cole. *I'm* nervous about Cole. Ellie's too excited to have this all taken away. It wouldn't be fair.

It wouldn't be right.

She trusts Dallas. And as much as it would be out of his control—he'll lose that trust if he lets this happen.

If *we* let it happen. I'm here to help him keep his daughter. Nothing else. No matter what.

Even if his texts do make my stomach flip for no apparent reason.

Dallas: What do you like?

Willow: A bit forward, but all right. Fragrant baths, limes, the occasional chili pepper, strong coffee and extra shots of tequila.

Roxanne Tully

Dallas: Let me rephrase. I'm at the grocery store.

Willow: Oh. My original list stands.

Dallas: Spicy tofu that makes your eyes burn it is, then.

Willow: Chicken, lots of greens, kale maybe? Watermelon.

Dallas: You call that a list?

Willow: And items two, three and four above.

Dallas: 😧

Dallas: How about wine?

Willow: Red.

I twist my emerald ring and play for a few more minutes, shifting to another song, letting the familiar tune calm me in a way I didn't know I needed.

My stomach has been in knots all day, ever since my morning with Ellie. And I can't quite pinpoint why. I can't be nervous about the nanny thing, right?

I mean, it's one thing to bring the girl her slippers and make her laugh, but I should be doing more, thinking of more. Do I need to stay on top of her mental health? Should I be asking about her favorite foods? Starting a recipe book that excludes all allergies?

This isn't babysitting, after all. There are . . . expectations.

I'm spiraling again, so I take a breath. Must be the conversation I had with Mom earlier. She always did know how to put a dampener on anything new or good in my life.

And this *is* good.

Or maybe it's Cole's visit stressing me out. And the damage he'd be doing, not just to Dallas for having to fight for a kid that's biologically his, but also to Ellie.

She doesn't need this.

I sure hope Dallas's instincts were right. *This'll blow over*.

The front doorknob twists and my fingers hop off the keys.

Dallas walks in, eyes sweeping over me once. He's in a black T-shirt, biceps straining against the sleeves, arms so solid and tanned, they look carved out of stone.

I attempt to look away but my gaze only travels down to his jeans . . . low on his hips and worn in all the right places.

Good heavens, does he keep getting better-looking or have I just been in dreamland too long?

"Hey." His eyes drop to where my fingers hover above the keys.

"Where's Ellie?" I ask, panicking a bit because he did say he was picking her up, didn't he?

He blinks, seeming slightly out of it. "Uh, Rose has a painting class at the cottage on Mondays and Thursdays. Ellie likes to go."

"Oh right," I breathe. "Rose's class."

He props the door open with a stopper and brings in bags of groceries.

"Need some help?" I push off the bench and head to the porch, where I watch him lift three bags and carry them toward the kitchen.

"I did," he grunts. "Not anymore."

I lift the last one up and follow. "What's that supposed to mean?"

"List you gave me was pathetic." He takes mine from me. "How do you not know what you need?"

"Well, you know I was here all day, did you think to maybe ask me to come with you?" I help him unload groceries onto the counter.

"Fine. The three of us can go shopping again later this week. Ellie isn't all that helpful either—always remembers what she wanted *after* I get back," he mutters, setting his hands on the counter and blowing a breath. "Sometimes

I wonder if she's testing me—to see if I'd know without her asking."

Damn if that doesn't pull something in me. Because I get it. I was just there a few minutes ago. I should be freaking out that neither one of us knows what the hell we're doing. But right now, I want to comfort him. To reassure him that as long as he's feeling this way—he's giving her everything she needs.

I wonder if the same rule applies to paid help.

I rest my elbows on the counter beside him. "Or," I start, with a murmur, "she might just still be pretty shy."

"Nonsense. She's been living with me for three months. I'm her father."

"For the last three months," I remind him. "It's possible she didn't get to ask for certain foods at her grandparents'. Maybe she just ate what they ate—she may still be getting used to *having a choice*, Dallas."

He straightens, eyeing me like I'm actually making sense. "Thought she was just being difficult."

My chest gives a little tug of defeat. I think it's the touch of vulnerability in his voice. I release a breath. "I'm not going to pretend to know much about kids, but I don't think she's being difficult at all. I think she's trying to be as easy as she can to make this work."

He frowns.

"She wants this as much as you do, Dallas." I spell it out.

"How can you tell?"

"By the look on her face when she told me she's moving in here with you." I shrug. "And the fact that she loses slippers in your room. It's a comfort thing." I used to do the same at Grandma's house—leave little bits of myself behind. A book, a hair tie, an occasional sock. It wasn't me being sloppy or careless. It was just home to me. Comfortable. Safe.

He watches me like I really am strange. But seems to accept what I'm saying, dragging a hand over his jaw. "Maybe you're right. I've convinced myself that I'm going to be getting it all wrong."

My stomach flips at his honesty. And I want to tell him something that's both comforting—and just as painfully honest.

I touch his arm lightly—but there's nothing light about it. It sends another current through me—starting at my fingertips and traveling all the way down to my toes. And it's almost as if he feels what that did to me, if his scowl at my touch has anything to say about it.

But I'm starting to be less fooled by his scowls. Especially when he's opening up about his insecurities about being a father. OK, opening up is a bit generous. Letting me drag it out of him is probably more what's happening here.

"You've done more for this girl in four days than I'll see in a lifetime."

His gaze darkens, a crease etching between his brows as he studies me.

I pull back. "Why don't I . . . make that list—for both of us—and then we can take her back to the grocery store and ask if there's anything else she'd want."

There's a beat before he blinks away, nodding like it's a step in the right direction. "OK."

I glance around, feeling like I could be doing more than just standing around pretending to know what he's going through. "And look, I tried to tidy up here, but everything's pretty much—"

"You don't have to clean, Willow." He catches my gaze, eyes and voice raw with exhaustion. "You're already doing more than you know just by being here."

"I'm pretty sure I'd go crazy if I don't do something."

He rubs the back of his neck, glancing past me toward the living room. "Maybe you could . . . teach Ellie to play? She's wanted to learn."

I smile. "Already planned on it."

His eyes linger on my face, that thread of tenderness making its scarce appearance. Or maybe it's the fatigue. "It sounded nice. Whatever that was. Heard it through the door."

I blink, fighting a strange urge to tuck my hair behind my ear like I've never received a compliment before. "It was my grandmother's favorite. She'd always ask me to play it for her. Actually, she taught it to me. It was all she knew, but it was how I started playing. It's not good, but she taught me the beginner version, so . . . I kind of kept with it."

He watches me. There's no nostalgic smile, no imagination in those eyes—the way you'd figure someone might get when you share something like that. His eyes are more . . . quietly uncertain.

I blush, giving in and pushing my hair behind my ear. "Sorry—sometimes I take small-talk compliments too far. What I meant to say was, thanks."

He shakes his head. "It's a fond memory. No need to apologize for it." He runs a hand down his face. "Guess we did kind of start off on the wrong foot."

I glance down to his thigh. "Or high kick."

He laughs and it's so real and hearty, it breaks something in me. "Definitely wrong high kick." He agrees, stepping closer, but I don't think he meant to. It's almost natural. Pulling.

But now, he's so close, I have to lift my chin to look at him. I must have moved too because my back hits the counter edge.

"Willow," he starts. "It's not that I don't like you. In fact, I think I've made it pretty damn obvious I'm attracted to you."

Good lord, I could have sworn it was the other way around.

He's definitely tired and I'm likely the one who's worn him out.

My heart skips as if a man in my life is something I could ever even consider again.

Especially not a man like Dallas. He might not be deceptive or manipulative like the others. But the man has heartbreak written all over him.

"Too damn attracted," he growls low, eyes flicking to my lips then back up to meet mine. "But I know this is the last thing either of us want or need."

I frown up at him.

"Think it's pretty damn clear you're over the hearts and flowers. Least of all from someone like me."

"That's one way to put it," I mutter.

He nods and looks around the house as if remembering who it was all for. What he's lost. What he never wants to go through again. But he doesn't define his need to hold back. Dallas would be the type to suffer in silence.

"So . . ." He scans me, jaw working like he's pained, then meets my eyes. "You're going to have to help me if I look like I'm about to cross some line."

I want to swallow but he's too close.

Do I want to help him—or even remind him—if he's about to cross some line? What if I want to see what's behind door number two—or seven?

What if I choose to be reckless—just for a moment? With *him*. What if he needs it? What if we *both* need it? Would I really be helping either of us by pushing him away?

I swallow. Yes. I would. I swore I'd never hand my heart over again. Wanting and allowing are two different things. And he's trusting me not to let either win.

I nod. "That won't be a problem, Spout."

He winces and grunts. "And you . . . *can't* call me Spout."

"It's the most unsexy name I can think of—I'm sticking with Spout."

There's a knock on the door.

This time, Dallas swallows. "That's probably Rose with Ellie."

"We should probably get it then."

I follow him as he marches across the living room and to the front door. I close the piano lid, eyes scanning the space like a seven-year-old cares if it's clean or not.

"The hell?" I hear Dallas mutter before he pulls the door open.

My heart tugs and I'm afraid it might be Cole again. But Wilder steps in instead. And he's not alone. A good-looking man in a suit—definitely no cowboy, perfectly trimmed beard and dark tousled hair—steps inside. His eyes immediately land on me, but he doesn't bother with an intro.

Rude much?

Wilder, on the other hand, does. He smiles softly. "Hello, Willow."

"Wilder, nice to see you again."

"Noah Reeves," the other man says sharply.

I smile politely. "I recognize your voice from Dallas's speaker last night."

Noah turns a hard glare on my boss. "Never have your attorney on speaker."

Dallas rolls his eyes. "Why are you here?"

"Checked in with Rachel at social services. Cole's not dropping it. He's got himself a lawyer on it." By the sharp edge of Noah's jaw, I take it he not only knows this lawyer—but doesn't like her.

"Yeah, I know—Glenda Lost."

"One and only," Noah confirms like she's something to be feared.

"That's an unfortunate name for an attorney," I chime in.

Noah steps inside, tossing his briefcase over the piano. I eye it with clenched teeth. "Well, she's about to prove you wrong, because she plays dirty. She's also on the school board, so—all too conveniently—she was helping with dismissal today and decided to flat out ask Ellie who 'the woman' staying with her is." Noah stretches his arms out like Dallas and I did something against his advice. "And Ellie said, 'My new nanny.'"

I wince.

But Dallas doesn't. He moves over to the piano and pulls the briefcase off carefully, resting it on the floor. "I'm not lyin' to Ellie. Willow is her new nanny, so—"

"Hope you plan on paying her off the books because she's *supposed* to be Ellie's stepmom."

"I never said that," Dallas snaps.

"It was implied," Noah growls back. "Rachel told me what went down here last night. Cole came over to talk, and you ambushed him with a sudden bogus engagement. He said the ring on Willow's finger couldn't possibly be real."

"Is Glenda Lost even allowed to talk to my daughter?"

Noah cocks his head. "She asked a kid a valid question at dismissal. I told you, the woman plays dirty. I don't even know how Cole's affording her, but my guess is she's doing it for pennies just to come after the biggest name in Blue River."

Dallas sighs like he doesn't disagree and I—want to practice my high kick on this woman.

I bet she's a blonde. I hate blondes.

"I don't care. Tell her she can't talk to my daughter and that she doesn't scare me one—"

"What can we do?" I ask, like the true New Yorker I am. We problem-solve like we walk the streets of Midtown, with purpose and efficiency.

Noah glances at Wilder as if to say, *here's where I drop the bomb*. "Because of what Ellie told her, Glenda's now going all the way. She'll use the fake-fiancé line in court and it'll be a strike against your character, make you look like you're hiding something."

"That's ridiculous," Dallas bites out.

Noah releases a heavy breath. "As your attorney, I'm strongly advising you here."

Dallas runs a frustrated hand through his hair. "Advising what?"

"Get hitched. For real."

"For real? Are you fucking with me, Reeves?"

"It's the only way to prove y'all weren't full of shit." He tosses his arms up with a shrug. "I'm sorry, Dal. I can't confidently help you unless you do."

Dallas cranks his neck as if to say, *then that's that*.

"No," he says flatly—at the same time as I say "Yes."

14

Dallas

Yes.

She said yes?

Has everyone lost their goddamn mind around here?

"Willow, stay out of this," I tell her, my voice low and hoarse.

"Right, 'cause you're doing so damn well on your own there," she mutters back, then turns to Noah. "What would we have to do besides, you know, signing some papers?"

"You'd need an announcement—several, in fact. In the paper, the Blue River Ranch newsletter, invite as many people from town as you can." Noah looks at me. "You'll need to invite family—make it look real."

Willow bites her bottom lip, making me wonder about her family. I know enough that she wasn't looking forward to staying with her mother. Her father's estranged. But what about the rest of her family? Does she have anyone else? I shake my head. I shouldn't want to know about her family or anything else about the woman who's somehow planted herself in my world. Invited or not.

Noah exhales. "Look, think about it. *Talk* about it. Act like you like each other and for God's sake, get your damn story straight." He runs a hand through his hair. "I'll call when I hear more. I don't know when that'll be, could be any time, so get on the same page soon."

Wilder and I exchange looks and he crosses his arms—coming to my defense. "Didn't I hear something about you helping out Levi and Tessa with a fake marriage certificate?"

Noah's jaw works. "I did no such thing." He glances at Willow like she's not to be trusted. "And even if I had, such an illegal act would have been warranted only if the bride was, say, held against her will in protective custody." He grits, "Which is not the case here."

Wilder nods in understanding. "Of course—I must have misunderstood."

I roll my eyes. "Thanks for stopping by, boys. If you'll excuse us."

Noah nods. "I can take a hint. In all seriousness, Dallas. This is your daughter. The marriage would be temporary—can be as short as three months—until we can finalize the custody transfer."

I nod back, my jaw tense. "And what the hell you suppose I tell Ellie? I'm not lying to her."

He looks me in the eye. "If it were me? I would. She might slip up to the wrong person."

I swallow. Lying is not an option—not to Ellie.

He closes his briefcase. "I've got a call scheduled with Glenda and Rachel on Thursday. Call me Wednesday and let me know what you decide."

I walk them both out with nothing to think about. There's no doubt in my mind that I'm not lying to my daughter about her having a new mother. Nobody—least of all Ellie—needs to lose a mom all over again.

I glare at Willow silently until the door shuts. "You said yes. How could you do that to Ellie?"

Her brows snap. "You said no. How could *you* do that to Ellie?"

"I'm not about to—"

"We don't have to lie to her."

"Then how do you propose I do this?"

"*We*, Dallas. How do you propose *we* do this."

"Right," I exhale, then clench my teeth.

She sucks in a breath, pacing the living room. "We start by asking her what she wants. If it's the same as what you want—that you want to be together—then we gently explain how that needs to happen, softening the truth."

I swallow. "Willow. This is a legal marriage. We'd have to . . . get divorced. That's no light commitment."

She barely blinks. "Well then, you might as well drive me back to the airport now. Because unless you're willing to do whatever it takes to keep your little girl with you, with her father—where she belongs—then you're going to lose. This Glenda Lost woman sounds like she plays hard. Let's give her a real fight."

"We can barely go ten minutes without a fight. How are we supposed to make three months work?"

She smirks. "With patience and a lot of heart."

I know she means for Ellie—but something about the way she poses it to me is . . . hauntingly alluring.

"I don't have much of either of those left," I mumble to myself.

But she overhears. Frowns. "I know. Millie, right?"

I clench my back teeth.

"Sorry," she breathes. "I'll just lock that away with all the other subjects we don't talk about."

"It's fine. And yes. That was her name."

"I guess this would have been a much easier decision if it were her you were marrying instead of . . . well, some stranger."

My stomach twists painfully. But it has nothing to do with my late fiancée. It's the flicker of something raw in her voice. Maybe even a quiet ache. Like she's some consolation prize.

I look at her. Willow's hardly been a stranger. In fact, since the day we met, there's been a connection that feels anything but strange. Not saying it feels right either. More like a puzzle that fits—but doesn't quite match the picture.

I don't want to insult Willow by leaving her assumption unanswered. In fact—I'm not sure if Millie would've taken so lightly to becoming a mother overnight. Especially to a child we didn't make together. But Willow—no loyalty or connection to me. Zero obligations. Didn't even blink twice at the thought. Her mind's on Ellie. On keeping us together.

Where mine should be.

I run a hand along my stubble. "I'm not so sure that would have worked out well either," I tell her honestly, and that's all she needs to know.

She narrows her eyes at me with a soft smirk. "I do. I think one look at that little girl and that's all it would've taken."

My chest lurches with that familiar ache. And I need to change the subject. There's no point in wondering how Millie would have reacted.

"Tell me about your family. I'm . . . going to need to know about them—to some degree."

A hesitant but curt nod. "I'm an only child. My father was in and out of our lives all through my early childhood until he finally left when I was ten. That's when my mother's career as a romance author took off. Singing *does not* run in my family. But my grandmother did teach me to play piano. I met Rose four years ago and she's the closest to family I have."

I smirk. "We were pretty quick to adopt her too." I rub my hands together, staying on track. "How'd we meet?"

"At the Lock Bar in Manhattan, of course. I was wearing your hoodie which I stole from Rose because it smelled *so* damn good. And knew exactly who it belonged to when its owner walked through the door in the matching cowboy hat."

I chuckle, wondering how much of this will be made up. "And how'd we fall in love?"

She smirks. "Easy." Then she turns and starts pacing the living room again. "Sparks started flying the moment I went back to finish my set." She glances back at me. "I felt your eyes on me all night."

Damn. "Fair enough." I cross my arms. "What happened next?"

"I came here for a visit. Fell head over heels for your daughter. Ran into you without your shirt on and I was a goner." She feigns a swoon with the back of her hand against her forehead and I hold back another laugh.

"So you fell first, huh?"

Her head snaps back up in shock. "Well, of course. You couldn't possibly. Your first and only priority is Ellie. No time for love."

I cross my arms. Getting too invested in this story. "Until . . ."

She smiles, satisfied she's got my attention. "Until you saw me with her. We spent a passionate night together—we'll of course give folks the U-rated version—and when I was about to leave town forever, you stopped me. Confessed your eternal love and asked me to stay."

"Should probably dial it down a bit if you want anyone who's ever *met* me to believe that story."

She scans me head to toe. "Unless you've got a better story, we're sticking with mine."

I grumble. "Fine. But you're going to get a lot of people calling bullshit if you use that 'eternal love' crap."

She crosses her arms. "Fine—when we get to it, I'll just hand it over to you." She slaps my arm as if to demonstrate. "Oh, Dallas *loves* this part of the story. You tell 'em, dear."

I roll my eyes. "Eternal love it is."

Her eyes light up with the win and it makes my stomach fizz because . . . I made her happy. Even if it is for a bullshit reason.

I shift my focus, checking the time for Ellie's return. "You'll help me tell her?"

Her grin is soft when she shrugs, meeting my gaze. "Where else would I be?"

Wilder: Sorry for the ambush earlier.

Dallas: It's fine.

Wilder: Y'all talk?

Dallas: She did most of it.

Wilder: I would've guessed. And?

Dallas: We'll do it. But keep it quiet until we talk to Ellie.

Wilder: Goes without saying. What about Willow? You're both in agreement?

Dallas: It's just for three months—give or take. She's fine with it.

Wilder: And you?

It's a loaded question. If you'd asked me a day ago, I'd have said no goddamn way I could live with this woman.

Dallas: I'll do anything for Ellie.

Wilder: Willow hardly classifies as *anything*.

Fallen Willow

> **Dallas:** Try spending a weekend with her.

My heart turns to shreds when I see Ellie walk through the front door just a little before supper time. Her usual smile is upside down. Her eyes meet mine for half a second—enough for me to see she's sad—then dip back down to the hardwood floor.

I lift my gaze to Rose. A faint twitch of her lip. Uneasy and unsure.

My mind races at what it could be. Bad day at school? Was it something Glenda said to her that could make her hate me?

Like the fact that I barely knew her mother? That I have no idea what I'm doing now that it's just the two of us?

I'm so stunted in my fear, I forget to greet my girl.

"Hey sweetie, welcome home," Willow says, crouching to her level. "How was your art class?"

Rose steps in. "Um . . . we've had better days, right, Ellie?" She flips over a sixteen-by-twenty canvas covered in scribbles.

Ellie glances at it without a response.

"I would have dropped her off earlier today but Wilder said to . . ."

I nod then shake my head. "It's fine, thank you." I reach for her art. "And . . . I'll go hang up this thing of beauty."

Willow straightens and reaches for it, then Ellie's hand. "I know just the place. Come on, Slippers."

Rose and I watch them disappear into the kitchen. "I don't suppose that was the assignment today?" I mutter low.

Rose winces. "It was to draw your house and your favorite thing in it. I'm sorry," she sighs. "I thought it was fitting, given . . ."

"I know, thanks. You know I always appreciate everything you've done."

She glances over my shoulder. "She's been like this since I picked her up."

"I'll talk to her." *About a lot of things*. My heart hurts at the thought. All that stuff Willow was saying about Ellie not really being difficult but actually trying to meet me halfway in this relationship—is about to blow up in smoke.

There were times Ellie's acted out a little, but she's never downright avoided my eyes, or given someone a hard time.

How do I find out what it is without being pushy or demanding? Rose always talks about gentle parenting but I didn't exactly get the handbook on that from my parents. When I acted out, Dad yelled and Mom hauled us out for yard work.

"Dallas!"

My head snaps up. "Yeah."

"You've got her tomorrow, right? I've got an early class in Denver. Maybe I could leave Willow my cart?"

"Cart," I grumble, shifting my attention. "She know how to drive that thing?"

Rose smirks. "Who do you think walked me through it when I drove it out of your lot?"

I scoff, feeling a strange ease in my chest. "Shoulda guessed." I glance over my shoulder, wondering what I'm about to walk into, and thankful she's here to help me through it. "Other than aiding in auto theft, she trustworthy?"

I don't know why I ask. Maybe it's a reminder that Willow's still a stranger. A stranger I'm counting on helping me through a tough moment with my kid.

But her response makes me glad I did.

Rose smiles softly. "Trust her more than myself most days."

"Thanks for your help with Ellie today. See you Thursday?"

"Definitely." She winks.

I close the door and go find out what garbage Glenda—or anyone else—has been feeding my child to make her come home sad.

Willow and Ellie are sitting beside the kitchen counter, Ellie's legs wiggling as she watches Willow trace her scribble.

I tread carefully. "What's going on?"

Willow's got her tongue out, eyes fixed on the canvas. "I'm teaching Ellie to make 3-D art." She stops and admires her work. "OK, so now you shade it in."

Ellie pushes it back. "You do it. I'm going to ruin it," she snaps.

"Ellie," I call and am immediately annoyed at the tone I just took.

Her eyes widen with alarm and my heart stops a little. She recovers quickly with a shrug of her shoulders. "Hi, Dallas."

I glance at Willow. She doesn't seem surprised that my daughter is on a first-name basis with me. And by the look in her eyes, she's not judging either.

I release a slow breath, crossing the room toward them. I rest my elbow on the counter. My voice tender and low. "Something wrong, sweetheart?"

She nods.

"You want to tell me about it?" I wait for it. The accusations that I never wanted her. That she wasn't made with love. That—

"I think I did something bad today."

What? Her?

I glance at the art—clearly an act of rebellion. And the next thing comes out easy. Naturally. Because hell, it's all I want to do. "Maybe I can help?"

She meets my eyes for another half-second. "A lady asked me about Willow and I told her she's my nanny."

I glance at the woman behind her. "Why is that bad?"

"It *felt* bad. Like I shouldn't have said anything. Like maybe it was just a secret between the three of us for now."

Kid's got my instincts.

And while I should be proud, I don't want to raise a child who doubts everyone.

I look at Willow again, if only as the anchor I need to keep me grounded so I don't blow a fuse. Glenda used my kid and left her feeling guilty for it. There's only one way I can see of fixing this.

And that's to make it OK. To make sure she knows she didn't betray anyone.

I glance at Willow and it's clear she's giving me the choice here. A subtle nod to let me know she's on board with whatever.

And that kind of support—is exactly what I didn't know I needed.

Shifting my focus to Ellie, I push a loose curl from out of her face. "You didn't do anything wrong, cupcake."

She looks up at me, blinking. "I didn't?"

My insides tumble over themselves at the hope in her eyes. I release an easy breath and shake my head, taking a seat on the chair next to her.

"You know how we're working on getting you to live here with me all the time?" I press my forehead to hers. "Because I'm your dad and you're my favorite girl?"

She smiles and gives a small nod.

"Well, some people might think it's not good for you to be here if it's just you and me. Some people think you might need . . . more."

"Like a mommy."

"Well, yeah. But I know that you and I would do just great, right?"

This time—the nod doesn't come. Her eyes drift to the space between us.

I swallow hard. *Fucking this up already.*

I look at Willow and she doesn't miss a beat, running a hand down Ellie's arm, grabbing her attention. "Ellie. Why did you bring your stuffed animals here from your grandpa's house?"

"Because Grandpa can't take care of them like I can. And I'll miss them."

Willow scrunches her nose. "So some people think that your daddy can't take care of you the way—well, a nanny—or someone *like* a mommy—could."

"What people? Rachel and Ms. Glenda?"

"Yes."

Ellie's head snaps back to me with a gasp. "I know. We can tell them that Willow's my mommy." She perks up and this is where I see the conversation going exactly where I didn't want it.

Willow wraps a loose arm around her shoulders, leaning in to whisper. "We were thinking the same thing, Slippers." She holds up a finger. "Just as long as you understand that it's not going to be—well, it'll only be for a short while. I might . . . eventually need to go home."

"Why? Is your house bigger?"

She laughs. "No."

"Is it better?"

Willow rolls her eyes dramatically. "How can it be?"

Ellie shrugs. "Then why leave?"

Willow's brows jump around, eyes skittering like she's close to panicking. "All I'm saying is, after we . . ." Willow winces, "finish playing house . . . I might just go back home. Do you . . . understand?"

Ellie smiles and hops off the stool, racing to the play area in the living room with a spring in her step.

Willow bites her bottom lip and I twist with doubt over the seed we just planted. "What do we do if she tells the wrong person that this is only for a *short while*."

Willow huffs like that's the easy part. "You tell them that it's our way of easing her into this. In case it doesn't work out—she won't be disappointed. I lost count of the number of times my mother would tell me, 'Daddy's staying with us again for *a while*,' in case he took off again."

Something about this still doesn't sit right with me. I don't want Ellie's heart broken. Running a hand down my face, I march out into the living room.

"Ellie, you heard what Willow said, this . . . isn't forever. Willow will be going home."

The girl doesn't even blink. "No, Daddy. She said she *might* be going home." She grins wide and grabs her backpack, then races up the stairs. "Be right back."

"Where are you going?"

"I'm going to draw my favorite part of my house like Rose asked."

My stomach squeezes and I pinch the bridge of my nose. "Shit. Did you hear that?"

Willow grins, leaning casually against the archway. "I did. She called you Daddy."

15

Willow

The soft notes of the piano fill the house on Wednesday afternoon. I've been working on a new song. No lyrics yet, but I'm in love with the melody. I didn't set out to write something new today. Not with Ellie coming home any minute, so I'll need to switch to nanny mode. I started with something familiar. A tune I've played in almost every set—just to get my fingers moving. But somewhere along the way, the rhythm shifted. Like it's taken on a life of its own.

I like it.

I pause for a moment to write down the notes the way they spilled out of me, grinning to myself as I try to come up with a name for this rendition.

But a prickle on the back of my neck tells me I'm no longer alone.

I smile without turning. "Hey, Slippers, when'd you get home?"

She pads across the room. "That was so pretty."

I scrunch my nose since I don't think I was going for *pretty*. "Thanks." I slide over on the bench. "Want to try?"

She nods and settles beside me, her little hands hovering over the keys like she's ready to pounce. But she doesn't, she waits for me.

"Go ahead. It doesn't bite if you don't know the notes. Just press some keys and listen."

Her eyes widen like I've just told her it's OK to break some rules, but then light up with excitement. Ellie taps tentatively on one key, then a few others, speed picking up as if she'd just discovered a new power.

"It's like . . . different voices."

"Talking to each other," I agree. "You don't have to know what they're saying to stay and listen." I nudge her.

Her grin fades. "Grandma used to play."

"I know. This was hers, wasn't it?"

Ellie eyes it and nods.

I bite the corner of my lip. "Did she tell you she was going to teach you?"

She shrugs a shoulder. "That was a long time ago."

My chest tightens and I flip through the pages toward the front of my songbook I'd brought with me. There was no way I was leaving it in storage with all the rest of my things. I turn to the first song I learned and wink. "This one's special. *And* pretty."

Resting my hands over the keys, I let them fall into the pattern that would never change. It comes as natural as breathing.

"This is the one that got me playing when I was a little older than you."

Something in her expression hits me hard. Bright warmth lighting up her face as she listens to the notes. When my throat tightens with the threat of tears, I stop, releasing a sharp breath.

She stares up at me. "Was that the end?"

I shake my head, watching her. The glow in her eyes pulled me right back to that afternoon at Grandma's. "No. I just . . . I remember the first time I heard it."

She smiles. "And you liked it?"

I smooth her hair. "It was the prettiest thing I'd ever heard." Straightening, I motion for her to mirror my posture and the position of my hands.

She does, bouncing into place.

"Let's start. Copy what I do on your side. It'll sound a little different, but that's OK." I press the first few keys a little sharper than usual, in slow succession.

Ellie waits a beat like she's repeating it in her head, then tries on her side.

With each new note, her face is less twisted, and more like she's discovering secrets to a superpower.

"That's it." My smile is wide and I can tell this girl grew up with an ear for music.

I can't wait to hear her sing.

I'm about to move on to the second verse when I hear gentle footsteps—or as gentle as those cowboy boots can sound on wooden floorboards—behind us. I glance back, catching him lingering in the archway against the wall.

His jaw is soft, eyes warm. The usual rough lines of his face mostly faded. I turn back almost too quickly. As if staring too long would ruin it. It's not often I catch him . . . unguarded and almost gentle. A part of me wants to hold on to that look. To the fullness it left in my chest. Because I know it won't last.

There's a soft knock on my bedroom door after my shower. Ellie's been asleep for over an hour. I slip on a short cotton bathrobe over my pajamas and pull it open.

Even though I know it's him on the other side of the door, my heart does some kind of somersault as I pull it open. He's standing there like James Dean in his black T-shirt and faded jeans. His signature get-up, from what I can tell. The dim light shadows him, catching the perfect cut of biceps I have to keep reminding myself to tear my eyes from.

Not that it matters . . . because Dallas's deep blue eyes are raking over me, slowly. Sweeping over my damp hair, flushed cheeks, bare legs.

"Hey," he starts on a gravelly breath.

I open my mouth but he cuts me off.

"The engagement announcement went out a few hours ago."

My heart rate kicks up. "That was . . . quick."

Even though Noah gave us until today, Dallas and I called him Tuesday morning together to confirm our agreement. And that Ellie's on board—with the truth. After he reamed into us for taking such a "dumb risk," he moved forward with his plans to take Glenda on in family court.

Then, not so gently, instructed us to move forward with our part—the public announcements. *The bigger the better.*

Dallas rubs the back of his neck. "It's easy when you got the pros on it. Ginger drafted the ranch newsletter and Rose handled the social media stuff."

I hold my breath. "You're worried about something." Is he worried about lying to so many people? I haven't even considered what he's risking if people find out.

"No. I just wanted to let you know things might be moving pretty fast from here—things I'm not even sure I can keep up with. I don't want you to feel overwhelmed by it."

I tilt my head. "Do you?"

He shakes his head, looking off to the side for a brief moment before meeting my eyes. "Not yet."

I grin at him. "Let me know when you do, I'll remind you." It's my way of telling him I know how important this is. And I'm not backing down. We're in this together . . . for Ellie.

He nods, his eyes warmer than usual but not entirely convinced as he watches me like he doesn't know if he should trust me—or if he could do this without me.

I hold his gaze because there's more in them.

"You taught her your grandmother's song."

My lips part because he remembered the melody. But I don't call attention to it. "She's as eager as I was to learn it."

Fallen Willow

He considers that for a moment. "I like that." He takes a step inside my bedroom and freezes, head dropping like he's crossed some invisible line. Then with one last sweep over me with his eyes, he takes a step back. "Thank you for that. Good night, Willow."

16

Willow

I smooth my palms down the sides of my dress, shifting nervously in front of the full-length mirror. It's a deep green knee-length cocktail dress. Ellie picked it out because she liked how it matches my ring. She's in a short yellow one, sleeveless and frilly at the shoulders.

I inhale a deep breath. "So, should we head down to say hello to everybody?" I ask, hearing the shakiness in my voice. Still hazy on how I went from being tossed into a truck and off to the airport, to hosting a house-warming slash impromptu engagement party for sixty people, in less than a week.

I'd clearly underestimated just how big the Thorne name is in this town. Because the response to the announcement came strong—and hard. Folks from town screaming for more information on the wedding, an engagement party, a reason to celebrate with us.

Hence tonight's housewarming. One Dallas and I felt cornered into hosting. It's supposed to be an open invitation to celebrate his new home—well, *our* new home—and upcoming nuptials. Simultaneously dodging the need for a bogus engagement party.

"Yes, I'm ready," Ellie squeals. She does love a good crowd. I only like a big crowd when it means more tips.

Another car crunches over the gravel outside, the tires grinding slowly to a stop. Ellie peeks out my bedroom window. It faces the ranch, unlike Dallas's, which faces the river and mountains. "It's Uncle Silas and his friends," Ellie announces giddily.

I narrow my eyes, having been given the family tree earlier this week. "*The* Silas Thorne, huh?" I mutter. I'm not as big a hockey fan as Rose so I don't expect to be star-struck or anything. But who can ignore members of the Denver Kings when they're right there in your living room?

Ellie smiles and nods. "He's funny. And he always brings me Swedish fish." She skips to the door. "Let's go down."

I bite my lip. "You go ahead. I'll be down in a minute."

Once she's gone, I close my eyes and exhale, trying to tune out the light music and chatter floating up.

The irony isn't lost on me. Downstairs, dozens of strangers are waiting to toast to a future I have no intention of living. A future I've cut out of my five- or even ten-year plan.

Now I need to plaster on a smile and let everyone believe that it's all I want. That marriage, trust . . . forever . . . are things I actually believe fit with who I am.

They don't.

They're things I've shaped myself to live without.

And tonight is just about pinning on another smile for just another crowd.

Except I can't hide behind a piano and keep my head down.

My heart rattles around inside my ribs as the house fills with even more unfamiliar voices. Louder, the house growing more excited.

I haven't heard Dallas's voice in a while and I'm wondering if he plans to look out for me tonight. Likely not. He's about as thrilled as I am about all this and will no doubt disappear every chance he can.

There's a knock on my door and my stomach flips, hoping I'm wrong, that Dallas *is* checking on me. This morning over coffee, he grumbled something about sneaking off upstairs to make it look like we can't keep our hands off each other.

I'm about to pull it open to ask if it's that bad already, but Rose sticks her head in. "Are you decent?"

I frown. "In what context?"

Her eyes scan the room before pushing the door wide open. A petite blonde female is with her, bouncing inside uninvited, like Goldilocks. "Hi there. Oh, you're a pretty one. I'm Charlie."

I perk a brow at Rose and she answers my unspoken question. "Noah's wife."

I look down at the ray of sunshine with a chuckle. "No, you're not."

Her grin is wide. "Almost a whole year now. Noah sent me up here for quality control."

"Quality what?"

She pushes me aside and opens up my closet, looking horrified. "What's all this?"

"My clothes," I tell her.

Since I'm staying a while, Dallas took me and Ellie shopping the other day. And Rose was right—money's no object for the man. He practically let Ellie and me go all *Pretty Woman* in that mall.

"I see that. *Why* are they in the guest room?" She glances back at Rose and cocks her head. "Help me out here." She grabs two handfuls of hangers.

Rose winces, pulling me aside. "Why don't you let us make it look like you're a couple up here while you head down."

I point a finger at her. "That woman seems intense, watch her."

She rolls her eyes. "She runs a children's bookstore—she's as harmless as they come."

I nod, still unsure about all these people. But if Rose trusts them, I suppose I could—for now.

The two of them haul my clothing and a few random articles of mine into Dallas's bedroom.

I shake my head, huffing out a breath as I smooth my dress once more and turn toward the stairs.

I stop short when I find Dallas standing at the top of the landing. His eyes roam down my figure.

"You look nice." The words escape with a raspy breath and a hard swallow.

I don't comment that I could certainly say the same for him. Dark jeans, light blue shirt, that black cowboy hat. And a bowtie with a dark blue emblem. Instead, I stand there and suck in a breath, wishing to God all those people would just go away.

And as hard as I try, I'm having trouble putting Dallas in that category.

Because the last thing I need right now is for him to be watching me with those blue eyes like he's saying the same damn thing.

You're going to have to help me if I look like I'm about to cross some line.

I've had to replay those words a few times this week—but more as a reminder to myself.

Because he hasn't so much as hinted at crossing some line. The minute he realizes he's been staring too long or we're in the same room *alone* for longer than your average small talk, he bolts.

Not that I can blame him—the stakes are high.

No room for screw-ups.

Me included.

I get a whiff of his cologne—or whatever this man does to smell so damn good. A mix of cedar and fresh-cut wood, layered with warm spice. "Thanks, some say green's my color."

His eyes roam over me again with a subtle nod that tells me he agrees. Either that or he's undressing me with his eyes.

Something fizzes in my belly. And my hand—by its own accord—presses against his chest as if to physically stop him from breaking down any more of my walls—which I realize aren't made of steel, but hell, they're crumbling to the floor like a pile of mulch.

My eyes fall to where my hand lands, expecting him to back away or set it down like a gentleman.

Goddammit. You had *one* job.

To my surprise, Dallas grips my wrist, holding my hand where I had it, and gives it a gentle tug, pulling me close. Making my pulse spike. Then without another word, he rakes his hand through mine and walks me down the stairs.

His voice is soft against my ear as we hit the bottom step. "Don't leave my side."

I turn my chin up. For the first time tonight, the knot in my chest eases. And maybe just for tonight, I can trust that I'm not alone. "That goes for you too."

Nearly every corner of the lower level is filled with guests. I smile knowingly at several like I'd do with any bar patron I don't recognize but accidentally lock eyes with.

"Do me a favor and squeeze my hand if I'm supposed to look like I know someone we start talking to."

He doesn't respond. Not with words anyway. He nods at a few people and squeezes my hand as he guides me toward a dark-blond male. Tall, light-skinned, and handsome. I don't know my hockey players as well as Rose does, but I know this man is a Thorne. He smiles back at me with a familiar smirk, glancing at Dallas as if to say he's got this.

"Silas," I say with a soft breath, trying to suppress the question on my tongue.

He sets his drink down and I step into his embrace. He's got a good grip, strong, confident, and a little bit playful. "Great seeing you again. Thanks for coming."

"Hey, no worries, sis. But listen." He points a finger. "I want a rematch next week. And this time, I'm bringing my own deck of cards. Can't trust you city girls." He winks.

A brunette swats at him like she's offended. She's pretty—beautiful in fact, with warm features. She also looks vaguely familiar.

Silas winces, rubbing his arm. "Oh please, you lived in Manhattan for less than a decade."

She shrugs her shoulders. "Always a city girl at heart." Then she smiles brightly at me. "Hi there! I'm Pepper." She tugs the arm of another broad-shouldered man, grabbing his attention. "This is my husband, Chase."

Now *him*, I know. Captain of the Denver Kings hockey team. And now I remember why Pepper looks familiar. It was on national television when Pepper Woods—supposedly Chase Reeves' fiancée—dumped him in the middle of a big game after going missing for days. The clip only showed her appearing on the sidelines and handing him back a massive engagement ring. Apparently, they worked things out.

I glance up at Dallas, who's busy looking over my head at some other guests, which means he's not so concerned about these two.

Chase stretches out a hand. "Congratulations and thanks for having us. Impressive place you got here." His brow twitches at Dallas. "Quite a surprise, Thorne. Can't decide if I should hug you or stage an intervention."

Another swat from the brunette. "He's kidding. Marriage is a beautiful thing. "

Tell that to the fifty percent divorce rate.

"But don't just take our word for it," she continues. "Ask my best friend, Charlie. She married Chase's brother Noah last year. They're really happy."

I laugh because somehow the words Noah and *happy* don't work for me, but fine, I'll take her word for it and smile like I could just picture it. "Well, we're excited—despite all the warnings." I squeeze Dallas's side playfully. "Right, babe?"

Dallas sucks in a breath. "Right." Then he nods at Chase. "If I could get a list of dos and don'ts when you get a chance . . ."

The five of us laugh—less than half of us genuinely—grabbing some attention from a few guests.

At that, we make a few more rounds, but there are no more subtle squeezes, which means most of these people are supposed to be exactly what they are . . . strangers.

Finally, Dallas pulls me aside.

"Did I say something wrong?" I ask immediately.

"You're a natural," he assures me, leading me toward the kitchen. "I just need a drink." He glances back. "And to tell you that Glenda just walked in."

I pause mid-stride, but know better than to turn back for a good look at her.

Sensing my dilemma, he twists me under the archway, wrapping his arms around me as if we just stopped for a private moment.

He leans down to my ear. His breath is warm, sending shivers everywhere. "She's the freakishly tall blonde looking this way."

I smirk like he's telling me something naughty and, ever so subtly, sweep my eyes over her but don't let them linger. Instead, I twist into him, my forearms pressed between us. It feels so natural, so good, being wrapped up in his arms. And the way he's looking at me now, like he might feel it too, makes my chest ache.

"I think I need a mental break," I whisper. "And to check on Ellie."

"She's fine. And maybe things are different in the city, but around here, a mental break doesn't include checking on others." He lifts an eyebrow. "Come on, let's get you a drink."

I deadpan him. "Ellie's not *others*." Then I give him a small smile. "But I won't turn down a drink."

His chest rises as he takes me in again. As if I've changed over the last few minutes. "She's in the kitchen." He glances back as if to make sure. "Everyone in there right now is a safe space. Including Noah's father—Aiden Reeves. He's the one talking to my dad."

My eyes stretch. "As in world champion wrestler Aiden Reeves?"

"He's not easy to get one over on, so Dad told him our plan. You can trust him."

I nod and follow him into the kitchen, our hands splitting when I head toward Ellie. She's propped up on the island, picking off the spread Wesley prepared.

Dallas steps over to the self-serve bar, where Connor, Aiden, Wilder, and Noah are talking. I watch as Dallas pours himself an ounce of whiskey and mumbles something to the men. Noah's eyes trail to the front door as if looking for someone.

"What kind of cheese is this?" Ellie asks. "It's not yellow."

"An expensive kind." Wes plucks it from her and replaces it with cheddar. He hands me something too. Something cold and delicious. "Margarita, if I recall?"

"Thank you. I either need four of these tonight or none—keep my mind in check."

"Let's start with one, but eat something too. There's enough food to feed a small town—"

"Why the hell do I need to give a speech?" Dallas suddenly hisses loud enough for us to hear.

Wes lifts a tray like it's his cue. "Hey kid, come help me refill some platters."

He helps Ellie down with his free hand and they step out into the living room.

"They all know why they're here," Dallas continues, and I move to stand beside him.

The man Dallas pointed out as Aiden smiles warmly at me, stretching out a hand. "Willow, pleasure to meet you." He looks about a decade younger than Connor, similar height and a total silver fox. "Congratulations."

"Thank you. And it's wonderful meeting you too. I'm pretty sure my mother stalked you to be a cover model for one of her books."

He chuckles. "My daughter-in-law owns a bookstore in Hideaway Springs. Would have been very awkward if I ended up on one of those shelves."

Dallas shakes his head, leaning down toward me. "Remember when we talked about saying things in your head rather than out loud?"

I nudge him with my hip. "You said this was a safe space."

Aiden's eyes flick to Connor. "Thought you said this thing's a sham?"

Connor grins, gaze shifting between Dallas and me. "Thought it was."

"Can we focus?" Noah snaps. "First off—" He points between me and Dallas. "Don't make Charlie and me give you two lessons on affection—"

"Someone's still gotta explain that one to me," I mutter.

"Second, you're giving a speech, Dallas, because they're all expecting one."

Aiden sighs. "What my son is trying to say is, just thank them all for coming and tell them when and where it's happening."

I blink.

Dallas glances down at me. "Um ... we haven't thought about any of that yet."

Noah checks his watch. "Well, you've got thirty minutes to figure it out and let everyone here know."

Fallen Willow

Dallas runs a hand down his face. "I need air."

Aiden, Wilder, and Noah step aside to give him space, but Connor doesn't. He stares at his oldest son like he means business. "If you *do* get up there, remember who you're talking to. This is your town. Your friends. They'll smell bullshit. They'll know you're not being real. Don't give them a reason to doubt this."

17

Dallas

Glenda's wearing a tight navy dress, leaning against the piano, and chatting to a few guests, a thin smile on her lips.

Her neck twists and our eyes meet.

No doubt about it—this woman's aiming for mayor or something, and she's making sure everyone knows no one's above the law, no matter their land or money.

I turn to Willow. She's been amazing tonight. Patient, easy, responsive to my every subtle gesture. She doesn't question anything. Doesn't go off-script. Instantly likable.

I'm about to give her a warning that Glenda is heading this way, but she cuts me off. "Let me do it."

"What?"

"The speech. Look, I know it's the last thing you want to do, but I don't know these people—or I won't for long anyway. I can say a few words and we can call it a night. Just give me the cue when."

It takes me a minute to respond. My eyes scan this woman who keeps surprising me. I grin. "Slow down, superwoman. I don't doubt you can say all the words. But I think it needs to be me."

At some point, she needs to stop being my hero and let me be hers. She's done enough this week—and tonight's been trying for her. I can tell by the slump of her shoulders as the night went on. That bright smile starting to dim. The fidgeting with her ring less aggressive—like she's lost the energy.

She smiles up at me weakly.

"What I was going to tell you was—"

"And when do I get to meet the blushing bride?" Glenda's voice is sharp, but her perfume carries something stronger.

Willow doesn't flinch. She shifts closer to me. Her fingers brush mine. I catch the signal and slide my hand into hers like it belongs there.

Willow puts out her hand, her smile not quite reaching her eyes. "No blushing here," she says, the smooth confidence back in her voice like she's been saving it.

Glenda takes her hand. "Congratulations, I guess?"

Willow feigns confusion, then laughs. "Oh, I get it. OK, bring on all the 'married life' comments, we can take it. But we're not worried, are we, my love?"

A ball catches in my throat, jaw tightening as I suppress the swallow. For a second, I forget we're pretending. Forget there's anyone else in the room at all. They're just two words. A line. An intention to sell this. But my chest goes tight regardless. "Not at all," I manage to say. "I do like myself a good challenge."

Glenda glares at me. Then turns a fake smile on my fiancée.

My very real fiancée, because apparently—there's going to be a very real wedding.

"So tell us about yourself, Willow." She looks around. "Is your family here?"

"Think you misunderstood the invitation, Glenda," I start sharply. "We invited folks who want to celebrate our union—not question it."

Willow grazes my arm. "It's all right." She turns a tight grin toward Glenda. "The *Thornes* are my family, now. So if you'll excuse us . . ."

"That sure was fast, wasn't it?" she muses. "The announcement."

Noah steps beside us. "If you're here to ambush an innocent little girl again, you're asking for a restraining order."

"Don't be silly, Noah. I'm on the school board. I was merely helping out the dismissal staff. They were low on—"

"In other words, if I were to subpoena records such as timecards and policy on minimum staff for dismissal, I'd find that someone called in sick and you were their last resort?"

She smiles tightly. "I respect your dedication to your friend—"

"My client."

Her jaw ticks. "But this isn't about me."

"It is when I'm your opposing counsel. Now do us a favor and let the happy couple enjoy their night without you breathing down their necks."

She smiles. "Fine. But since you're here, I'm doing you the courtesy of letting you know that I've petitioned for Ellie to move back in with Cole, as he still has legal custody."

Noah doesn't flinch. He keeps his piercing blue eyes on Glenda. "Guys, if you'll excuse us for a moment."

I don't hesitate to lure Willow away. I suspect Noah's about to drop some unethical threats against the vulture.

I pull her behind the stairs, finding those pretty brown eyes swimming with tears. All at once, I'm outraged, concerned, and filled to the brim with a whole new level of protection.

But it's not for my daughter right now.

"Don't tell me she scared you, Sunset." I swipe a strand of hair behind her ear to get a better look at her face.

"She's going to take Ellie back to Cole," she whispers, her voice cracking. "Who would do that? What kind of person, what kind of court would let a child be bounced around—"

I press my finger to her mouth as her voice grows loud. And it was a mistake—feeling the soft tremble of those lips.

They part slightly and it's almost like a kiss to my flesh.

"She's not going anywhere. Not for any longer than a short visit, I promise."

She's breathing hard. With fear or desire—I'm not sure either of us know. A tear slips down the slope of her nose and I swipe it with my thumb. I'm not a shusher, but I find myself shushing her, my fingers stroking her jaw like they've got a mind of their own. She's slipping and I feel helpless. She's been so strong, so willing, but one threat against my little girl and she spirals like it's a personal attack.

One I'm feeling with her.

"How can you know that? What are we even doing here if I can't do the one thing that—"

Hitting my breaking point, I cover her mouth with mine, sliding my hand into her hair, gripping the back of her neck, anchoring her to me as I kiss her with an intensity I can't comprehend.

Her throat vibrates with a moan and my body reacts, plastering my hips against hers. I can feel her pulse drumming beneath my thumb. Fast. Alive. Wild.

The seam of her mouth opens, giving me a taste of tequila, lime, and something out of this world.

Something that's all Willow.

God, she's soft.

Every inch of her responds, fits like that damn puzzle piece.

When whistles and applause roll in like a rough wave, we break apart. Our eyes stay connected for no more than a second. I might not know what she's thinking, but I know we're both done with this crowd.

Noah wraps an arm around my shoulder, a rare smirk on his face. "Nice touch, Romeo. But Glenda was already out the door."

"What did you say to her?"

He glances around. "Is Ellie about?"

"Rose took her upstairs to bed when Glenda showed up."

"Good. And don't worry, she's going to convince Cole not to petition for Ellie to be returned to him in the interim. But it can still happen."

"How'd you do it?" I ask again. Normally, I don't care for details on his tactics, but Glenda isn't easily manipulated. I need to make sure his threat is rock solid. And legal.

"Courts generally have strict protections against minors being approached or manipulated. All I had to do was tell her how much she upset Ellie that day, and she knew enough to know I'd use it should my client decide to sue her personally." He smirks.

"You're worth every penny."

He slaps my shoulder twice and nods to the stairs. "Now, while you've got their attention."

I sigh and let go of Willow's hand. She stands aside with a tentative grin. "Good luck," she murmurs.

I swipe my bottom lip, then move up a few levels on the stairs, making nearly every head in the room turn. "Thank you all again for coming. We are . . ." I glance at Wilder, who's wincing on my behalf. ". . . overjoyed, with such enthusiasm for . . . this wedding."

Crickets.

I stare back at the same faces I last saw at Millie's funeral barely seven months ago. The same faces the two of us imagined watching us with happy tears and wide grins as we danced at our wedding.

My gut twists.

My lips burn.

I fight back a swallow and scoff at the crowd. "Frankly, I think y'all must be pretty bored to make such a fuss over us. Guess there was no game on tonight?"

One . . . maybe two laughs.

Tough crowd.

I catch Dad leaning against the back wall, his head shaking lightly.

Be real.

The hell does he expect me to be real about? This isn't how I pictured it. The pressure, the lies. The consequences. This isn't even the woman I—

My eyes sting and I pinch the bridge of my nose. "I'm sorry." I suck in a sharp breath. "The truth is, Willow is a . . . beautiful soul." I swallow the lump, glancing at her. "Who saved me." A chuckle escapes and I sniff. "Think we all know this wasn't the wedding y'all were expecting this fall." I watch their faces, the sad subtle shakes of their heads. The motion takes me back to the dark day I buried her. These same heads lowered with sorrow and grief.

"Neither was I." I grip the stair rail like I might fall over. "I'll always love Millie," I breathe, my nose tingling again. "Y'all know that. But life had other plans. In the shape of a seven-year-old, who many of you—all right, all of you—know came to me when I thought I'd lost everything. She not only got me back on my feet, but she showed me a new kind of love, with just her voice, her trust, her eyes." I press my hand to my chest. "One

I'd no doubt die without." A handful of guests glance at Willow—a gentle reminder that they're not here to celebrate the life I'm building with my daughter. They're here for her—and me. They're all waiting for a reason there's a wedding after all—and I need to give it to them. "Just when I thought she was all I needed . . ." I release a breath and shift my gaze to Willow for a moment. The woman who's been breaking down the iron gates I've locked my heart inside. "My heart made a little extra room."

A soft murmur ricochets around the crowd. It's almost deafening and Willow blushes at the sudden head turns.

I take advantage of the momentary pause in their attention to look at Dad.

His eyes are misty and he's nodding with approval.

"If you remember Millie, you know she loved people, loved a good party just like this." I smile at her memory. "And while Willow's not big on crowds . . . she's got a big heart, with plenty of room for all of you."

"Just not all at once," she calls out, that voice growing a little raspier, that smile not quite meeting her eyes anymore.

Still, her response gets a laugh from everyone in the room.

When the heat of everyone's eyes shift back to me, her shoulders ease, her stiff smile falls.

And that does it.

I'm done letting her burn herself out for a crowd of strangers.

I turn back to everyone, as if there's anything left to say. "But as you all witnessed a few minutes ago, my bride and I do need to say goodnight to y'all."

The room erupts in more laughter and someone shouts, "Where's the wedding?"

That's an easy one. "Right here. On Blue River Ranch."

"When?"

I hold up my hands. "If we knew that, you'd all be getting a formal invitation today. But I can tell you one thing." I look at Willow. "It'll be at sunset."

18

Willow

"Bachelor party. Next Saturday. I'll round up the guys. You just show up," Silas states, slapping his oldest brother's back.

Wilder, Rose, Silas, Wes, Noah, and Charlie stayed back after everyone left to help clean up.

Dallas wipes a platter dry and hands it to Rose. "You can give it up, bro, everyone in this room knows this isn't real."

"The way I see it, you're still getting married," Wilder adds. "Which means the wedding will be real. And every *real* wedding calls for a *real* bachelor party." The two younger brothers high-five each other.

Dallas grunts. "You all enjoy yourselves. I'll pass."

Charlie gasps. "If y'all are having one, then Willow gets one too." She raises her hand, still barely meeting the height of most men in the room. "I call planning Willow's."

Rose glares at the blonde. "Put your hand down, I called dibs on this years ago."

I purse my lips. My instinct is to turn this down the way Dallas did. But, instead, my stomach fizzes with excitement because when will I ever get to enjoy something like this again? One carefree night with new friends, and Rose, in a new town I've yet to explore.

I smile. "I'm in."

Charlie and Rose cheer.

"You're in?" Dallas asks, his voice low but prominent.

I lift a shoulder. "Wilder makes a good point. We *are* getting married. It may be temporary, but why not enjoy the perks of this phony matrimony?"

The guys roar in the background but I can't make it out because Dallas is watching me like he can't figure me out. One more thing to add to the list of things we'll need to discuss when everyone leaves.

The first being the kiss behind the stairs.

"Fine," he grits. "I'm in too." He turns a lazy gaze to his brothers and Noah. "But it can't be the same night as the girls. Someone needs to stay home with Ellie."

I lift a finger. "I agree. I'd want Ginger to come too, so we won't have a sitter."

Dallas meets my eyes for a brief moment—and I don't linger long enough to make out his unreadable expression. All I caught was a faint crack in his armor.

"We can get on board with that." Charlie nods at Rose like they're keeping a mental list.

My eyes flick back to Dallas. His eyes are trained on me, soft, smiling. A moment of shared understanding passes between us.

This sense of union, friendship . . . family. For a sliver of a second, it's almost like this whole thing is real.

This might not be new to him. But it's an entirely foreign concept to me. Being surrounded by people who show up, plan parties, *fight* for each other.

"We could make it the *following* week," Charlie says, looking at her phone. Her husband stands next to her, his phone out too.

"Fine," Noah says. "But you need to come up with a wedding date soon." He flips his phone to me and Dallas. "I've got a feeling the first hearing will be set soon. We'd be in a better position if you and Willow made it official before then."

And just like that—we're back to all-business. And it's just as well.

No one leaves until the kitchen is spotless. But eventually, Noah, Charlie, and Wes head out while the brothers share a cocktail on the back porch. Rose and I are sitting at the kitchen island with cups of tea.

I stare through the kitchen windows to the back porch, which is basically pointless since it's pitch-black outside and I'm staring at my own reflection.

Rose glances back. "It's unfair, isn't it? We can't see a single thing through those windows, but they can see us."

"Wonder what they're talking about," I muse.

She sips her tea. "Oh, I don't know, maybe that kiss you two shared this evening."

I laugh. "They are not talking about that. And how'd you hear about that anyway? You were with Ellie."

She shakes her head. "Caught you when I was upstairs. Was going to come down, but then Dallas started his speech and I started crying and it was a mess."

I swallow.

His speech tore at me too, in ways I hadn't imagined it would. He's so gruff and grumpy, it's hard to imagine him loving anyone so much. It's hard to imagine any man loving someone so hard.

He built a home for Millie brick by brick, exactly where and how she wanted it. He gave up his job, family obligations, and probably loving ever again because of it.

Not until that speech did I really consider what he went through. How badly he's been hurting.

The high from our kiss quickly melted away. The desire to do it again, and again, and again, faded too.

It would be selfish.

And wrong.

To go after a man whose heart is still broken. Who's never imagined kissing—much less marrying—anyone else.

"It was for show," I say.

Her brows perk. "Well, that's just not true, and I'm offended you think I'd buy that."

I glance away. "Well, the next one will be," I tell her, an unwelcome disappointment coiling in my chest. That quiet unease the moment Dallas broke our kiss—then told a room full of people that I wasn't the one.

Of course I'm not.

And I don't want to be.

Another pang of heaviness settles. It's deep and almost bruising. The kind you know is going to take a while to heal.

"Neither one of us is looking for love right now," I add as a reminder to both Rose and myself.

She pouts. "You're right about that. But you can't blame me for daydreaming about how it would be if circumstances were different. It would be perfect, wouldn't it?"

"I don't know about that . . ." I wave her off as I push down the bubbly feeling in my stomach at the idea of Dallas and me. "I'm a city girl. I've got . . . dreams. Ones that don't involve dive bars and lousy tips. I want to play, sing, record, make my own brand of music for people who get it."

Rose watches me with a quiet wonder, even though she's heard all this before. "And a commitment to stay single, apparently."

"Not forever. Just until I get myself settled. Get my career going. You can't figure any of that stuff out when you're tied down."

She shrugs. "I did."

"I'm not you. After Eric, I realized where my focus needs to be right now—and it's on me. What I need, and how and when I'm going to get it." My tone is sharper than usual and it's almost like I'm reprimanding myself. Like I've forgotten all this.

She smiles softly but it's laced with concern. "Honey, I know. But now you're four years closer to that life goal of taking care of yourself first. So, why not move up the romance timeline too?"

I frown. "What?"

"Your money, Willow. You're getting married. Which means your inheritance will be released."

Chills run down my spine and I shake my head. "No, no, I don't think this counts. I'd have to—" I try to think of the stipulations. And I can't think of any. "Surely there has to be some kind of provision that I'd need to stay married for—no, it doesn't matter. I've made up my mind. I'm waiting."

She laughs. "Willow, what is the matter with you? Just ask Dallas to stay married for however long it is and that's it."

My eyes bulge. "No. No, I'm not even contacting the lawyer about it. I'll wait until I'm twenty-eight. This is to help *him and Ellie*, not me."

"Why can't it be both?"

I try to think of a valid reason, knowing Rose won't drop it until she gets one. "I know this won't make sense, but I chose to stay for a father and a little girl who's been kept from him her whole life. For a chance for them to be together. Dallas is a good man—he deserves this time with her, to raise her. To catch up on the relationship they should have been building all along. Taking this money would feel like . . . cheating myself—cheating my grandmother. I won't do it."

Rose leans back with a breath. "Wow, I never looked at it that way. I'm sorry."

"No, please don't be. I guess I've kind of set my mind about it in my head, so I haven't even considered claiming my grandmother's money."

"So I take it you'll be keeping this wedding a secret from your mother? Because once that woman finds out—"

I sigh. "Noah asked about family—to make it look as real as possible."

Rose winces. "I doubt she'll see your view on this."

"She's going to have to."

Rose glances back as the brothers' laughter carries through the door.

She turns back to me. "I know it feels like you're failing if you give in. Like it's some endless cycle of falling in love and getting hurt that you're trapped in."

My heart sinks. Way to hit it on the nose.

"And while I'm proud of you for choosing you first . . . I'm afraid you might miss out on what could be your happiest years."

I want to burst into tears, because I know she's right. And I felt it in an overwhelming wave when he kissed me tonight. The way he stood by my side, burning with protection. The way our hands found each other's when our eyes were on the crowd. The way he held my gaze, searched my eyes when I was spiraling over the possibility of losing Ellie.

I *do* want him.

More than I should.

And much more than I can help.

Everything in me is ready to let go and give in. But my best friend is forgetting one frightfully important thing here.

"Rose." My voice cracks. "I can't fall for a man who still belongs to someone else."

I hear Dallas downstairs as he shuts the front door after walking our guests out. I sit back on the soft pink velvet chair in Ellie's room—where I escaped after saying goodnight to everyone.

Admitting I want him wasn't as hard as I thought it might be. It's what came directly after that packed the bigger punch.

Can I really have him?

And am I willing to risk getting hurt finding out?

My heart pounds when I hear him coming up the stairs and down the hall. Stopping somewhere near my room, then making his way down to Ellie's. The door creaks open slowly. And he finds me on the other side of her nightlight.

I look up at him, feeling restless. "I don't think she's moved all night," I whisper.

A grin slips out with a soft exhale. "She had quite an exciting night."

I watch her breathing, the glow of her skin in the soft light. "I didn't like all those people pinching her cheeks and playing with her curls."

He steps inside. "I didn't really notice." He peels his eyes off her and looks down at me and I know what he's saying with that one look. "Thank you for tonight."

"It was just as much *fun* for you as it was for me."

He holds his hand out. "Let's get you to bed."

I yawn at the thought of a good night's sleep and groan as he pulls me to my feet. As he does, my balance slips and I fall into his chest. His grip tightens instantly. His chest warm, solid, and steady as he momentarily holds up my weight.

I blink up at him before straightening, swallowing under his heated gaze. We're still for a moment as his eyes drop to my lips.

"I think . . ." he starts, voice catching, low and raw. "I think we need to set some . . ."

"Boundaries?" I guess, suppressing my disappointment since it's clear he's fighting the urge to kiss me again.

He glances at Ellie over my shoulder then takes my hand, walking me out of the room and gently shutting her door. "Ground rules," he breathes, as he puts some distance between us in the narrow hallway. Twisting to face me again, he holds up his hands. "For me, mostly, I . . . I think I crossed that line tonight." He rubs the back of his neck apologetically.

Another pang of disappointment and it's exactly why these *rules* are a damn good idea. *He's so noble . . . honest.* Breaking down more of my walls, making me trust him.

But it would be wrong to let him take the blame for that kiss tonight. I wanted it too—but I'm not apologizing for it. "Is it crossing a line if I let you?"

He meets my eyes. Strong and unwavering. "It is."

Right. Because you're emotionally unavailable and I should know this.

Can't get mad for the painful truth. I nod, clearing my throat since it's clear he means business. "Is there a ground rules handbook? How do we do this?"

He scoffs. "If there were, I'd have thrown it out, but," his eyes drop to my lips again like some sort of magnet, "we most certainly need one." He blinks, rubbing his eyes like he's condemning them. "Rule number one. You can't let me kiss you again."

I almost laugh, but it's mostly at myself. "Veto. I can't make any promises."

"Willow."

I cross my arms. "Oh what, you can have self-control and I can't?"

"Fair enough." His mouth curves, but he fights that smile. "We both make an effort on . . . rule number one."

I nod.

He gestures to me. "Your turn."

I narrow my eyes, assessing him. That heated gaze might be controlled now, but it's coming back and then I most certainly can't be held responsible. "You can't *look* at me like you want to kiss me."

"Veto. I don't know what that looks like."

I laugh, my tension easing. "All right." I pace the small space. "No walking around without your shirt on."

"What, you're not even going to try on the looking thing?"

I smirk and shrug a shoulder. "You're doing it now, what would be the point?"

"I am not."

I laugh.

"Shirts on when walkin' around the house. Done. Three." He sighs. "Think it's safe to say neither one of us needs to worry about seein' other people, so we'll skip that." He runs a hand down his face. "Last one and then I think it's all I can handle for one night." He meets my eyes, all humor gone. "Exit plan."

"What do you mean?"

"Noah insisted you . . . sign a contract of sorts . . . I said no. I'm not tying anyone down to my problems. You stay at your will, you decide when you go, I won't hold you to anything."

I frown.

"But if at any point you change your mind, I'd like some notice. A chance to come up with a plan B." He swallows, then grins awkwardly. "Or hell, maybe a chance to change it back."

My stomach flips.

And that pretty much seals the deal for me, contract or no contract. How could I walk away from a man who doesn't believe in locking a woman down, temporarily taking away her freedom?

Even if it would mean losing his daughter.

"I'd have signed anything you wanted me to," I assure him without a doubt in my mind.

He watches me. "I appreciate that. But even if you did, I'd never hold it against you if you wanted out. So . . . it's sort of a moot point."

I close the distance so there's no mistaking it. "Dallas, I don't want you to worry. I'm not going anywhere."

His features flatten.

"Yet, I mean. Until . . ." I shrug. "Until Ellie's safely, *legally* yours." My eyes drop to his chest. "And until Noah feels there's been a safe amount of time before we realize this," I point between us with a sheepish grin, "didn't work out."

The idea makes my heart hurt a little.

Which is insane, because it's nothing personal. It's just what it is. A temporary arrangement. A pre-planned departure. A closed heart.

"I believe you," he says, his eyes sturdy and warm. "You know, it's not often someone does anything selfless for me." He pinches the bridge of his nose like he can't wrap his head around it. "Hell, it's not often I see that at all." He smirks. "You sure there's nothing I need to know about? They didn't find a dead body in that apartment of yours, did they?"

I shake my head. I don't even laugh along.

Should I tell him about the inheritance? What if I change my mind? What if Rose is right and I'm only hurting myself by not taking it?

No. Dallas is paying me plenty, enough to afford a decent apartment in the city for a few months while I work on booking those high-end venues so I can afford some decent recording equipment.

Fallen Willow

I won't cheat Grandma on what she wanted for me. I won't lie to myself that I earned that money.

In the end, I'll respect myself that much more.

"No dead bodies," I confirm. And make the decision that he doesn't need to know about something that isn't happening. "Just doing what feels right."

He nods, a sliver of a smile forming on his lips. "How's a week from next Sunday?"

"For what?"

This time he gives me an almost-full grin. "Our wedding."

19

Dallas

"What's your problem today?" Silas asks, like I'm the one who's making a production out of coiling up a rope. He's wearing jeans that probably cost too much, spotless sneakers, and a white long-sleeved shirt that looks brand new.

"You, showing up dressed like that. Give me that." I snatch the rope away and roll it up like it's second nature, then hang it up on the peg in the barn I built just outside my house.

"Nothing wrong with clean clothes," he says dryly, voice distant like I've offended him. But Silas doesn't offend easily, so I'm suddenly on alert. He also never offers to stick around for a weekend to help with land work. He rolls his shoulder back, looking off to the side. "What's next? Is it indoors?"

I blink, glancing at the house. *It can't be indoors.* Willow's in there with a yoga mat spread out and an outfit that definitely should have gone on the ground rules list.

Did we even make a list? The hell is even on it? It was only two nights ago—fresh off the high of our kiss, exhausted from faking, smiling, and stressing—that we came up with said list.

I bet she doesn't even remember it.

I turn back to Silas. It's hockey season and he was back at my house Saturday morning to help with some finishing touches. Then insisted on staying the weekend to spend some time with his niece.

Not the worst thing.

Kept my hands—and mind—busy enough to keep them off Willow. Not to mention Ellie was over the moon having him around. So I didn't question it.

But my big-brother senses are tingling.

"Shouldn't you be at practice or a game or something?"

"Told you, took a weekend off for family matters."

I narrow my eyes at him but he avoids me. "Family matters, eh? Dad sick or something?"

He didn't spend any time with Dad this weekend, so we both know that's not it. But from what I understand, the league doesn't just *give* you a weekend off. There needs to be a problem. Either with family—or *him*.

Silas shrugs, then flinches. "Well, you know how he is, always acts like he could ride a bull on demand, but struggles to pick up the paper on the doorstep."

I nod, even though I'm pretty sure Dad's not the one struggling here. I lift a shovel. "Hey, do me a favor, and put this up against that wall." I toss it to him.

He catches it with his left hand—which is strange, considering he's a righty.

"Something wrong with your right arm?"

"The hell you doing throwing a shovel at me?" he shouts.

"Be happy it wasn't a pitchfork," I bark back. "What's wrong with your shoulder? You injured?"

"No," he snaps. "Just—" He sighs. "Tired. Stiff." He rubs under the blade. "Where'd you get the mattress anyway? A flea market?"

I shrug. "Old man Norman's got some great deals, you ought to stop by his table on Saturdays."

He sets down the shovel and sits on a barrel.

I leave it alone for a minute and fill the stalls with straw where I intend to stable Trouble and two younger horses our trainer's bringing over soon.

"How'd it happen?" I ask, tossing empty bags aside.

His jaw tightens. "Season opener, few weeks ago."

"Shit. Anyone know?"

He shakes his head. "I was checked out but—it wasn't bad then. Played just fine, till one night it . . ."

"Got worse?"

He shakes his head. "Snapped or something. I figured a few days off the ice might help. I've been starting every game."

I release a heavy breath. "I've noticed."

"I haven't told Chase."

"He's not just your captain, he's your best friend," I point out.

"Just keep this between us?"

I glance at his shoulder. "So long as you get that looked at. Physical therapy should do the trick, no?"

He nods but doesn't confirm it.

I roll my eyes. "You don't need to tell anyone at the league you're hurt to get treatment." *At least I don't think so.*

Silas shakes his head. "It's not that easy."

"Come on, there's that doctor–patient legal crap, isn't there?"

"I'm fine. Just need a day or two to give it a rest."

I cock my head. "All right. Let's head inside. I'll make you a cup of tea and spoon-feed you like a child." I chuckle, slapping his good shoulder as we step out of the barn and into the daylight.

Halfway toward the house, he stops short, distracted by the steady rhythm of hooves echoing across the path.

I adjust my hat and squint, following his eyes. "Ah. You bringin' me Trouble?" I wink at Storm, our horse and riding trainer. Don't read me wrong, I don't wink at just any employee—but Storm's always been like family around here.

The Thornes have known the Daltons for decades. In fact, when Tom Dalton and his wife moved to Blue River, Storm was only nine or ten. Blew us all away with her riding skills and just a love for the outdoors.

After coming home from college last year, she took a job at Callahan Ranch—a rival operation over on the other side of the river.

Wilder and I didn't ask questions when she came looking for a job here a few months ago. My guess would be the two bone-headed cowboys we lost to them this summer. Not the most respectful duo.

She smiles and swings off my horse in one smooth motion, her worn white boots hitting the dirt with trained ease. "Heya, boss. Meant to bring her and the other two along in the trailer, but she put up a fight," Storm teases, hand moving slowly over Trouble's neck.

I chuckle and take the reins. "Sorry you had to ride all this way." I point to the yellow sports car in the driveway. "Silas will take you back down. I'll help you bring the other two tomorrow."

She glances back at the car like I just asked her to walk across the river. Then her eyes narrow at my brother—who's been quiet behind me.

He steps forward, gaze locked on the blonde. I almost laugh and try to remember the last time he saw her. Must have been years. Since before they both went away to college.

Storm's eyes don't linger on him for more than a beat. "That's all right, I'll walk."

"What's the matter, you don't take rides from strangers?" Silas smirks and I wince.

"Don't tell me you don't remember *Storm*. You guys probably went to—"

"No—I don't ride with strangers." Storm's response is sharp, ignoring me and keeping her eyes on my brother. "Plus, I might get your pretty interior all dirty with my boots and clothes."

Silas frowns, confusion flickering to recognition. "Storm *Dalton*? I remember pigtails and freckles." He scans her once. "Can't say I recall the attitude."

She rolls her eyes. "See ya tomorrow, boss."

She starts walking and I nudge my brother. "Look, I'm not going to try to figure out why she doesn't like you—but give the girl a ride."

He watches as she makes her way down the sloped path, blonde hair braided on either side.

"Unless, of course, you want to be the one to get Trouble settled in the new barn, and I take your car."

He glances back at the horse. "I don't know what's more dangerous."

"You've got to be kidding me. Hell happen to you two?"

"Nothing. She was just . . ." He shrugs. "Not part of my crowd."

"But you two were close, weren't you? Wilder and I'd trail Dad around the ranch, while you two climbed fences and built forts out of hay bales."

He lets out a laugh, short and without any real humor. "More like tryin' to keep up when she did all that."

I smirk. "So, Trouble or Storm?"

He yanks his keys out of his pocket. "All one and the same to me." He starts toward the car. "Kiss Ellie for me, I'm gonna head back to Denver after this."

I chuckle. "Good luck. But don't think I'm not askin' questions next week."

It's after midnight and I can't sleep. Willow and I called it a night shortly after Ellie went down. I cleaned the kitchen and started the dishwasher while she tidied up the living room.

Both of us finding some reason to steer clear of one another—without my brother as a buffer.

Barely forty-eight hours since we laid down the rules after our kiss. One damn weekend. And I'm already losing it.

I try to focus on the version of Willow when she's around Ellie—a damn sweet version—natural, funny, caring, passionate.

But instead, my mind zeros in on the sound of her raspy morning voice. The light moans that come with that first sip of coffee. The swollen lips I'd like to kiss senseless. Then tell her where she can shove those dumb rules.

At some point during dinner, she was quiet. Unusually quiet, so I took a page out of her book and started rambling. Topic of conversation: my brother and his run-in with Storm. It was the only thing I could think of to talk about in front of Ellie.

Willow's eyes brightened. "Another chick around here *and* she's got attitude? When can I meet her?"

More moments like that. Safe moments.

I growl and push off the damn covers, feeling like they're suffocating me. I sigh at the twisted mess at my feet and shake the duvet cover. A little black thing goes flying and I jolt out of bed.

The hell was that?

I make out the flimsy object almost instantly in the moonlight.

Panties.

Black. *Lace*. Panties.

I bring them to my nose and inhale. Logic, question, source—out the window. They're *hers*. There's no doubt—no other. They're hers. From one of the nights she slept in my bed.

My eyes flick back to my bed as if I'd find her in it. Picturing every scenario of how these ended up buried in the covers. I stuff them in my pocket and step out into the hall without thinking.

The hell you going to do, asshole? March into her room and ask when she got naked on your bed? If she intentionally left them for you to find?

I start pacing the hall like a lunatic. Then turn at the sound of a door creaking. Willow steps out into the hall. Barefoot in a crop top and a pair of flimsy shorts.

My breath catches at the sight of bare skin under the dim light. Anger and frustration simmers to a whole new kind of heat. Temptation. And the gnawing guilt and fear that comes with it.

She freezes when she spots me—staring like a deer in headlights.

The only light filling the space is the plug-in motion sensor I put in for Ellie. It's just enough to catch Willow's brown eyes as they dip to my bare chest.

"Doesn't count," I say, voice lower than I mean it to be.

Her eyes dart back to mine quickly, like they'd just betrayed her. She releases a shaky breath in an attempt to say something that catches in her throat. As she composes herself, she squares her shoulders, a smirk playing on her lips. "I say it does."

My head tips to the side, gaze sharpening. "You don't play fair, Willow." There isn't a playful bone in my body as I step toward her, slow enough so she could walk away. But she doesn't. Instead, her wide eyes follow me as I advance, rising with each step. "Fine. I broke a rule. What are you gonna do about it?"

My challenge comes out of left field. Like I've caught the ball from a team player I don't particularly like.

Chin tilting up, she challenges, "If you're implying I break rule number one so we're even, you've got another thing coming." She perks a brow. "I've got self-control, Daddy."

The organ between my legs throbs at the nickname.

I didn't even know I had a kink for it.

My voice is like gravel. Because I'm damn sure I'm about to break another rule. "Do you now? 'Cause I've got something in my pocket that says you don't." I'm too close. The soft scent of rain and crushed petals hits me. But it's not enough to cover the arousal that still lingers from her panties.

She frowns. "Is that a—"

I slide them from my pocket and lift them for her to see. Black lace dangles from the hook of my index finger.

Eyes wide and lips parted, she flushes. Then blinks slowly like she's coming down from temporary shock.

"You sleep naked, Sunset?"

With a swallow, her eyes flick to mine—heat simmering behind them, but she doesn't speak. Almost as if she's calculating her words—or how I might react to them. "I did that night," she breathes.

I clench the back of my teeth. Biting back a curse. Then stuff them back in my pocket, like I own them now.

Her gaze dips to where they disappeared.

I close the small gap between us and place my hands on her hips, backing her against the landing rail. Her chin lifts but her body is still. Not an ounce of tremor. No panic or protest. Not even a surrender. Just a flicker of something deeper. Not quite an invitation to whatever the hell I think I'm about to do.

But trust. She trusts me.

Pulling my hands off her, I wrap my fingers tightly around the baluster, like I'm afraid to lose what she's giving me.

Her head drops back without a sound. Just a soft breath.

It's painfully pretty—the way she breathes me in. The way she watches me.

I need to stop. Need to step back. Instead, I grip tighter, like there's a chance my hands will wander to that bare skin.

Focus.

"Why that night?" I ask, lips dipping to ghost along the smooth line of her jaw.

"Because I was hot." It comes out in a soft whispery breath. Eyes rolling like she's ready to beg for me to touch her. I want to ask more. Taunt and tease. Find out exactly how many times she felt *hot* in my bed. But I'm not playing fair. I should make a confession too.

"You smell sweet."

She bites the corner of her lip, chest rising with each breath, long hair brushing against my arm.

My eyes drop to the curve of her neck, hungry to taste the flesh there. "Stop me." I exhale, meeting her gaze. I'm not sure if it's a challenge or an order, or if I'm talking to myself. Because the warning lights in my mind are flickering out—reaching the end of their battery life.

Every boundary we've set be damned.

I don't remember what they are, and in this moment—I don't care. "Dallas . . ." She swallows so hard I hear it. "You have my underwear in your pocket. Your hands on me that night is why they came off in the first place. And judging by the wood poking my hip right now, I don't think either one of us cares to stop you."

I bite back a chuckle. Realizing I like this version of Willow too. Daring, sexy . . . honest.

I smirk. "Always with the words . . ." I sweep my thumb along her chin, back and forth like I'm testing the waters of a brand-new island. "A simple *I don't want to* would've sufficed."

She exhales like she needs more and I break, sliding both hands beneath her jaw, fingers curling around the sides of her neck.

Willow's eyes flutter closed before I kiss her lips, slow and firm, her back arching for me. The way I imagine kissing her on our wedding day. In front of witnesses.

A kiss that would fool just about everyone watching.

Willow melts into me with a moan, hands sliding around my back as she deepens the kiss like a woman who likes taking control. Or a woman who's just as desperate to taste me as I am her.

Our tongues tangle together. Mouths moving in a dance we've never practiced before, but know by heart.

Another sexy noise slips from her and it sets me ablaze. My hand slips down to her ass, cupping the bare skin beneath her cotton shorts.

Her body reacts. Her throat vibrates with need.

She's so sexy it hurts.

She's . . . *perfect*.

All too suddenly, a lump forms in my throat—in my gut. It's distractingly loud and . . . painful.

It hits me sharp, like a cold wind cutting through our fire.

Willow gasps and pulls back, eyes wide with shock and a flicker of hurt.

I bite back a curse. This time at myself. I run a shaky hand down my face. How do you explain guilt from a ghost I simply can't put to rest. "I'm sorry, I . . ."

Willow's eyes dip to the side with a frown. And before I can finish the thought, she covers my mouth. "Shh. Do you hear that?"

I blink. The house is quiet except for some faint shuffling. We both flick our eyes to Ellie's door. It opens slowly and we jump three feet apart.

Ellie steps out, sleepy, holding her pink bunny. She blinks, finding us in the hall. "I need the bathroom," she whispers groggily, then pads on into the hallway bathroom.

Willow looks up at me sheepishly. "I'll see her back to bed."

I press two fingers to my temple. "No. I've got it. You were probably on your way down or . . . something?"

"For my Thermos. I got caught up reading and my tea went cold."

I nod and switch on the light to illuminate the stairs for her.

"Goodnight." She glances at my pocket. It's not until the toilet flushes behind me that I realize I've lost focus. And it's about time I get it back.

20

Willow

> **Willow:** He kissed me last night.

> **Rose:** He kissed you Friday night too.

> **Willow:** It was different. Hotter.

> **Rose:** Hope the kid wasn't around.

> **Willow:** Can you be real for a moment?

Rose: Don't ask me to be real, Wil.

Willow: Why not?

Rose: Because "Real Rose" would tell you to be careful.

My stomach twists, fingers paralyzed over the screen. Not because I expected anything different from Rose. She'll forever have my best interests at heart.

But because she's dragging out that little voice in my head, saying the thing I've shoved aside. That I'm off the market. Done handing my heart out like it's got an open return policy.

And I'm at risk of doing it again.

Rose: He's had an intense year. And fighting a scary battle right now.

My chest tightens and I blow it off. For both our sakes.

Willow: It was just a kiss.

Fallen Willow

Rose: Fine. Kiss all you want. Just don't go . . . you know.

Willow: Falling?

Rose: Yeah.

Willow: I'm done falling, remember?

Rose: I do.

Willow: Then what are you worried about?

Rose: He's a Thorne. If there was ever a man worth the fall, it's him.

I sigh as my stomach drops. *I know.*

"So where's this Bones place you were raving about?" I ask Rose on Friday night.

She hadn't actually *raved* about the place. But I know it's where she ended up causing a major bar fight on her first solo night out in Blue River Springs. And I assume it's where we're heading for drinks this evening.

I know what she's doing. Finding out where I stand since that kiss with Dallas.

And she can go ahead and grill me all she wants. I couldn't care less that Dallas's bachelor party is tomorrow night. Including what he may or may not do at such a thing. Nor have I rationalized that since the wedding is technically all for show, the bachelor party must be too.

I suddenly feel nauseous.

Which is stupid, because Dallas has been grumpy about the whole thing all week.

"I'm not taking you to Bones. Not tonight anyway. That's more of a weekday kind of bar. It's Friday night, we'll level up a notch."

"Gee, thanks. Can't wait to see what 'level up' means around here."

OK, so maybe I'm a bit grumpy too.

The texts with Rose earlier this week were disheartening—even if she is right.

Just before I pulled back from our heated kiss a few nights ago, something shifted in Dallas, something that threw me off. Almost like his body was acting before his mind caught up.

And sure, those make for the best kisses, but is that what I want? For him to *lose* himself in me?

Would it be too much to ask for a man to *find* himself with me?

I've been wondering if maybe I'm overthinking it. Maybe he'd heard Ellie too. And this is all just my history with heartbreak creeping in. My trust radar going off. They say parents have that natural instinct . . . or prediction when their child is about to wake up.

Judging by his avoidance this week—I'm going with my first suspicion.

He's closed off.

Emotionally locked away.

Or worse . . . still haunted by grief.

And I'm either falling into my old ways—or I've found something that's worth giving a chance.

Whatever this thing, or non-thing is with us, we're sort of . . . back to normal.

Even if my underwear is still enjoying its new life in his possession.

He still has that fancy coffee machine running a little extra for me each morning. Makes fun of my knitted socks. And still cuts in on my bottomless rambling just when I'm about to get to my point.

The things that *have* changed are the things I've found myself longing for. His gaze doesn't linger anymore. There's no flirty banter when Ellie isn't around.

To him, I'm just . . . the under-table paid nanny. The one to make his problem go away.

Way to make a girl feel irresistible.

Rose pulls her golf cart over to the side of the street and hops out.

I take in the stretch of bars and storefronts lining the dimly lit street. "So," I question, stepping out onto the uneven pavement. "We can just *leave* this here?"

She shrugs. "It's got my name on it. Who's going to take it?" She reaches for my arm as I start toward one of the bars. "No, come on. It's this one here."

Rose steers me in the other direction through a black door under a dark awning. It's warm inside, a nice change from the cool night. The place is big for a small-town bar. Round tables fill the floorspace and there's a large built-in bar taking up most of the back wall. Vintage signs hang from the remaining exposed brick walls and strings of naked bulbs illuminate the room in a muted, warm light, drawing my eye to the wooden beams that run along the width of the bar. It's a mixture of rustic, chic, and . . . "trying too hard," if that was a style.

But the thing that draws my eye the most is the black grand piano perched on a wooden platform at the front of the room, where a woman is playing.

"What is this place?"

"It's called The Blue Branch. It's our version of a jazz club or wine bar."

I narrow my eyes. "But?"

"But it wasn't getting much business being that, so they let a few fights start up to get people talking."

I slide onto a seat along the bar. "To give it a *good* reputation?"

Rose reaches for a menu. "That's what Wes tells me."

"So this isn't a you-and-Wilder spot?"

She huffs out a laugh. "If Wilder comes out with me, he takes me *out* of town." She glances around. "Besides, there are particular regulars here the Thorne brothers prefer to avoid."

"Sounds juicy."

"That's what I thought when I first heard about the rivalry between Blue River and Callahan Ranch. But it's pretty serious. Goes way back to when Connor ran the ranch. Lost his wife because of it."

"Dallas's mother?"

She nods, eyes shadowed with regret but pinned to the menu. "Learned the hard way just how deep the feud runs. From what I hear, Ricky and Dusty Callahan are worse than their dad. Play dirty. What started as a battle over a river, turned into a clash of egos."

"Who's in the lead?"

Rose shrugs. "Ricky's probably the only one keeping score. He and his crew have stopped going around Bones much anymore since it usually ends in one of ours winning a brawl *they* started." She glances back. "They sort of migrated here recently. And it's for the best. Anytime Dallas and Ricky are in the same room—there's blood."

I scan the menu like I'd get anything other than my usual. "How are the margaritas?"

Rose smirks. "Not as good as mine."

We applaud the woman playing her second set. And I'm *impressed*. Her fingers are fluid along the keys, her gaze trained. She doesn't care that she's got an audience. Or at least it doesn't seem that way.

It usually takes me one margarita to get to that point.

She's also gorgeous. Dirty-blonde beach waves, high cheekbones, strong build.

Bet no one messes with her around here.

She finishes her glass of water and moves behind the bar for a refill. She chugs it halfway then sets it down, eyes pinned on me. "Can I buy you a drink?"

I blink. "Me?"

"Least I could do, you watched my entire set. I'm Laurie."

I exhale a laugh with a wince. "Sorry, I didn't mean to stare. You sounded amazing."

Rose leans in, shouting over the crowd, and points to me. "Willow plays *and* sings."

"Oh, sing too, huh? Carl's been begging me to add words. You got a gig around here?"

"Oh, I'm only in town for—"

Rose punches my leg.

"New. I'm fairly new in town. Left a decent gig in Manhattan because I . . . fell in love." I say the words tightly.

"How romantic," she says with little enthusiasm.

I clench the back of my teeth because I know what she's thinking. Some artist I claim to be—dropping everything for a man. "It is. But it's not stopping me. I'll be back out there soon. I miss playing."

She gasps, then glances at the bartender. "Well, you're in luck. Fill in for me tomorrow."

I frown with a sideways glance at Rose. "Wait, like here? Are you serious?"

"Dead serious. I've got another gig tomorrow night and Carl won't let me off. Hey, Carl." She waves the bartender down. "I've got you a player for tomorrow. *And she sings*."

Carl's brows shoot up. "You don't say." His eyes dart to mine. "Be here at nine. Your last set's midnight."

"Oh, no. I wasn't offering."

"You said yourself you miss it," Laurie argues. "Plus the tips are amazing on Saturday nights."

Carl sets a whiskey bottle back on the glass shelf. "Then how come you always callin' out sick?"

"Because it's *Saturday* night, Carl." Then she covers the side of her mouth and mutters to me and Rose, "Plus the tips for my *other* gig are usually better."

"What's your other gig?" I ask.

She winks and shakes her shoulders. "I'm a dancer."

Rose mutters an "uh-oh" and takes a sip of her wine.

Laurie leans in. "Tomorrow, Blue River's most eligible bachelor is having a party, and let me tell ya, I'd work *that* one for free."

My heart clutches. *Dallas*.

The man who's been acting like I barely exist all week. The one who kisses me like I'm the one he's being waiting for and then pulls away like I'm the plague.

And maybe I am. Just another woman who's trying to lock him down when he's got a town full of Lauries to pick from.

"I'll be here." I assure them both. "Tomorrow. And every Saturday night, if you like my set."

Rose seems conflicted by my promise. Grabbing hold of my arm, she leans in. "Shouldn't we check with Dallas and maybe even Noah on this?"

I brush her off like she's with the enemy, smiling tightly as Carl and Laurie drift off to the side. "Why should I?" I hiss. "I'm a free woman. I make my own decisions."

"I don't disagree. But even as a courtesy, or just to make sure there's no issue with—his situation."

"I guarantee you, Rose," I mutter, taking a sip of my margarita as I watch the gorgeous blonde liven up the crowd once more. "Dallas will be too distracted tomorrow to even *care* where I am."

21

Dallas

I'm not surprised to see Rose coming over with Wilder on Saturday night. In fact, I expected her. *Hoped* even that she'd come to spend the evening with Willow while the guys drag me out on the town for a dumb pre-wedding ritual.

What I *am* surprised about though—is that Rose is dressed for a night out herself and Ginger is stepping in behind them.

"Where's that cupcake of mine?" Ginger starts. "We're going to watch movies and make popcorn—"

"Hang on." I glance at Rose as if I'm missing something, then turn back to Ginger. "What's going on here? The girls' party is *next week*. We don't need you watching Ellie tonight."

Ginger's grey eyes beam. "Oh, I know, I'm goin' to *that* party." Then she frowns, turning an accusing glare at Rose. "You didn't tell him, did you?"

Rose bites her lip.

I don't wait for her response. Flipping around, I move to the stairs, gripping the banister with a tight fist. "Willow," I howl like a father of an out-of-control teenager, fully aware I'm making everyone in the room uncomfortable and not giving a shit.

The steady sound of heels moving across the floorboards overhead. My jaw hardens as I lift my gaze to the top of the stairs.

"Thank you so much, Ginger. She's just upstairs, drying off her bath toys." Willow's voice is soft, calm even, as she comes downstairs, ignoring my outburst.

She's in blue jeans and a black sequined top, hair down, eyes made up in a smoky purple. Lips red.

"I'll just heat up dinner for you two." She disappears into the kitchen.

"Did I miss something?" I call out to everyone in the room.

Wilder sighs, chin tilting toward his girlfriend. "She didn't tell him?"

"Tell me what?"

The doorbell rings again. Noah and Silas let themselves in. "Reservations at eigh—whoa." Silas frowns, glancing from my hard glare to Wilder. "What's up with him?"

Wilder cocks his head to the couch. "You boys should have a seat for now. Might be a while."

I run a hand down my face in frustration. "Don't get comfortable. This'll only take a minute." I march to the kitchen just as Willow locks the back doors and shutters.

"Something you need to tell me?" I try to keep my voice down, I really do.

"Yes," she answers without sparing me a glance. "I'm going out. So I asked Ginger to watch Ellie. She's more than happy to."

"I know she is. Not the point. When were you going to run that by me?"

She jerks, brown eyes widening at my tone. "Run that by you? I don't owe you a—"

"I've got two paychecks that says you do," I snap back. She looks too damn good and I'm picking up all kinds of bad vibes with her not telling me about this.

I hear one of the guys grunt in the background at my comment and my stomach twists. But I'm not a fan of being caught off guard.

Willow continues to clear the counter. Her silence pounds against my chest, indicating I might've crossed some line with the *I'm your boss* move.

I'm about to take it down a level—or three—but then she answers.

"I got a job," she says flatly.

I stare at her, heat rising again. "What do you mean, you got a job? You already got one."

"It's only Saturday nights. Playing at . . . a spot right here in town."

"There's over a dozen—which one?"

Her eyes flick sideways with no answer.

"Oh, you don't want to tell me." I move around the counter to her. "Think I'm going to show up and cause a scene?"

My focus shifts from being annoyed that she kept this from me until the last second, to comparing me to one of her exes.

She rolls her eyes and glances over my shoulder. Where I'm sure we've got an audience. After all, there's hardly a wall between the living room and kitchen.

"Gee, why would I ever think that . . ." she mutters. "Willow."

Another voice cuts in behind me. "Actually, Dallas," Noah starts. "If she's got a job, especially one in town . . . no one can say *you're* paying her for . . . anything else."

Wilder steps in, a little more tentatively than my lawyer. "He's got a point, Dal. Let this one go."

My jaw tightens as I pull my gaze off my bride-to-be to my brother. "Next time Rose gets a wild idea, I'm supporting it," I mutter.

Wilder shrugs, glancing at the tiny brunette at his side. "I probably would too after I bitch about it for a day."

I glare at him.

"We'll be outside," my brother says, then practically shoves the others out to the front porch.

I turn back to Willow, barely taking a moment to breathe. "What time will you be home?"

She crosses her arms. "Why do you care?"

I jerk at the question—and the attitude. "What's that supposed to mean?"

Her jaw clenches and she shifts her gaze momentarily. "I'm here for Ellie, right? I got her a capable sitter—who'll have her in bed in an hour anyway. So, what does it matter where I am or what I'm doing?"

She's being a brat. Why is she being a brat?

We're eye to eye for a moment. "Fine. You got a job doing what you like, I get it. I won't stop you." I step closer, into her space. "But I want to know why you didn't tell me."

She lifts her chin. "Because we're not a couple. We're living under the same roof, but let's be real, I'm *no one* to you. You don't tell me why you kissed me—or why you're acting like it never happened. I don't tell you that I found a life outside of it. Something else to do once a week—other than *not* being the woman you thought you'd marry." With both hands, she presses hard against my chest and I step back, letting her pass.

Something twists in my gut. Something that shouldn't be hitting me so hard. But it's sharp. It's heavy.

And this time, I can't ignore it.

I hurt her.

"Willow." It's barely a whisper—not enough conviction to stop her, but I want to. I *mean* to. "Willow," I try again, my feet moving this time, catching her arm as she crosses into the living room.

She flips around, eyes glancing up the stairs where Ellie and Ginger quietly pad across the landing from the bathroom to her bedroom.

I swallow, reading the message. "This every Saturday night?" I ask as softly as I can manage, the gruffness in my voice still lingering.

She blinks. "If they like me, yes."

Then I'm screwed.

I sigh. "That's when all the weirdos are out." I don't know what I'm saying. I'm not even sure I know what "weirdos" is supposed to mean. What I want to say is "single men."

"Don't be silly, weirdos are out every night. Least in my part of town," she mutters, rolling her eyes.

Her last words should serve as the reminder we likely both need right now.

She doesn't live here. This is temporary.

But all it does is twist me up a little more.

This is temporary.

I couldn't tell you what I like about this little arrangement—but what I can say is, I don't like the idea of Willow being anywhere else in the world but here.

I'm not ready to tell her this. Hell, I'm not even sure I'm ready to try and make sense of it myself.

"Fine," I relent. "Call me when you're done. I'll pick you up. That's not up for discussion."

She smirks. "Nice try. Rose is my ride. She'll have me home by one . . . ish."

"Midnight." It's a challenge because even when I'm still simmering down from our sparring, I enjoy this fire between us. The push and pull.

"Or what? My clothes will turn to rags and my heels to slippers?"

I shove my blazer on with a smirk of my own. Because my comment doesn't come out of nowhere. "Something like that. You won't make it past midnight."

Fallen Willow

If there's one thing I noticed about Willow the past two weeks it's that she's no night owl. About an hour before midnight, she starts to fade, makes her tea, and starts her nightly routine.

Her eyes soften for a second. Shimmering with something uncertain before her defiance returns. "I'm a musician. Staying up late comes with the territory."

That might be true, but doesn't mean she likes it. "We'll see," I tell her, then grab my keys and head for the door. "Have fun."

As much as I might grumble about it, I do mean it. Wherever she's performing—and I will find out just where—I want her to enjoy herself. She's been selfless since the day we made our arrangement. She should get to do what she loves without anyone getting in her way.

"You too," she says, in a dragged-out, half-hearted way.

I don't know who won this round.

I'm not even sure it was a round or if this is just us.

But I can't wait for the next one.

The music is too loud. But the whiskey's smooth, so at least there's that.

Silas—who planned the whole thing—promised low-key. Which I naively believed, since we're just outside of town. There's a mile-long night-life strip here. A go-to spot if you're looking to get out of Blue River but not committed enough for Denver.

We're at a place called Salt Rim. Which is no strip club, thankfully, but the place is still too loud and busy for my liking.

Still, for Silas—and the typical rituals I've heard the hockey team do when someone's getting hitched—I'll take it.

I'm sitting at the bar with Wilder, who slips his phone away when I look over.

I twist my neck. "Gotta say, I'm surprised. Not like you to let Rose be out on the town without you knowing where to find her."

Wilder pauses mid-sip. He doesn't look at me when he pours down the amber liquid.

"What was that?"

"What was what?" He sucks his teeth, twisting the glass like he's inspecting it.

"You know something?"

Wilder glances behind us. "Will you relax and try to have a good time?"

Silas and Chase all but jump us from behind. "Grabbed us a table in front of the stage," Silas shouts. "Come on."

The stage? There's a stage?

I'd laugh if I weren't already annoyed. "No goddamn way. You boys enjoy."

The teammates exchange a look like they expected this reaction and walk away—which should probably worry me.

I twist back to Wilder. "You know where the girls are."

Another casual sip with no response.

Noah stretches an arm between us, lifting his drink. "Course he knows. *His* wife tells him where she's going."

"Girlfriend. And she only tells me because she knows I'll always find her."

Least she *wants* to be found—even if she pretends not to. Willow made it painfully clear she doesn't want me coming for her. And that's fine. I'm not about spying or keeping her from doing something she loves. But then I think of Rose's first night on the town—and Ricky Callahan slipping his arm around her and offering her his smoked sausages.

And it doesn't sit right with me. Leaving her to fend for herself in a town that works nothing like the one she's from.

"Tell me where they are." I say calmly, but there's a bite in my undertone my brother wouldn't miss.

He chuckles. "I would, but something tells me you're about to change that thought to *Willow who?*"

Unlikely.

"Ladies and gentlemen." A female voice comes over the microphone. "It is a *very* special night."

I flick my eyes over to the vaguely familiar blonde on stage. "Just tell me."

"You're not married yet, now let it go."

"Y'all know what I'm talking about, *Dallas Thorne* is getting married next week, folks. So my girls and I are here to give him something special."

I clench my teeth. "I'm leaving."

Two other women bounce up on stage with a mix of joy and sex appeal, working up the crowd—who cheer them on. Theme dancers—not strippers. All in matching fringe jeans, sports bras, boots, and cowgirl hats. The blonde one comes up to me and takes my hand, leading me to a chair—I'm too busy registering her face to resist.

"Laurie," I say as I remember her. We had a minor stint right before I met Millie. Barely remember it or why we broke up. But . . . here she is. I move my head back, needing distance to take her in. "New gig?"

The dance isn't erotic. It's showier and meant to entertain.

Which is a relief.

She smirks, gripping my shoulders and sitting on my lap facing me, smelling like a sweet cocktail and perfume. "Special occasion."

"Right."

"Don't worry." She winks. "You can still catch me at the Blue Branch each night—except Saturdays."

She doesn't dance at the Blue Branch. Plays piano there, I think. Last time I was there, I got into a fight with Ricky Callahan. Our parents might've started the rivalry—but Ricky keeps it alive. Using anything and anyone he can to get to me.

Ever since he ripped two of our best cowboys from us this summer, Ricky's been hanging out at the Branch instead of Bones—our usual spot.

Which is for the best—the less that evil man is around my family and crew, the better.

"Good to kn— Did you say *except Saturdays*?"

"That's right. You planning to visit me?"

I lift her off me and stand. "Thanks for the dance, Laurie. But I've got to run."

She steps back. "You coming back?"

"Probably not."

Wilder stops me halfway to the door, hand to my chest. "All right, all right. We pushed it with the dance. But it's over now, will you come and finish that drink with me?"

"You let them go to the Branch? Really?"

He glances over my shoulder to Laurie. "I didn't let them do anything. It's where Willow got her gig—what was I supposed to do? Besides, it's a non-issue—Rose and Wes go there all the time."

"That's because Wes's got it bad for Dusty Callahan. There's always a ninety percent chance she and Ricky are there."

Wilder's jaw tightens like he's second-guessing his decision. "Dusty likes Rose, she's not going to mess with her."

I nod curtly. "Fine. You keep telling yourself that while I get my ass over there. Because the only Ricky Callahan I know is the one who loves nothing more than to fuck with me. And if he saw the announcement, he's going to ride that for all it's worth."

22

Willow

"That was beautiful. I swear, I could listen to that voice of yours all day." Rose praises me as she always does after one of my sets. Then shoves a margarita in my hand as I step off the stage.

Laurie gave me a quick rundown of the crowd here. And so far, she's been on point. Most of them buzzing for the jazzy entertainment, light meals, and cocktails. But then there are some that totally give off predator vibes. But chances are they're more brood than bite and I should ignore them.

And whilst I've heard from Rose that the crowd itself can get pretty rowdy, Carl has assured me he's never had any trouble between the crowd and the talent.

That *may* have been true until now. But I'm picking up some major trouble vibes from the tall dirty-blond man with the beard and ponytail on the far right. He's been staring at me like there's no one else in the room. And not in a romantic way.

I'm wary of him, if I'm honest.

Aside from that, everything else has been incredible. This crowd's different. They're alive and fun. They make me want to sing. Not feel like I *have* to.

"Hey, I missed three calls from Wilder. I'm going to step outside and call him back. Have fun on your next set, I'll be right back."

I wink at her and take a few more sips of my drink before stepping back up on the stage. I'm a few minutes early, but I'd rather be up there playing music than in my head about Dallas.

Mr. Ponytail watches me with that look again. I want to say something to Carl, but it doesn't feel right. I'm trying to convince myself that I'm overreacting. But I've been in situations like this enough times to know when a patron is harmless . . . and when I should watch my back.

That guy—is definitely making me think the latter.

Eric's words are in my head. His threats and the implication that I'm helpless surface overwhelmingly, to the point my hands quake as they hover over the keys.

Deep breath. There are too many people here.

Nothing will happen.

I do my best to shove aside the gut feeling that Eric was right. That I need someone to protect me because I'm defenseless on my own. Rolling my shoulders back, I focus on the *rest* of the crowd.

I start slowly, fingers steady over the keys and voice low and soft. I close my eyes. The moment I do, a shadow appears and they fly open again, my voice pausing for a split second. Ponytail man puts a hundred in my tip jar and then lifts my drink, taking a long sip from the side stained with my lipstick. Then places it down in front of me and winks.

Nausea fills my insides. I glance to see if Rose has returned, but she hasn't.

Left on my own, my heartbeat thunders in my ears, overpowering the music.

I glare up at him. He's got a strange scowl, like he doesn't like me.

But I'm a professional. And I'm a New Yorker. And I won't be intimidated. "Take a seat, cowboy," I manage, now focused on the keys.

He does—but it's beside me on the bench. "Laurie likes it when I stop by."

There's a beat before I respond, "I'm not Laurie."

"Don't be shy now," the guy murmurs, leaning in close enough that I catch a whiff of cheap cologne and beer breath. I stiffen, shifting to force space between us. My heart stills in my chest.

I glance up to see if Carl's around. When I do, I catch Dallas at the door. Relief washes over me instantly. The hammering in my ears and chest subsides. And I start to feel more in control.

Dallas's scowl is firm, his eyes only briefly meeting mine before they shift to the man I'm about to spring away from.

I don't finish the lyrics. But I wrap up the notes, letting the final chord fade. I barely have time to hop off the small riser they call a stage before the blur of motion.

Dallas is on stage, boots thudding hard against the wood. Then comes the blow. Sharp and solid, leveling the guy off the bench and onto the floor. He falls hard with a grunt and the surface cracks under him.

The rest of the place turns into a ripple of voices and scraping of chairs.

I watch in horror as my future husband bends down, lifting Ponytail by his collar and growling into his face. "Hell do you think you're doing, Callahan?" Dallas grits.

Callahan?

Anytime Dallas and Ricky are in the same room—there's blood.

This isn't about *me*. This is the never-ending feud Rose was telling me about.

"Just welcoming your new bride to town. Got quite the taste, cowboy. Helluva lot better than—"

Another punch and my heart starts to hammer against my chest again.

Callahan sneers, wiping blood off his lip. "I was going to say Laurie. Christ, man."

Two, maybe three men jump in and I can't tell if they're trying to help or making it worse.

The speakers shriek and I cover my ears, then flinch when someone grips my arm.

"Come on." Rose yanks me away just as Wilder jumps on the stage to help.

When I look back, I notice Ricky isn't the only one getting it bad. Dallas's cheekbone is red, his lip cut and bleeding.

I have the urge to jump between them and practice that move Dallas showed me. But I'd knock myself out cold.

Before I have a chance to decide, Carl and a bunch of others rush past us onto the stage and tear the guys off one another. "Get out. All of you. Dallas—I'm sending you my bill."

Despite being restrained, Dallas's glare is unrelenting, voice lethal. "Come near her again and I'll end this between you and me for good."

"Get out. Both of you, out," Carl shouts at the bruised and bloody men. He hops off stage and hands me an envelope. "Great job tonight. Please don't come back."

My mouth falls open at the painfully familiar blow. My hands are shaking. I don't even defend myself. I can't find it in me to lash out at Carl for my feeling unsafe on his stage.

This is just my life. A sign that I really am on my own. Defenseless.

And right now, I can't find it in me to prove Eric wrong.

I shove the envelope at Rose, who's standing beside me, then storm off, stepping out into the cool night air with a gasp.

Dallas is one step behind me. "Willow."

I spin toward him, but only in time to see Callahan stumbling out of the bar with two men at his side. He peers over at us with a sneer. "Call yourself a man,

Thorne? Puttin' your woman to work? Ranch sufferin' that much?"

To his credit, Dallas ignores him. His eyes only on me.

Ricky mumbles something inaudible to his friends and the trio disappear into another bar across the street.

My chest rises and falls with each second we're alone. Before either of us have a chance to speak, Rose and Wilder step out. "Gonna head home in Rose's car. You two be all right?" Wilder tosses Dallas his car keys.

Dallas tears his gaze off me, nodding at his brother. "Thanks. I'll get the truck back to you tomorrow."

Leaving Rose behind, Wilder crosses to fetch her car from where we parked it.

Turning his eyes back to me, Dallas tilts his chin toward the truck. It's double-parked like he owns the damn street. "Get in."

"Get lost," I bite.

He sighs like I'm an inconvenience. "Can we do this later? Get in."

I cross my arms stubbornly. "I didn't need your help in there."

He's quiet for a moment, like he's biting back a comment. "I wasn't waiting for you to ask."

"I was waiting until the song was over," I snap defensively.

"For God's sake, that wasn't about you, Willow. Now can we please go?"

I swallow at his honesty.

He doesn't wait for me to follow, instead he circles the car and hops into the driver's seat.

Rose steps up behind me. "He's right. That was Ricky Callahan—the rival I was telling you about. He must've seen the announcement."

I shake my head, keeping my voice low. "Of course it's not about me, Rose."

"Wil."

"This isn't a good time to rationalize with me, Rose," I whisper harshly. "I'm all sorts of messed up. I was scared up there. I felt alone and helpless. It just . . . it came out of nowhere. I've *never* felt that way."

She grimaces like she understands exactly what happened. "You can't let Eric get in your head. You've got this. You always had."

"If I really believed it, I wouldn't have ended up taking self-defense classes like my life depended on it." I laugh at myself. "And I still don't know how to defend myself, and I've lost another gig because of it."

She glances over my shoulder where Dallas and Wilder are waiting. "It's not the same thing."

"Maybe not. But it's still a man taking out his insecurities on someone else, and leaving me without a job."

She bites her lip and I know she can't argue with that. Then she slips the envelope into my purse. "I think you can do better than this place anyway."

We're a few minutes into the drive when Dallas starts. A deep breath with a slow exhale. "I'm sorry, Willow." He shakes his head like this all spiraled out of his control.

"When I heard you were there—I had to come. It's where the Callahan crew always hang out, so I had to make sure you were safe."

"I can handle myself." My voice is flat as I stare ahead, trying to figure out what the hell I'm really upset about.

Is it the fact he came looking for trouble? The gig I lost? Or how badly Eric still fucked with my head.

Dallas runs a hand down his face like he's trying not to yell. "I wasn't about to stand by and let him taunt you."

"He could have been standing off to the side and I'd have still lost my job tonight."

"But that wasn't the case. Because he *was* taunting you. And he did it because you're *mine*."

"Your what? Your fake fiancée? Your responsibility?"

He sucks in a breath, but the words get caught. Instead, he stares at the road like it personally betrayed him. "You're going to be my wife. For whatever short time that may be, that makes you mine to protect. And I'm going to do that the only way I know how."

I scoff. "With your fists."

"With the only language Ricky Callahan understands," he snaps. Then sighs. "I'm sorry . . . I'm sorry it ruined your night. I'm sorry you got caught in the middle of it. But I'll never be sorry for setting that asshole straight and certainly not for keeping you safe."

My mouth opens but nothing comes out. My tongue feels useless against his words. So I stay silent for the rest of the drive home.

And so does he. Swiping his hand through his hair as if he's trying to figure out a way to fix this.

No, exactly like he's trying to figure out a way to fix this. I don't know how I know that, but I do. It's the part of me that trusts him. That knows he's a good man.

Deep down, I know that Dallas did nothing wrong tonight. And his attack on Ricky Callahan—it *was* about me.

Eric did such a number on me that I completely lost my way at the first sign of trouble. Granted, it was the worst I've had in a while—but it still rattled the shit out of me.

The words "thank you" are on the tip of my tongue by the time the gates spread open to the ranch. But I don't say them. The other side of me is still angry. But it's not at him.

It's at myself.

Because I want to be more than his responsibility to keep safe. I want to be his *reason*. For letting go of his grief and guilt. For believing in second chances. For finally letting his walls fall.

Mine have.

And I'm tired of pretending I can fight it.

Rose is right. If there's a man worth falling for, it's Dallas Thorne.

A few minutes later, he holds open the front door for me and I tense as I pass him.

I hear him exhale roughly behind me. "Willow, what the hell did you want me to do? Sit back and watch you try that high kick on him?"

I flip around, furious that he doesn't get it. "What went through your head?"

"What?"

"When you saw me tonight. You were frozen by the door. For a few seconds at least, you were watching us. I want to know what went through your head."

His jaw tightens. "Why does it matter?"

I shake my head. I don't know what I want him to say or . . . confess. I just want to know if he was measuring how fast he could tackle him. Or if he . . . was looking at me.

His eyes search mine as he steps up to me and he doesn't wait for a reason. "I just—when I saw him near you . . . my instinct was to storm in swinging. But something locked me in place. I've heard you sing that one before. It didn't sound like that. That's when I focused on you. Caught that stony look on your face. Your voice tight. Like you just wanted the damn song to end so *it* could end . . . I saw red, Sunset."

My chest squeezes. But I have one more question.

I meet his eyes. "And what did you see when you pulled away from our kiss last week?"

His eyes dip and I have my answer.

He saw—her.

23

Dallas

I slam the tailgate shut, clenching my teeth as I do because the sound cracks across the quiet Sunday afternoon like a warning shot.

Shit. It's Wilder's truck. All I need right now is for him to pester me about damages when that's *my* damn job. I huff out a breath, fisting the coiled whip, and head for the bullpen.

It's just past the south pasture, surrounded by steel panels bolted down tight. Bruiser isn't dangerous, just . . . unpredictable. It's breeding season and Wilder and I need to do a temperament check before we turn him out to the pasture.

I step inside, watching Bruiser as he paces, his thick muscles covered in dust, his nostrils flaring. "Hey buddy." I don't crack the whip yet. Don't need to. He's not showing signs of aggression. I step toward the middle of the pen, struggling to focus when my mind keeps drifting back to last night.

Guilt ate me up all night and I don't even know why. I don't regret anything. I don't regret kissing her last week. And I'd certainly never regret protecting her by any means necessary.

But I regret upsetting her. Making her feel like she's a consolation prize. Willow's too damn smart. Too smart and . . . *in tune* with me. She knew exactly why I broke off our kiss last week. Why I haven't brought it up and have avoided her like the plague.

And she didn't deserve that.

I also regret costing her something she enjoyed because I couldn't be mature enough to tell Ricky to step outside—and *then* beat him to a pulp.

Still doesn't give her the right to tear into me just because I made her safety my business.

Bruiser snorts, pawing at the dirt, then turns away from me.

"Not you too," I mutter.

A sneaker scuffs a few feet behind me. "Talkin' to yourself or the bull?"

I don't take my eyes off Bruiser. "What are you doing here, Silas?"

"Wilder said you'd be here. Wanted to check on you after you ran out last night."

"I'm not exactly in a position to chat right now," I say, voice low but enough to be heard.

"Look, I'm heading back and I just wanted to make sure you're all right."

I sigh with one last look at Bruiser before stepping back to lean against the fence. "Thank you for last night, Silas. I mean it. The dinner was nice, the bar after was—well, something to appreciate, I guess. I'll make it up to you for skipping out early. Now will you go so I can get back to work?"

He squints up at the sun. "Heard about The Blue Branch. Rough night?"

"Rough night." I rub my jaw. "Rough morning." I think about Willow in the kitchen. Eyes averted. Shoulders tight. Cheeks flushed. But she didn't look angry like I'd expected. More lost. Eyes fixed on the swirl of her coffee.

Silas shakes his head like he doesn't understand. "Then move on and apologize. Or are you forgetting how important it is that she stays?"

"I'm not holding anyone hostage. And I didn't do nothing wrong." My jaw clenches. "She's the one who didn't tell me where she's working, making me play guessing games all damn night. Didn't *ask* me for the night off. Then had the nerve to lash out because I wouldn't stand back and watch her get assaulted," I snap, noticing Bruiser square his stance.

Silas raises his arms in defense and steps back. "Dude, you might want to step out of the pen for this conversation."

I shake my head. I don't know what's more tiring—unruly bulls or redheads I can't seem to say the right thing to.

But it's not going to be another fucking apology. Said enough of those last night.

It's a hot reminder of some spirited arguments Millie and I shared. Had some grit in her too. Couldn't stand those rows. One step in the danger zone and I'd pull back. Put up my white flag. Whatever it took to stop it in its tracks. Because I hated leaving her mad at me—regardless whose fault it was.

But God help me, I *like* the way Willow looks at me when she's mad. The fire in her eyes. The sharp, snappy wit. There's passion there that makes me want to whip her around and kiss that mouth shut. Pull a desperate whimper out of her instead. And then there's the stubbornness, the distance she sets almost instantly—like I'm the last man she should trust.

And that's the part that keeps me waking up feeling the way I did this morning.

"OK, fine," Silas continues when I refuse to abandon Bruiser for this conversation. "But one piece of advice—don't throw the *I'm paying you* thing at her—nothing pisses off a woman more than feeling like she's owned."

"I know that." In fact, that piece of advice would have come directly from me in any given circumstance. I clench my jaw. "Now if you'll excuse me, I need to get back to work."

Silas steps back but doesn't leave. "All right, well, I'm going to stay and watch . . . in case she knocks you unconscious and I need to call someone."

"Bruiser's a *he*." I adjust my hat and step toward the bull before he becomes restless. His ears twitch and he tenses. I crack the whip once into the dirt. He barely jerks.

From the corner of my eye, I catch Silas as he leans over the fence. "I meant the redhead that just pulled up in your truck."

"What?" I look over my shoulder, cursing under my breath when I catch Willow jumping out of the driver's seat. Freezing when she spots me inside the pen. She's wearing a cream-colored floral sundress under a denim jacket, with brown boots, and that sunset hair falling down around her worried face.

I bring my eyes back to the bull. Fix them on his shoulders, hooves, muscles, kicks. Making sure I stay within his field of vision. "That's right, over here," I mutter.

I hear the car door shut and her boots crunching against the rocky ground.

"Ellie all right?" I ask when she's within earshot, keeping my voice calm.

"She's with Cole at the house. Ginger's with them."

Right. It's Sunday. Cole visits on Sundays. "Fine. Why you here?"

Silas clears his throat and shakes his head in a warning. I don't mean to be dismissive. But I'm not exactly in a friendly environment over here.

"I need to talk to you," she calls, a hint of urgency in her voice.

I circle slowly, whip dragging beside me in case Bruiser charges. By the looks of it, he's not convinced I'm worth the effort. "You leaving?" I call back. It's the only thing I can think of that might be so urgent.

She's had enough.

"N—no."

Relief settles in my chest.

"Got my hands full, Willow. Say what you came to say and go."

She grunts restlessly behind me. "Well," she whines, then pauses for a moment. "Can I come in there?"

"No," Silas and I bark at once.

Bruiser snaps his neck around and I crack the whip into the dust again. "Easy now," I murmur, stepping closer.

"Is he dangerous?" I hear Willow ask. Silas wouldn't particularly know the answer to this, other than the sheer fact he's a bull.

"He can be," I breathe steadily. "Knowing how this usually goes between us, Sunset, think it's best you say what's on your mind and go."

She's quiet and I can't tell if she's holding back from yelling at me some more or deciding she's got me exactly where she wants me.

But something about the desperate look on her face when she showed up tells me I'm way off base.

I hear metal shuffling behind me. The distinct sound of a latch falling loose. My heart rate kicks up and I snap my head back. "Willow, don't."

She's already inside, pressing her back and arms along the fence, watching the animal with wide eyes.

Christ, this woman.

I take a breath, then extend a gloved hand toward Bruiser's shoulder, palm flat. "Willow I'm going to ask this once . . ."

"I'm sorry," she calls in a burning yet steady tone. Not loud though. She keeps her volume in line with mine. From the corner of my eye, I see her rounding the fence to get closer.

"Willow, not now."

I crack my whip in the direction I want him—away from her. And this way, I'm facing her, meeting her eyes.

One look is all it takes to know she's not going anywhere until she says what she came to say.

I glance and signal at my brother and he reads me like a book. Saluting me, he takes off in that yellow sports car of his, dust swirling in its wake.

Turning my head back, Willow shifts her gaze from the bull to me. I catch her swallow. "I was out of line last night. I should have told you about the gig." She closes her eyes, takes a breath then opens them again. "I should have *talked* to you first."

My chest constricts at her sincerity, but I cock my head and stay focused. "With the understanding that you'd do it anyway, right? Permission or not?" I couldn't help adding that last part. I glance at her with a smirk.

She shrugs, her voice a little shaky. "Probably. I wasn't trying to be a brat or difficult. I was . . . frustrated about something."

I meet her gaze. Her brown eyes are penetrating, carrying a need that damn near undoes me.

Her eyes flick to the bull, lip pulled between her teeth.

I sigh, the corner of my mouth tugging to ease her tension. "Fair enough, Sunset."

Her eyes soften and it's everything I didn't know I needed.

I don't know what to do here. Except abandon the damn bull and go to her. Find out what the hell this thing is between us and if she's feeling it the way I am. But my movements are limited and I can't *do this* here.

I'm not . . . ready to.

Chest tight, I turn back to Bruiser. "I appreciate the apology, Willow. But I need you to step outside the fence."

She doesn't move. "You're still mad."

"I'm standing in front of a twelve-hundred-pound bull. I literally *can't* be mad right now," I say calmly.

"Oh," she sighs, eyes flicking to the animal. "You going to ride him?"

"No." I step back to give him some space, eyes still locked on him. "Checking to see if he's ready to be around others."

"And?"

Bruiser huffs, drops his head, and steps back. A sign of submission.

You and me both, buddy.

I exhale, stepping back and muttering low. "And it's about time I stop fightin' it."

I meet Willow at the fence and guide her out slowly. The moment we're through the gate, she forces out a breath. "God, you're stubborn."

"I'm stubborn," I say flatly. "You follow me into the bullpen for something that could have waited till later, but *I'm* stubborn." I start toward the far end of the fence for my lasso.

She shrugs. "Not like I was in there alone. I trust you."

I pause mid step, breath catching in my throat like she'd knocked the wind out of me. I turn back to her. "That just might be your biggest gamble yet, Sunset."

She barely blinks. "I'll take my chances."

I shake my head, fighting the ache in my chest. The one begging me to do the same.

Like the kind of man she doesn't need, I walk away. Grabbing the lasso off the hook, I swing it around my shoulder. "You're a real handful, you know that?" A grin somehow works its way into my voice. I start the walk back to the shed uphill. "Back in a minute."

I needed things from the equipment shed. I know I did. But for the life of me, I can't remember what. I just know I need a minute.

I barely make it halfway before I hear her trying to keep up behind me, slightly out of breath. "I overreacted last night. I'm sorry. But you have to understand why I was so upset."

I keep walking, jaw tight, her voice trailing behind me like a damn hook. "I get it, Willow. It's why you broke up with your ex."

"No. Well, yes. But I also want to be able to defend myself."

"Which is what he said you couldn't do, right?" I don't stop. I don't turn. I don't understand what's happening between us, but I know that the next time I look at her, I'll be done for.

"Exactly," she breathes. "I swear, I'm usually in control a lot more when I'm up there playing. I don't know what got into me with that guy. But between Eric getting in my head, you intervening and me losing my job, I lost my . . ."

Behind me, her footsteps slow before stopping completely to catch her breath. "Can we . . . can we go back in the bullpen?"

That makes me stop. "Why?"

"Because . . . you can't walk . . . away from me there."

I turn and stare at her. Her hands are resting on her knees. She straightens slowly. "I'm *sorry*, Dallas."

"Stop saying that," I mutter.

"Why?"

"Because I don't know what to do with that," I snap.

She frowns. Then closes the distance. "You say you're sorry too, you buffoon."

"I already did."

"Well, you say it again." She pouts. "Then you look at me and tell me that I don't know what it's like to lose the love of my life. And that expecting you to be in the moment with me and not think about her was unfair." Her voice cracks.

My stomach twists. "Willow."

"Then maybe you call me out on being petty and blindsiding you." She sucks in a breath.

I take a step closer. "You're going to have to help me, Willow, I still don't know what to do." My voice is rough.

She blinks up at me. "You're not . . . talking about the apology anymore are you?"

I give a slow shake of my head.

She takes a breath like something is finally settling. "I understand. You just want time." She nods once before turning back.

"Willow, I don't want that."

She holds up her hands like it's no sweat. "You're working and I'm . . . too much." She shakes her head at herself, like this is all too familiar, then continues downhill.

"Get back here," I call on an exhale. Hands itching at my sides to go after her, I lower the lasso off my shoulder and narrow my eyes, assessing the distance.

She's a little over ten paces away before my rope goes flying, snaking through the air smoothly. The loop lands softly around her.

She freezes, head dropping to her middle. She twists to face me, eyes wide, lips parting before she speaks. "Did you just . . . lasso me?"

I keep my eyes on her, tugging gently, gathering the rope as she comes closer. "How's it any different than stepping into my bullpen?"

"Oh," she breathes. "Well then, are you apologizing too?"

I pull her the rest of the way to me, holding the loop tight like she's a flight risk. "No. And I really don't believe that's all you came to do either."

She shakes her head with a smirk. "You really don't know what to do when a woman apologizes, do you, Spout?"

"Don't get me wrong. I know what I *want* to do." My eyes drop to her lips. "I know I've wanted it since the day

I laid eyes on you." I release my grip and let the rope fall to the ground. Then I take her hand and move her against all the new hay bales we got stacked outside the shed. "But since we're being honest, Sunset, I didn't pull back because of Millie." I swallow. "Not in the way you think."

"You don't have to explain."

"I pulled back because it was different." I push her hair back. "The kind I wanted more of that night. The kind I haven't been able to stop thinking about."

"More of . . ." Her voice trails off, eyes hooked to my mouth.

I lift her chin. "Stay with me, we'll get there." I drop my hand, careful not to touch more of her smooth face with my filth. "More of what I felt with you in my arms. Things I never thought I'd feel again. Hell, things I didn't *want* to feel, because Millie was supposed to be . . . it for me." I remove my hat and set it over the hay. Then, like it's the most natural thing in the world, I press my forehead to hers.

She inhales, breathing me in.

"I'm going to mess this up," I tell her. "I don't want to hurt anybody."

Her eyes are on mine. "You have a history of breaking hearts?"

The thought of breaking Willow's heart guts me. But losing her might just destroy me. "Don't think so. But it's not just mine and yours on the line here."

She wraps her arms around my shoulders. "I *don't* have a history of breaking hearts, cowboy. And I sure as hell don't plan on starting with yours or Ellie's."

There's a fierce light in her gaze, hot and unyielding. It knocks the breath right out of me. Even if I know it's not a promise anyone can make, I believe her.

In an instant, I'm lifting her face to me and crushing her mouth with mine. I'm not careful or sweet. It's hungry and desperate. It's for us. Her lips part with equal wild urgency. A moan tears from her throat and she pulls my shirt, tugging me closer, starved. This time neither one of us is pulling back. The longing, the ache is too strong.

It's a kiss of surrender . . . and one heck of a risk.

A faint buzzing sound tries to pull me back, but I'm not ready to let go.

Willow draws back with a breath, eyes blazing with heat. "Dallas," she murmurs. "There's a . . . vibration in your pants."

My lips are still parted. I'm ready to curse the damn thing but the amusement in her eyes has me huffing out a laugh. "I was hoping you wouldn't notice."

She drops her head with a smile, and I tuck loose strands behind her ear. Then I dip my hand into my pocket, and answer my phone.

24

Willow

Dallas and I arrived at the house minutes after Ginger called letting us know Cole was getting ready to leave and had one request.

"No," Dallas barks as soon as he walks in.

On instinct, I grasp his arm to tame him. It's one thing to come in attacking an innocent, broken, elderly man. It's another to do it in front of a little girl.

Cole stands up off the couch, giving me a polite nod then turning his eyes on Dallas.

Ellie jumps from the carpet, pulling on a piece of paper from the coffee table. "Look what I drew today."

I scan it as she holds it up for us. The crayon is faint in the light, but it appears to be a yard with a house in the background and several stick figures in front of it.

Dallas dips his eyes. "That's beautiful, baby. That's a lot of people."

"We have a big family."

I notice another figure on the far right of the page. "Who's this?"

"That's Grandpa."

Dallas and I exchange a look and I glance at Cole, knowing she means him, since Dallas's dad is "Grandpa Connor."

Ginger stretches out a hand. "Ellie, let's go pack up some of those pumpkin cookies for Grandpa before he goes."

Dallas glares at Cole. "Let's talk about this outside."

"That's a good idea." His eyes flick to mine briefly. "Alone."

"She comes too. Willow's going to be Ellie's stepmother."

"Dallas," I warn softly.

Cole runs his eyes over me like he's got no argument and my heart goes out to him.

"Dallas," I whisper another warning. "Let's step outside before we upset someone."

The three of us step out on the porch, Cole shaking his head the entire time, eyes scanning the fields before turning to us. "I don't buy it. This whole thing is a lie. And you're doing it to keep me from my granddaughter. I know it. Glenda knows it and she says all we need to do is give the courts a reason to doubt your integrity."

Dallas steps forward. "This is about *Ellie*. Not Willow and me. And I'm not keeping you from her, *you're* trying to take her away from me. As if six years wasn't goddamn long enough."

Cole drops his gaze, jaw tight. My heart breaks for him, and as right as Dallas might be here, I wish he'd stop.

As if reading my mind, my fiancé exhales with a step back. Voice low. "This is bullshit, Cole. Call it off and we can work it out like grown-ups. Like the two people she's got left in this world who only want the best for her."

"Grown-ups." Cole laughs and pulls his phone from the inside of his jacket. "I'm not the one getting lap dances from an ex a week before my wedding." He holds the phone out to us with a picture of Dallas on a chair and Laurie on his lap. He's leaning so far back he looks like he's about to fall backward.

Dallas doesn't say a word. But the tension radiates off him.

I'd laugh if I weren't so disgusted. Not at what's happening in the photo. But at what a decent man like Cole Hartly is ready to do just to win. "You're using your visit with your granddaughter to threaten us?"

"It's not a threat. It's proof you two are a sham."

"It's a *bachelor* party. That's what happens at these things. And any judge looking at that will know that Dallas clearly wanted no part in it."

Dallas's head dips sideways to me. But I keep my eyes fixed on Cole. His tired, kind, green eyes. He clearly hates all of this.

His pain is almost a look into what Dallas went through not all that long ago. And if I screw this up—he'll lose his daughter too.

Cole puts his phone away. "That's just one. There're others of you last night at The Blue Branch. Glenda's got it all."

"Then she should be sending them to my lawyer. Not sending you here to taunt us."

Cole frowns at the word. It's just as I thought. He's not evil. But he is hurting and letting a ruthless attorney get in his head.

"What makes you think I'm going to honor your request to spend time with Ellie on your own tomorrow now?"

"The request was a courtesy. She's still legally—"

"Until our first hearing she's still staying here. With us."

"I just want to take her out for ice cream after school. I'll have her home by six."

"She has her paint class tomorrow at the cottage with Rose."

"Tuesday then. I'm just trying to not be the estranged man in the corner of the page."

"You put yourself there. Now get off my property."

"Dallas," I warn again. Because despite his coolness and threats, I feel for this man.

He merely glances at me, then walks back into the house.

I give Cole a tentative smile. "Maybe leading with the photo wasn't a good idea. But I'll talk to him about taking her out for ice cream. I think she'd love that."

Cole runs a hand down his face. "Don't you think I know how this story ends? You two are going to like playing house a little too much and I'm going to lose my little girl."

His words make my heart ache and break all at once.

"She's also Dallas's little girl. And no one is losing anyone. It's not too late to call this off."

He smirks. "I'm willing to bet that if I do, you'll be straight back to where you came from. And my granddaughter is going to be raised by that man and that man alone. With all his lap dances, bar fights, and . . ." his eyes dip down, "grief." The last word trails off like he can hear the hypocrisy in it.

I stare at him for a moment, trying to will the anger, but it doesn't seem to come. This man means no harm. He's just scared to be alone. "We'll see you next Sunday, Mr. Hartly," I say softly, then turn toward the house.

"I'm not coming to the wedding."

Confused, I flip my head back. "What?"

His brows shoot up. "Oh, you meant the visit. Well, that's interesting. Never met a bride who forgot her own wedding day." He tips his hat. "Have a good evening."

I close the dishwasher, eyes scanning the marble counter for any speck of dust or crumbs. I hear Dallas's footsteps above as he shuts Ellie's door softly and heads down.

One look at me and his brows come together. "What's wrong?"

"Am I pouting again?"

He smiles, dims the lights in the kitchen, and comes around the counter. "Yes, but this time I don't have to resist wiping it off your face."

When he closes the distance, I press a hand against his solid chest. Wishing I could focus on seeing it bare soon, but knowing I've got to get something off mine. I lift my eyes to his. "I slipped up."

He freezes. "What do you mean?"

"I told Cole we'd see him next Sunday for his visit."

"And?"

I cock my head. "He had to *remind* me we're getting married next Sunday."

He grins and snakes his fingers around my neck, his thumbs sweeping my jaw gently. "You need to relax."

I pinch the bridge of my nose, my stress levels heightening. "I'm going to ruin this for you."

He lowers my hand. "Then stop talking, Sunset," he murmurs against my lips in that gravelly tone. Then kisses them tenderly. "By the way, I'm sorry about the photo with Laurie."

I laugh.

"What's funny?"

"You were one breath away from falling off that chair and crackin' your head open."

He chuckles, but there's little humor. Instead, he pokes my stomach. "Liked you stickin' up for me tonight."

I'm about to blow it off with a comment about blondes, but it catches in my throat when I see how serious he is. And nervous. "He's got nothing on you, Dallas. And I'm prepared to tell anyone who questions it that I was being harassed on that stage and you jumped to my defense."

He sucks in deep. "I hate this." He runs a hand down his face. "The lies, the fights, putting Ellie in the middle of it all. I just want to give her a good life. I want a chance to be her daddy. To raise her. To make up for lost time. Last thing I want to do is take someone else away from her."

I cup his face. "We won't. If he doesn't drop this, we'll do everything we can to win and then reason with him. Show him that it doesn't have to be this way."

He watches me like he's not sure about any of it anymore.

"Dallas, all you're doing is getting the rights you and Ellie deserved, the ones *he* promised you from the very beginning."

He nods, a slow resolve. "You'll help me make things right when this is all over?"

I smile up at him. "Unless you're kicking me out."

He growls low, hand sliding back into my hair. "Good. Now where the hell were we before all this?" He dips his head, kissing my jaw.

I'm already melting from the heat of his body when Dallas hikes me up onto the island. The skirt of my dress bunches around my thighs as he spreads my legs apart and steps between them.

I gasp and he's barely touched me—which means I'm in trouble. I'm even more aware of this fact when he brings his hands to my bare thighs and gently squeezes as he works his way up. Stopping when he reaches the warm inner part between my legs.

I toss my head back with a shudder. "Don't be a tease, Dallas."

He responds with a throaty chuckle as he brings his hands back to my face, brushing my lips with his. "It's only a tease if I don't follow through." He presses a kiss against my neck and works his way down. "I'm not teasing anyone tonight."

I tug on his shirt. "We're done with rules, right?"

"Damn right," he rasps, then reaches back and peels the shirt over his head and tosses it to me.

I drop it beside me on the counter, and he inches me forward. I yelp, then exhale a laugh as my hands dig into his hair, still damp from his shower, then stroke his sexy stubble. "This beard turns me on."

His brows knit like he thought I might have said something else. "You like it?"

I nod, flustering.

A slow grin spreads over his face as he watches me. "Then lie back, Sunset. So you can feel it between your thighs."

He lowers me flat on my back, my hair spread around me, and bends my knees. His hands stroke the side of my thighs, rough and sure. He taps my hips gently when he reaches the lace fabric. "Lift. I need to see how wet you are for me."

My stomach squeezes and I do as he asks, my panties peeled off me in seconds. I can't see where they go, all I hear is another husky command. "Wider."

Lip pulled between my teeth, my knees can barely fall further apart. I want him. I want this so badly, but what if he has another moment of doubt? What if I'm not the *good different* he felt from our kiss?

What if I fall in love with this feeling? With his mouth. Or worse.

His finger strokes me gently, slowly. And suddenly his face is in front of mine, our eyes locked. "Willow," he starts in a husky whisper. "Stay with me," he tells me for the second time today, voice low and rough against my skin. "Because I promise there's no one else here."

I lift my fingers to cup his jaw. "There isn't?"

"Hasn't been since the night I found you in my bedroom."

My heart swells. My center throbs and I whimper, letting my knees fall.

His eyes stay locked with mine for a beat and he grins with unspoken praise. His arms flex as he wraps them around my legs.

My head falls back and I stifle a moan as his beard brushes my inner thigh. I suck in a breath when he does the same to the other side, closer to my pussy this time, rubbing that stubble along my skin.

I writhe with need for more, but enjoying every second of this foreplay, this torment.

"Need to taste you," he growls, then presses his lips to my pussy in a feverish French kiss.

My mouth falls open in a silent cry, hand seeking out his shirt to muffle the sounds I know I won't be able to control for much longer.

I'm breathing hard, writhing as pleasure builds and builds, intensifying by the second.

"You taste like heaven," he says, his praise vibrating in just the right spot. He licks and sucks tirelessly. Impressing the shit out of me with not only his talented tongue but the tenderness of his hands that explore everything within reach.

I moan, rock, beg with my hips, catching my voice every time it slips. I nearly laugh when the shirt lands on my chest.

I inhale his scent, my head falling back like it's the drug I've been waiting for.

He chuckles against my wetness in a brief pause before his mouth takes hold of me again. Hard. Fast. Like he's been holding out this whole time—catching my clit between his lips, flicking and sucking. My legs shake as an orgasm slams into me, shattering me into pieces. I cover my face with his shirt and muffle my scream.

Dallas kisses below my belly button softly as I come down. "You're out of this world." He brings my knees down and helps me up.

I release a breath. "Sure feels like it."

He lifts me off the counter and brings me to my feet, the skirt of my dress falling back to my knees. His hands stay wrapped around me protectively—or reassuringly.

I smile up at him. "What now?" It's barely a whisper.

"I think we move this to my bedroom," he says, voice low, eyes steady.

"God, I want to," I breathe. "But—"

"But you weren't talking about tonight, specifically."

Way to read me. "No, I guess I wasn't."

He nods once, giving me space, his hand dipping into his pockets. "Now we . . . plan a wedding."

I nod firmly in agreement. "And focus on getting you Ellie."

Dallas cocks his head with a wary glare. "Sunset, we can focus on more than just my daughter."

I shake my head. "Dallas, I almost slipped up today. We just . . . need to be more careful."

He releases a heavy breath. "You're right," he rasps, then looks back down at me like this whole thing is unfair. "For the sake of Ellie, maybe we . . . press pause."

I don't realize I'm holding my breath until it's my turn to speak. "Right. A . . . long pause."

He steps close to me, presses his body against mine, sweeps my hair back, and snakes his fingers under my jaw. Heat flares in my stomach and the words "this isn't what I meant" and "take me up to your bedroom" jumble in my mind. His fingers grip my chin, thumb stroking and coaxing my mouth open as he kisses me. A deep, claiming kiss. So unrelenting, I forget how to breathe.

With a soft breath, he pulls back. "But I still get to do that."

25

Willow

On Monday evening, I sit in on Rose's art class at the cottage. Watching her do what she does best and teaching it to the kids in town.

Today's lesson was to draw something we love doing out in nature.

I don't sit next to Ellie. I want this space to be her own, without me looking over her shoulder. Instead, I sit in the back, with a blank canvas of my own.

Would it be too suggestive if I drew a picture of a cowboy catching a redhead with his lasso?

I chuckle to myself.

Rose might find it hilarious—and ask questions. Lots of them. The minute I walked in here, she noticed the difference in my mood. Telling me I looked "happier today" and a little more like I "belong"—whatever that means.

Least she didn't tell me I was *glowing*.

I told her the short version. Dallas and I made up. And then broke up. Agreeing to keep things strictly Ellie-focused for the time being.

She still had that concerned-friend look on her face. And I get it. I've got a track record for falling for what's bad for me. And then falling hard on my ass when it's over.

But Dallas is the kind of man who would never want to hurt me. But he's also the kind of man who would do it without trying.

After the kids get picked up, I hand Rose my wet canvas, where I painted streaks of pinks, yellows, and orange over a blue river.

"Oh, pretty, is this a sunset?"

"Well, it's either that or a strange-lookin' rainbow."

I reach out for Ellie, who's got her hand in the cookie jar. "Ready, Slippers? Your dad says dinner's almost ready and it's going to rain soon."

She grabs two cookies and gives me her picture to hold. "Ready."

I look at her art today, almost afraid of what I might find. But it looks innocent enough. Like a field of dandelions.

"How pretty," Rose comments.

Ellie beams. "There's one for all of us."

"All of us?" I ask.

She nods. "So you can all make a wish. You, Daddy, Rose, Uncle Wilder . . ." she goes on. I wait for her to skip Cole, but she mentions both grandpas.

"Where's yours?" I ask.

She shrugs and picks up her backpack. "I already made mine."

Rose pouts like that's the cutest thing she's ever heard. But I know this kid better. And I'm almost afraid to ask what that little wish was.

"Saving that cookie for after dinner?" I ask, walking to the golf cart.

She stuffs it her mouth. "Nope."

"Figured. Bring me one?"

She holds the other one up for me. "Yep."

We're at the house within minutes and I roll the cart under the low-roofed carport on the side of the house just as I hear thunder rolling in the distance. "Uh-oh, better hurry before we get that painting wet."

Ellie and I scramble toward the house, the strong wind tugging at our clothes and hair. We slip inside and shut the door against howls.

A warm, rich scent of lemon and garlic wraps around me, tugging a smile from my lips.

Ellie sets down her painting and kicks off her boots. I follow her to the kitchen. Dallas is in an oil-stained white shirt and jeans. Hair damp, a dishtowel over his shoulder. And for the first time in weeks—he doesn't look *all that* grumpy.

"There they are." Dallas glances over at us from behind the counter. "Dinner in five." He does a double-take at Ellie. "Hold up. Get over here."

She giggles as he comes around the counter and lifts her over it. "Are those crumbs on your chin?"

"Maybe." She chuckles.

He sniffs the corner of her mouth and gasps. "Chocolate chip." He tickles her tummy and winks. "Go wash up."

Ellie races to the bathroom but not before tattling. "Willow had one too."

Dallas tosses the rag down. My stomach flips when he pulls me close and presses his nose to the side of my face with a low growl.

I press my lips together and shake my head. "You can't prove anything."

His arms trap me, palms braced on either side of the island. "Oh, I think I can make you open your mouth for me."

My eyes shimmer with a warning, but I can't help the smiling, the teasing.

The sizzling of my skin.

"Smells good in here." I eye the table set for three. Dinner napkins, wine glasses, a colorful salad bowl, garlic bread. "What's the occasion?"

It's not his first time cooking dinner while I'm here. But it's rarely this . . . involved. This . . . homey. Usually he'd grill something outside or whip up Ellie's favorite pasta dish.

He shrugs, blue eyes meeting mine like he's got a secret. "Yeah, well. Suddenly realized, the kitchen's my favorite place in the house."

I fight a smirk as heat creeps up my neck.

Ellie steps out and he steps back—but not as quickly as I'd imagined. More like he's doing it for my benefit.

Like for him . . . it wouldn't be the worst thing if Ellie saw us this close. This . . . happy.

The oven beeps and I step around the island to wash my hands while Dallas plates up our dinner. My phone rings and I look at the screen.

Mom.

I ignore it. The clouds grow dark and thunder rolls. *How fitting.*

"You can grab that, we'll wait."

I shake my head and silence it. "I'll call her back. Let's eat."

As usual, during dinner, we're fixated on Ellie. But it's different today. There's stolen glances, smirks, winks, moments I forget to breathe because of how much I like this. How much I *want* this.

But even in my mind, I need to shift focus.

I love Ellie. I want the best for her. And I believe Dallas can give her that.

My stomach squeezes. My eyes mist as I realize what's happening.

What I can't let happen. Not now.

I can't fall for Dallas Thorne.

No matter how easy he makes it. No matter how right this feels.

Dallas sets his fork down. "All right, let's see what you painted in Rose's class today."

"It's still drying by the door, I'll get it." Ellie races out.

Dallas and I start clearing the table when my phone rings again.

This time, he sees the screen. "Any reason you're dodging your mother's calls?"

I purse my lips. "Guessing she got the digital invite to the wedding."

He frowns. "Those went out a few days ago."

I flick my gaze to his. "Not hers."

Understanding reaches his eyes. "I'm sorry, Willow. Look, if you want, we can take the call together after Ellie goes to bed. We don't have to lie to her."

I swallow, my heart plummeting a little, because this is still a lie.

"That's sweet of you to offer but—"

"Offer? Willow, we're in this together. You stood by me with my family and in front of half the town. However much you want to tell her, I'll do it with you."

I scoff because this is one conversation he *doesn't* need to hear. "I'll fill you in after."

He gives me a soft nod, letting me know he'll be here for me when I need him—however I need him.

Ellie returns with her dandelion painting.

I'd like to use my dandelion wish to avoid this phone call. Instead, I smile at them both and step out to the covered back porch, where my conversation with my mother can be muffled by the sound of the rain.

"Before you start, no, I'm not pregnant," I tell her before she has a chance to greet me.

"Of course you're not. You've been there three weeks, what do you take me for?"

I release a breath. "OK. So, you're calling with your RSVP?" I hold my breath.

"I'm calling to tell you I'm *proud* of you." Her tone too dry and flat to match the word.

"You are?" I ask warily, barely phrasing it as a question. For a second, I let myself believe she might be proud of my selfless act of kindness. Helping a good man—who has more than enough potential to be a good father—keep his daughter.

Then I remember who I'm talking to.

"Well, it's pretty obvious, dear. You saw an opportunity to collect your inheritance early and took it. That's my girl."

"It's not obvious, because it isn't true," I snap. "This is all for Ellie."

"Is someone listening to our conversation?"

I sigh. "No."

"Good. Then no need to fool me too. Sweetheart, this is *brilliant*. It's a two-way deal. Why should he be the only one benefiting from this arrangement?"

"Mom, we're talking about a custody battle for a man who didn't even know he had a daughter until a few months ago."

She releases an exasperated breath. "And I'm talking about you choosing to scramble for the next four years instead of taking charge now."

"Mom—"

"I know you don't realize this now, but life is short. Twenty-year-olds are making six, seven figures a year online while you're wasting precious years being noble."

My stomach gives a tight, aching squeeze. I hate how she finds ways to make sense.

A chill runs through me as I look over my shoulder at Dallas and Ellie. He can't see me out here in the dark, but he looks over anyway, as if he can sense me. "You're right. It would be . . . nice." Especially when I'm on my own again. "I'll think about it," I whisper.

A pause. Then another sigh. "I'll take it. And I'll see you next week. Do you want me to bring anything? Family heirloom or something to really sell it?"

"Please don't."

Her voice grows distant as she ignores me. "I'll have to see what I've got . . ."

"I'm going now. It's cold out here."

"Send me links to the best hotel in town."

"There's just the one inn here. But I think the ranch will be opening up their guest cabins for the wedding. I'll see if I can get you one."

"Sounds lovely." She doesn't sound convinced. "Keep me posted about the other thing. I'll call the lawyer in the meantime . . . you know, just in case."

"Don't call anyone. Case closed."

I step back into the house. The kitchen is clean and empty. I can't think. I can't even feel anything but that twist in my stomach. It feels a lot like betrayal.

A lie to my grandmother.

"She's all tucked up and ready for her bedtime story," Dallas calls as he comes back down the stairs, a grin on his face as he enters the kitchen. It fades quickly when he sees me. "Hey, what's the matter? Your mother can't make it?"

I shake my head. "No, no, she'll be here."

He backtracks as understanding hits. "She know about the . . . special arrangement?"

"That it's temporary? Yes. She's . . . happy about it in fact."

He nods slowly. "Protective of you."

I look off to the side. "More like my . . . future."

"Willow?"

I meet his eyes. Tentative and heartbroken for even considering betraying my integrity.

He steps closer, holding my gaze. "What is it?"

I swallow.

He lifts my chin. "I've been nothing but honest with you. And I'm respecting our deal to press pause on . . . this." He looks at the space between us, then tucks my hair away. "But I'd be lying if I said you don't look guilty as hell for something right now."

"I promise, it's nothing," I whisper.

Nothing that affects you anyway.

"Just answer me this," he starts, and I brace myself with a breath. "The marriage might be temporary, but . . . it isn't *fake*. That piece of paper, the officiant . . . as real as any other." He shifts on a pause. "Do you want out?"

I shake my head with a vigorous *no*.

He relaxes, but just barely, pinning me with those blue eyes. "When the pressure's off and Ellie's ours . . . think you might want in?"

Warmth spreads across my chest. I want *all in*.

He and Ellie are a package deal, I know that. But what about when the high is over? When he looks at me and remembers *her*. Especially in a home he designed based on what *she* wanted. When the pressure's off—who's to say he'll need me?

And how do I tell him I've been burned so many times that I'm on autopilot, doubting everything.

I *trust* Dallas. It's more like my curse I don't trust.

My eyes mist and I nod slowly.

His lip quirks up and he cups my jaw, pressing his body against mine. "Then that's good enough for me."

26

Willow

My bachelorette party wasn't nearly as much of a bust as Dallas's, but it left me feeling bitter all the same.

I was the only single woman out tonight. Rose, Charlie, Pepper, their sister-in-law Tessa, who's a fellow redhead and hilarious, are all married or practically married. And also Ginger, who has a not-so-secret relationship with Connor Thorne.

Rose, Charlie, and Ginger were the only ones tonight who knew this whole thing with Dallas is a farce, so I had to act like the blissful bride-to-be all night long.

It was exhausting . . . and depressing.

Rose and Charlie brought me home just before midnight and suggested a quiet drink out on the back porch. While they grabbed the glasses and a bottle of wine, I fetched a few blankets.

Now, the three of us are settled under the stars, wrapped up and sipping in the stillness—Rose and I on the swing and Charlie stretched out on the loveseat across from us.

"You're a real trooper," Rose tells me, words slurred, smile wide.

I snort. "Yeah, it was a real rough night. All those half-naked dancers. The free drinks."

Charlie giggles low. "And where you all been hidin' Ginger? She was the life of the party."

Rose laughs. "Did you see the look on her face when tassel-cowboy shook his junk in front of her?"

"Shh. There are innocent ears two windows up," I whisper and point.

Charlie hums and looks up at the stars for a long moment. "Nice digs you got here, Willow."

I'm about to absently thank her when reality slowly settles and my stomach sinks. "You know it's not mine."

She scoffs like she knows better than I do. "*Right.*"

I exchange a look with Rose and she rolls her eyes. "Charlie's a book nerd. She believes in happy endings."

"Excuse me, but I happen to be *living* mine and it didn't come from a book," Charlie argues.

"Oh yeah? Did you fall for your boss too, like Rose here?" I sidetrack.

"Noah, my boss?" she laughs. "Heavens no. We got stuck helping Chase and Pepper plan their wedding together. It was also the same week I was wrongfully evicted—so he practically kidnapped me to stay with him—after he threatened my landlord with a class-action lawsuit and somehow made the old man owe *me* money."

"Sounds like a fun recipe to me." I snicker and sip.

"Sure. If he hadn't dumped me three years before for cheating on him."

I sit up, nearly choking. "You cheated on Noah?" Somehow, I don't see a man as ice-cold as Noah forgiving something like that. And Charlie—just doesn't seem like the type. She's Little Miss Sunshine who owns a children's bookstore.

"She's exaggerating." Rose rolls her eyes, clearly knowing more about the story.

"Blame it on the drinks, but I've got to say, you two don't seem like a . . . likely pair . . ."

"Where's the fun in that?" Charlie goes on with her point. "All I'm saying is sometimes the best things . . . start off a bit messy." She takes a sip of wine and shrugs. "What if this is just the start of something that was always meant to be yours?"

I can tell by Rose's expression she doesn't agree. Or she's protectively wary. But she doesn't say as much.

Frustrated with her silence, I decide to let Charlie in on a little secret. "I'm not letting myself believe that. It's dangerous territory for me."

Charlie cocks her head at me. "First off—*interesting*. Second, how so?"

"I've got a track record for falling for the wrong guy. Toxic, unavailable, uncommitted. And a recent rock-bottom relationship had me swearing off men for a while."

I say the words I've been telling myself for months like a broken record no one—least of all me—cares to hear anymore. The words that seem foreign when the subject is Dallas.

Charlie hiccups, bringing her wine to her lips. "Boy, did you pick the wrong time to end that streak."

I take a slow sip, the wine suddenly bitter. Because the truth is, I can press pause on this thing between Dallas and me all I want. But I know in my heart—he's *not* the wrong guy.

I'm not blinded this time. I'm not seeing something that isn't there. I'm seeing something that's so right, so good and so rich with everything I've been missing—that it hurts.

I've fallen for Dallas Thorne.
Painfully hard.
Not in that over-the-moon, scream-at-the-top-of-my-lungs kind of love.

But a raw, aching kind that makes you want to cry. A lonely kind.

Because as much as we both want all in, he's emotionally charged with grief, loss, and fear of losing people he loves.

While I'm stirring with how deeply I've fallen. First for the girl, then this house, and now for the man.

I pour a glass of whiskey and head upstairs. My heart geared up to drop to my stomach if this goes sideways.

Dallas's bedroom door is cracked open, a habit of his I'd noticed, so he can hear Ellie if she needs him.

I swallow and knock. He's at the door in a matter of seconds, sleepy and sexy with his tousled hair, tanned skin. Boxers resting low at the hips.

He scans me. "What time is it?"

"Late."

He eyes the whiskey. "Thought you girls were drinkin' wine downstairs."

"We were. This is for you."

He inches closer, assessing me. "You all right?"

My eyes sting because I want to say no. But I nod. I nod because I am now. With the way he's looking at me. Like he'd kill anyone who might've hurt me tonight.

He wraps a firm warm hand on my wrist and brings me inside. "Stay here." Then he leaves me alone, walking across the hall to check on Ellie briefly.

I stare blindly at the dark room. The soft streaks of moonlight edging along the walls as they bleed through the window. Still no curtains. But just as warm and welcoming.

He steps back into the room, this time shutting the door behind him.

"I don't need this." He takes the glass from me and sets it aside. His hands return to me instantly, framing my face, running his thumb back and forth along my frown. "What is it, baby? What's wrong?"

I meet his eyes. "I want to unpause."

His grin is slow. "And you thought I needed liquid courage?"

I shrug innocently. "It would only be fair."

He sighs heavily, drawing back like he's obligated by some rule to turn me down.

"Dallas."

"Willow," he rasps, a strain in his voice.

"If I stand on one foot and press a finger to my nose for one whole minute, will you let me stay?" I smile coyly.

He huffs a laugh, taking my hands and pulling me toward the bed. He sits and holds my waist as I step between his legs. "How was your night?"

My lip quirks. "The girls had fun."

"And you?" He starts to tug teasingly on the hem of my dress.

I stroke his beard lightly with my fingers. "What do you think?"

He pushes to his feet with a low growl, covering my mouth in a hungry kiss, devouring me with his tongue. Breaking for a breath only to pull the dress over my head.

He cups my breast over the thin fabric of my bra, squeezing hard, dipping his fingers inside then yanking one cup down.

My head falls back in an invitation he reads like a book.

He sucks a nipple into his mouth, making me cry out. "You love my mouth on you, don't you, Sunset?"

"Hmm, yes," I gasp.

"Been thinking about it sliding into you all night, haven't you?" he murmurs against my lips.

I only whimper in response and he slaps one ass cheek, making me cry out. "Yes."

"Good." He runs his hands down my sides, hovering over my panties.

"Let me guess," I pant. "Last chance to change my mind?"

His fingers stroke back up my arms and he kisses my lips softly. "Never. You control that pause button."

I cup his jaw. "Strip me," I whisper harshly.

Another low curse before he all but destroys the last bits of fabric left on my skin.

"Look at you. You're so damn beautiful." His fingers dip between my legs and I shudder. "Soaked too."

He presses a sweet kiss to me again and I close my eyes. Half worshiping his tenderness. Half wishing he wasn't following all the love-making steps.

"Willow, turn around," he growls low.

I open my eyes, a glimmer in them as I meet his, now dark and lust-filled.

"Crawl on my bed and stay on all fours for me."

Aroused more than I've ever been, I turn, facing away from him, eyeing his massive bed with a grin before crawling over it. I don't feel exposed. I feel sexy, wanted. And that's all before I look over my shoulder at him. He tugs his boxers down, his big, hard cock springing free. I pull my bottom lip between my teeth, suppressing a gasp.

Our eyes lock as he strokes himself. I whimper, wanting him inside me. Unsure if I can take it all at once, especially starting with this position. But *fuck* if my pussy isn't throbbing for the challenge right now.

Pulling on a condom from his drawer, he sheathes himself and I turn my face, ready for him. His hands grip my thighs and I can practically feel his cock inside me. I'm dripping for it.

I gasp when his tongue plunges into me instead, fucking me with an impressive length of its own. With a closed mouth, I cry out, practically in tears as he sucks, licks, and fucks me with his mouth. In seconds, I'm shattering, coming so hard I drop my head into his pillow and scream.

I feel his weight on the bed as I come down, his arms wrapping around me and turning me onto my back. He brushes his thumb across my flushed cheek. "You good?"

I release a breath, grinning lazily. "You tricked me."

"Needed you to come first." He runs a hand around my breast and down my side then slowly between my legs. I jerk, still sensitive and still so needy for him. I can feel his cock—long, hard, poking against my skin.

I arch into him in a silent plea as he strokes me. "Dallas," I moan.

"Almost there." His breath is warm and soft against my skin. "Caught you eyeing me. You're not sure if you can take it all."

I dig my fingers into his hair. "I can."

"I know you can." He rubs slow circles. "And you will." His voice is firm yet tender, making me wetter, hotter. "Making sure it's easy on you."

I relax in his arms, tilting my head to kiss him. Deep, raw, the kind of kiss that doesn't scream *fuck me*. It screams *I've fallen for you. I trust you.* And as long as I'm in his arms, I'm *good*.

I hardly notice when Dallas stops working me. All I feel is the slow flex of his muscles when he pushes inside me. One. Long. Thrust.

I suck in a breath against his lips. Trembling because it feels so good. He's big, filling me completely. He doesn't ease in, he doesn't wait for me to adjust. There's zero resistance and I'm not even sure how that's possible. But he pumps, in and out, eyes locked on mine like he's reading every thought.

"There you go," he encourages. "Spread wider for me," he asks, but I barely move, he does it for me with the gentle encouragement of his knee.

I whimper, feeling the friction intensify as he rubs against me and I meet him thrust for thrust with my hips.

"You are the sexiest thing, Sunset," he murmurs.

My stomach coils with heat and my heart swells.

"So damn sexy, it hurts." His voice strains, he squeezes his eyes shut briefly before locking them with mine again.

I'm close. So close. Trembling with the need to come and the need to savor this. I palm his face. "It's so good," I whimper.

He holds my gaze. "I know." It's all he says, raspy and conflicted.

For a moment I feel like I might be losing him, but then he says, "You're going to be my wife." His pumps turn slow and hard.

"Yes."

He snaps his hips and I moan. "You and me."

"Yes, yes."

Thrust. "Against them all."

I gasp, trembling in his arms as another orgasm hits.

"For better or worse," he grunts as he thrusts one more time, shuddering through his release.

"God, yes." I detonate, coming hard, convulsing around his cock as he covers my mouth with his, swallowing my cry.

We're both panting hard as he eases out of me. Midnight-blue eyes roam over my face, saying so much and nothing at all. "Don't move, Sunset." He eases off the bed and slips into the bathroom.

My eyes sting with hot tears I can't explain and I blink them away. *What was that?*

Reckless.

It was reckless and desperate.

And quite possibly ruined me for life.

A life without him in it.

I hear the shower start and a moment later, he steps back into the bedroom. One look and I forget the argument I'm having with myself.

He steps toward the bed, lifting the whiskey off the nightstand and taking a sip.

"What was the name of that wine?"

I chuckle, shuffling up on my knees on the bed. "I'm not telling you."

His eyes roam over my body and he sets the glass down. "Guess I'm gonna have to buy them all." He lifts me off the bed and sets me on my feet, then sweeps my hair back. "Spend the night with me. Tonight, tomorrow. Every night."

I bite the corner of my lip. "And if I don't?"

"Then we're going to have to switch rooms. Because I'm not lookin' at that bed again without you in it."

27

Dallas

Willow's mother is stressing her out. It's no wonder she was dreading moving in with her weeks ago.

It's our *wedding* day. And I'm pretty damn sure there's some rule against annoying the bride right before the ceremony.

The ceremony site is set by the oak tree behind my property. Charlie, Rose, and a few members of our staff have been setting everything up. There are rows of white folding chairs, evenly divided by the aisle—worn grass lined with pink rose petals—and bordered by weathered barrels on either side. The tree is decked out in white mesh fabric interspersed with sprigs of willow.

It's a clear day in November, but chilly. No one seems to mind though. Ginger's got a station with warm cider for the guests to take a glass on their way in.

I adjust my collar, fighting the urge to step between Willow and Lucy Brooks—her mother, who introduced herself like someone I should know—and tear her away with an excuse.

"Leave them alone," Dad says, handing me a whiskey. He, Wilder, and I are standing under the roof of my back porch. "Nothing good comes from stepping between a mother and her daughter."

I frown.

"Remember Grandma Tilly?"

"Barely."

"My point exactly. Let it go. They'll work it out."

"Yeah, fine," I grunt and flick my gaze away from them.

We're not exactly being traditional here, with Willow wanting to be out in the open before the ceremony—greeting early guests and directing the setup, taking this on together.

She's stunning today, in a lace-trimmed knee-length white dress and a pair of cowgirl boots. Her hair is loose for the most part, with one thin braid on either side. Rose tucked what was left of the willow sprigs into her hair, like a half-moon crown.

I damn near died when I saw her.

"You doin' all right otherwise?" Wilder asks.

"Why wouldn't I be?" I take a sip.

My brother glances at Dad like it's obvious. "Like you said, this wasn't the wedding you were expecting."

I frown, nearly losing my grip on the glass. "I said that?"

Dad nods slowly, glancing at Willow.

The party seems such a long time ago, but he's right. I *did* say that. Right after I kissed Willow for the first time. The moment I realized I was healing. I was moving on. And felt guilty for it.

Dad puts a hand on my shoulder. "She's a good one."

I know what he means. That if anyone were to replace that hole in my heart, she's it.

I look at Willow again, her face lighting up when Ellie runs up to her. It's contagious.

I don't comment, but something tells me my look says it all.

She is it.

Noah steps onto my porch. He's in a suit, as usual. Also as usual, he's scowling. "Gentlemen." He nods respectfully, but it's mostly at my father. Then he pins me with those blue eyes. "Could we have a word?"

I take another sip, knowing what this is about. "No."

He draws out the folded papers from his inside pocket. "Dallas, don't be an idiot. Make her sign this."

Dad curses under his breath. "For Christ's sake, Noah, it's the girl's wedding day."

"That's why I sent it last week. Your *son* sent it back to my office—blank."

I see Willow shake her head and walk away from her mother, leaving the woman frustrated.

Hell is her problem?

I turn back to Noah. "Dad's not exactly big on prenups either, so you're barking up the wrong tree."

"Dallas, this is a *real* marriage. With *real* assets at stake. Which means she'll be entitled to half when you two split."

Sharp pain tugs at my chest, but I don't budge. "Put yourself in my shoes. Would you have made Charlie sign it?"

He jerks. "Charlie?" Then glances back at Willow taking pictures with Rose and Ellie. Her smile wide and real.

Understanding hits and he turns back. "No. It's not the Reeves way. But fine, so you two have something going on, doesn't mean you can't protect yourself. You still don't know anything about her."

Dad holds up a glass for Noah. "Pipe down and have yourself a drink."

"Oh good," Willow chirps, bouncing up the steps with a shiver. "Something stronger than cider."

"Keep you warmer too," I tell her, handing her mine.

Noah clears his throat. "It's getting a bit crowded here, I'll see you out there. Congratulations again, you two," he says flatly as he folds up the papers.

Willow gasps as she plucks the packet from his hands. "Is this our certificate?"

My heart plunges into my stomach when she unravels it. "Willow," I step toward her, but she turns.

"I'm going to go see if Rose needs help." Wilder races down the steps.

Dad follows with a heavy sigh. "I'll go . . . try that cider."

"*Not* the marriage certificate," she mumbles, flipping through the pages. She looks up at Noah. "Got a pen?"

He whips one out in a hot second. I watch her profile as she props the last page up against the man's chest . . . and signs it.

She doesn't look hurt as she hands it back. In fact, I'm not picking up much of anything.

"Willow, I didn't want—"

She presses her palm to the side of my face and lifts up to kiss my lips, soft and quick. "You worry too much. He's just doing his job."

I grip her wrist to keep her close for another moment. Kissing her a little more. "I'll see you in a few."

She grins back . . . but that light in her eyes has faded. She steps down.

I wait until she's out of earshot before turning a sharp glare at Noah. "Tear it up."

He laughs and tucks it into his jacket. "No way. You'll thank me for this."

"That looked intense," Silas says when I make my way over to him. He's standing a few feet behind the ceremony setup, watching Storm with Pickles, the pony Ellie chose to be the ringbearer.

I slip my hands in my pockets. "Do me a favor and help Storm tie these to the saddle. Think you can manage that without her stepping on you?"

"We talkin' about the horse or the trainer?"

"Just don't get trampled by either—especially while carrying these." I hand him the rings.

He takes them and smirks.

I squint around the growing crowd. "How's the shoulder?"

He stills. "Barely feel it anymore. Think it resolved itself."

"Liar," I rasp casually.

"Says the man about to walk down the aisle to win a custody battle."

I wince without a sound, keeping my eyes focused on the decked-out oak tree.

"I love her," I rasp out loud.

From the corner of my eye, I catch Silas glance over at me. Then he nods slowly, a smirk tugging at his lips. "I'm glad."

I scoff. "That's it? You're glad?"

"Dal, a few months ago I could hardly say three words to you. No one could." He shakes his head, still barely looking at me. "It was like you buried yourself with her."

The soft strum of a guitar drifts through the air, signaling it's almost time.

"Kid changed you," Silas continues. "Gave you a reason to wake up, show up, brought some life back to your eyes. But with *her* . . ." His blue eyes shift to the redhead feeding Pickles a carrot. "You're you again. Lookin' people in the eye, smiling, teasing. It's like she pulled you out of a place the rest of us couldn't reach."

"Couldn't agree more," Wilder adds, stepping to my left.

I glance back at the house. Then the end of the aisle. Wishing I knew how to tell Willow all this. "I don't think she's convinced," I mutter.

Silas slips his hands into his pockets, mimicking my stance. "Well, you're about to say your vows. If there were ever a time to do it . . ."

I shake my head. "No. This is between her and me."

28

Willow

I walk down the aisle in my white dress—it's simple, but elegant enough to feel like a bride. *His* bride. I grabbed this one off the rack a few days ago when Rose hauled me to the town mall. It caught my eye instantly. For its knee-length, mostly, to go with my boots. But also because it didn't make me feel like I was putting on a show. It felt comfortable, uncomplicated. *Right*.

The ache in my heart is still fresh. My pride—my confidence and my reassurance that this thing with Dallas and me could turn into something that lasts forever—torn a little.

A prenup should *not* have surprised me.

Having it handed to me while I'm in my wedding dress, moments after battling with my mother, refusing my inheritance to keep my integrity—that stung.

But like the stupidly in-love fool I am, my heart hurts for *him* more.

I know he didn't want it. And I know what it's like to have someone who's supposed to be rooting for you only care about protecting you financially.

Despite who it hurts.

Brushing the pain aside, I focus on the beauty of the moment. The sun dipping behind those pretty blue mountains. The same ones I've loved waking up to from his bedroom window. The setting sun casts a warm gold glow over the open field.

Heat lamps are lined up on either side of our seated guests, adding to the warmth and light.

A week ago, I would have been too nervous to look at anyone. Feeling like a fraud. But when I lock eyes with the man under the tree, the one with the cool easy grin, I don't feel like a fraud at all.

I'm a woman marrying the man I've fallen for.

He and I may not be forever. But I'm not lying to anyone today. And whether or not he feels the same, one thing is for sure—he's going to win his daughter.

And *that's* forever.

I glance at my mother with a small smile and she perks her brow. I know what she's thinking.

I inhale a deep breath, my heart sinking to my stomach. Then, I give her a subtle nod.

Fine. I'll do it.

Her shoulders rise proudly and she mouths, *That's my girl.*

I hand Rose my flowers and step under the tree to join Dallas. His eyes warm as he watches me.

He takes a couple of steps toward me, cupping my chin as we meet. "Just you and me, Sunset," he whispers low, an inch from my mouth.

At first I'm confused, frowning up at him. Then he adds. "Against them all."

I suck in a breath, my heart still pounding with confusion for my emotionally driven decision. "For better or worse," I say with a light shrug.

He watches me, reading me. "I'm all in, Willow. I'm not just ready to spend the rest of my life with you. I was meant to."

29

Dallas

"I thought she'd never leave," Willow exhales as I shut the door behind us, having said goodbye to her mother. Wes agreed to drive her to the airport, so Willow didn't have to.

I pull her into my arms. "She's not that bad."

From across the room, Dad gives me a pointed look and I glare at him to keep his mouth shut. Lucy lost him when she said we had a "cute farm."

The woman was here less than thirty-six hours—arrived Saturday morning—and when she wasn't on the phone with her agent or boyfriend, she complained about everything from bottled water to the crickets.

But I must say, the woman was in surprisingly better spirits after the ceremony. Still, it was no surprise to anyone that Willow didn't ask her to stay another night.

"I'm going to go check on Ellie. She's had a long night." Willow presses a hand to my chest and I lean down for a quick kiss before she pads up the stairs barefoot.

I look at the floorboards. The same ones that were thick with dust only a few weeks ago. When she walked into this property I had abandoned for too long.

Made it a home.

I feel Dad's eyes on me and I lift my gaze to his.

He grins. "You two have a minute alone yet?"

I shake my head with a sigh. "Plenty of time for it later." I nod toward the kitchen, moving us both in the same direction. "Thanks for sticking around and kicking everyone out for me." I hand him a beer from the fridge and we step out onto the porch.

He takes a sip. "Noticed Cole didn't show."

My heart sinks. It didn't bother me at the beginning, since the whole thing was supposed to be staged for the town's benefit anyway. For weakening the fight Glenda's preparing.

But it bothers me now that I'm pretty damn sure our vows were real today. And some day, it'll be even more real. Without prenups or people wondering if it's real or not. With Cole in the front row with Ellie.

"He should have. For Ellie." The fact that my little girl didn't ask for him today tells me she's smarter than I give her credit for.

It's quiet for a moment as we look out into the darkness, toward the large oak tree that sits along the river bend.

"She's the one."

Dad chuckles. "Well, I hope so."

"I mean . . . she's it. I barely had a chance to tell her that today."

He scoffs. "Tellin' a woman you love her when you're about to tie the knot is like sayin' it during sex."

"I didn't . . . tell her I love her."

He clears his throat. "OK, then what *did* you say?"

"I wanted her to know that this was real for me. That it's forever. That I'm choosing her over . . . a ghost."

He chuckles. "What every woman wants to hear."

"Dad."

"What? In other words—you told her she's not some consolation prize."

I pause . . . then take a long sip of the cool liquid.

"So . . . no longer a thorn in your side . . ." he muses.

"I get it," I snap. "I don't exactly have a way with words."

"They're three fuckin' words, Dal. Did you ever think you might've not said it because you're not ready to?"

I turn to him, a challenging glare. "I'll go tell her right now."

He coughs a laugh. "Like *I* matter in this equation."

"OK, Romeo, when are you and Ginger movin' in together?"

He waves me off, not bothering to act surprised. "We're too old for that."

"Why? You keep each other company, I know you spend the night."

His expression dries. "She was your mother's closest friend."

I nod. "I know. I'm sorry."

"We're happy just as we are." He stands. "Go tell that woman how you feel and ask her to stay."

My phone rings.

I growl. "It's Noah again."

"Put it on speaker, going to give that boy a piece of my mind."

I answer it and hit speaker. "You better be calling because you forgot something here and not as my lawyer."

"Dallas," Noah starts, car engine in the background. "Listen, I'm traveling for a case this week, but I'll keep you posted on a court date—should be soon."

"As long as Ellie doesn't have to be there."

"I don't think so. But you're in good shape. The house is done, you've got a legit partner in crime. It's just a matter of getting it over with, and . . . hoping there's no surprises." Concern laces his voice.

"What about the photos from the bar fight?"

"Took care of that. Turns out Carl's been trying to get Ricky and his crew to stop comin' around, causing too many problems and bringin' the wrong crowd. He's happy to be a character witness if it comes up."

"Always liked that man."

"Also said he'd take Willow back in a heartbeat if she's willing to give it another chance. Said the crowd's been askin' for her."

I chuckle to myself. "I'll leave that up to her." I sigh. "For now, we got more important things to tackle. And while I have you, do me a favor and tear up that prenup."

"Or what?"

I think about the one thing this man cares about. "Or I'll tell Charlie you ambushed a woman with a prenup on her wedding day."

There's a beat before he sighs, relenting. "Look, what do you know about this woman besides her being Rose's friend? What if she's hiding something? Broken the law or something. Imagine that coming out in court."

I glance at Dad with a smirk. "She checks out—told me she had nothing to do with the dead bodies found in her old apartment. And I believe her."

Dad and I chuckle.

"All right, fine, laugh. But this is how people get screwed. You don't do enough digging."

My smile fades quickly. "Noah. Whatever you're thinking, don't."

"I'm not just your lawyer, I'm your friend. Dallas, she showed up three weeks ago and didn't want to go back. You don't find that suspicious?"

"No, I find it convenient."

"Exactly."

"Noah. I'm going to tell you this once. Stay out of her business. Willow's personal life is not up for discussion."

"Fine," he tells me. "I'll call you this week."

I hang up with a frustrated sigh. Dad watches me.

"I'm not doing it."

"You afraid you'll find out she's not as perfect as she seems?"

"She's *not* perfect. No one is. But she hasn't had it easy. She's selfless, she loves Ellie, helped me make this place a home. I'm not repaying her by letting my lawyer look into her."

He holds up his hands. "Look, son, I get it. We trust until they prove we can't. That's the Thorne way. But we're dealing with Glenda Lost."

I swallow.

"I've never seen Noah get this rattled over a small-town case, have you?"

I shake my head.

"Then let the man do his job."

I flex my biceps against the fence with a harsh breath, pushing off. "I said no. Willow is off the table."

"I was about to give up on you," Willow tells me with a smirk when I step into my bedroom—our bedroom. If all goes right.

She's at the window, wearing one of my T-shirts and nothing else, staring out at the moonlit mountains, the river's shimmer dancing across her face.

I unbutton my shirt and toss it to the side, my expression humorless because of Noah's bullshit.

I trust Willow.

How could I not?

"Is that right? How so?"

She glances over, her eyes on my loosened buttons instead of my eyes. "Well, I thought about slipping off my panties and leaving them stuffed between your sheets, but . . ."

I rake my hand into her hair, pulling it back and kissing her wildly. She moans into my mouth. Relaxed. Something I haven't seen since her mother got into town.

I pull back, my eyes on her wet lips. "But you need fresh material."

She bats her lashes at me. "What I need, is my husband to get naked."

Something kicks in my chest at the word. "Like the sound of that."

Willow bites her lip and laughs. "I got more sounds for you if you're interested," she teases.

I should strip out of my pants. Tear off that T-shirt and toss her over the bed—make love to her.

But the tightness in my chest won't budge.

She showed up three weeks ago and didn't want to go back.

Of course I found that suspicious at first.

But I don't care now.

Perhaps I should. Because that hollow feeling in my chest I thought would never leave? I never want to feel it again. And I'd die a thousand deaths before I let Ellie feel it too.

Taking Willow to bed on our wedding night is all I fucking want to do. But knowing her—in and out, the good and the ugly—is what I *need* to do.

A pit forms in my stomach and I know I'm going to regret this.

"Willow. Why'd you sign the prenup?"

Her easy grin falls, her shoulders tense. "Because it doesn't matter. I wouldn't take anything from you."

"Why doesn't it matter?"

She releases a confused breath. "Well . . . why was it handed to me?"

"I never meant it to be, you have to believe that."

"But it was," she blurts out, then takes a breath. "I told you, I don't blame you. You don't know me. You have a daughter to protect."

"Yes, and you're helping me do it. I thought we were in this together."

Her eyes fill with liquid. "I want to be."

I close the distance. "Then be honest with me. I haven't kept a single thing from you since the day we met. But you have."

She stares at me. "I have never lied to you."

"What were you and your mother fighting about earlier?" The question probably sounds like it's coming out of nowhere, but she seemed equally upset when she was on the phone with the woman last week.

And I need to make sure I've got no surprises coming. Like another man she's been promised to or something.

Willow stills, wide eyes locked with mine. Shoulders tense as she brushes past me to cross the room, wincing as she says, "It doesn't matter."

I pinch the bridge of my nose and turn. "You got to give me something, Willow."

She flips around. "I've given you everything. I'm ready to give more. But I don't see why this matters so much to you."

I stare at her—beautiful, vulnerable, strong, and protective. Protective of the one thing all the men before me took for granted, used, manipulated, hurt.

I toss my gaze out the window to the spot where I wanted to tell her exactly how I feel about her. And realize now, I never did.

I lift my shirt off the floor and grab her hand. "Come with me."

Quietly, our bare feet fly down the stairs. She pauses when we reach the bottom. "Ellie," she whispers.

"She'll be fine." I button my shirt in a flash and duck into the coat closet, grabbing a long one for her while she grabs her boots from the front corridor. "We'll see the motion lights from the window."

"Window? Where are we going?" she huffs, but doesn't argue, slipping her arms through the coat.

I take her hand and lead her out the back sliding door.

Another sharp gasp. "Dallas."

I turn, alarmed she might've heard Ellie.

"I'm not wearing underwear," she hisses.

I grin. "I'll keep you warm."

Our boots thud softly over the grass, breaking the quiet of the night until we reach the tree where we exchanged basic vows a few hours ago. Where I had the chance to do it right, but I let it go.

I lean her up against the tree, away from the wind. I catch her as she glances up at the house, then back to me with a swallow.

I run both hands along her neck and into her hair. "You're safe here. Your heart is safe with me. I'll never let you fall."

I take her hands in mine and stare at them. "Cowboys, we don't—we're not good with words in a big crowd. But when I saw you walking down that aisle toward me—I lost my breath. Because I don't know when or how it happened, but I was marrying the love of my life."

Her eyes fill with unshed tears.

"I've fallen for you, Sunset. That's something I never thought I'd allow to happen again." I swallow. "I love it all, fighting with you, bantering, kissing, obsessing over you. You're it for me, and dammit, I'm it for you. Don't shut the door here because you're afraid of making a mistake, Willow—I'm not your mistake."

She shakes her head, tears spilling down one cheek, a cloud of air leaving her lungs. "No. You're not."

I step closer to her. "I promise to always love you, cherish you, protect you—" I press my forehead to hers. "And someday soon we're doing this again so that you can walk toward me without a shred of doubt and I can tell everyone how much I adore you."

"Dallas," she breathes, cold hands gripping my face. "I trust you. I *love* you. You and Ellie—and everything you've given me."

Resolve settles in my chest. "Then I don't need anything else."

Her eyes dip between us with concern but I bring her back, lifting her chin and kissing her. She melts into me as I step inside her coat, lifting the hem of her oversized shirt. She shivers at my touch. My hand moves from her bare ass to between her legs.

I hum with appreciation. "What'll it be, Sunset?"

She snaps my belt undone in a hurry and unzips my pants.

"Face the bark. Palms flat."

My girl doesn't hesitate. She turns, pressing her hands against the tree. Her body warm and ready.

I lift the coat, bunching it over her hips, and stroke myself. Willow watches me over her shoulder, licking her lips.

"You tryin' to help me, baby?"

"Can I?"

I keep stroking, desperate for her mouth but conflicted. "Your knees will be cold."

"I can take it," she breathes.

I bend and growl in her ear. "Then get down there and take me to the back of your throat."

She drops to her knees, a vision and a half. A fantasy I never knew I had, come to life. She takes my cock like it's something out of her fancy, lowering her jaw.

"Sunset." I dig my fingers into her hair. "When I say, I want you to let go and get back on that tree. Ass facing me."

She smirks and gets to work on my cock, taking me all the way. My hand flies up to the bark with a curse. I inch in and out of her slowly, then with a pained growl, I fuck her mouth. She gags but doesn't let go, sucking me hard.

My thighs start to shake. "Now, Willow." I pull out of her mouth and help her to her feet. "You good?"

"Yes."

"Good." I flip her and lift the coat again, sliding my thick cock into her dripping center.

She moans and gasps as I thrust hard, filling and stretching her, claiming her. Because she's mine. I praise her, taking me so good as I fuck her senseless. Maybe some residual anger over our fight. Maybe she brings the barbarian out of me. But I've never felt so alive. So wanted. So desperately desired than I do by this woman.

I grip the back of her neck, lowering to her ear. "So warm, so tight. So perfect."

"Dallas, I'm—I'm coming." She starts to shake beneath me.

I hold her still, snapping my hips brutally. "I'm going to spill inside you. That OK, Sunset?"

"Yes. Yes, please."

I let go, shuddering through my release. Grunting as I empty inside this perfect woman—then cursing myself for getting so rough with her.

On our *wedding* night.

We're both panting when I turn her to face me. Cheeks flushed, hair wild, a lazy smile on her smooth face. "Sunset," I start.

She strokes my cheek. "And I thought you ruined me the first time."

I grin at her, shaking my head. "I make love even better." I lift her off her feet and carry her back to the house.

30

Willow

I hiss at the sting, tugging my palm from his grasp.

"Hold still," Dallas urges, the alcohol pad dangerously close to my scuffed skin.

I'm lying back in a warm bubble bath. Dallas doesn't own bubble bath, but he swiped some from Ellie's bathroom on our way up.

I wasn't expecting this . . . what I can only describe as *aftercare*. But then again, I wasn't expecting to step into his bathroom and find red scrapes and dirt on my palms and knees either.

He swipes the pad again, gently, then blows against my skin. "How's that?"

I grumble and take a sip of the champagne with my free hand. "And was *this* really necessary?"

"It's still your wedding night. Tea didn't seem appropriate."

I finish the glass and hand it to him. "You going to get in with me now?"

He shakes his head and lifts the washcloth, dipping it in the soapy water then running it along the back of my neck and arms.

I groan. "Fine, I'm getting pruny over here anyway."

He helps me up and drains the water, turning the shower on for me.

I wince under the spray. Then cover it up with a grin.

He rolls his eyes and moves to the counter with the first-aid kit. "When you're done, I'm treating those knees again."

A moment later he makes good on his promise—or threat—and cleans up my scuffed knees again and dries my hair.

When he's done, I bring my hands to the back of my hair, forgetting he put some aloe over them.

"What are you doing?"

I look over at him in the mirror. "My hair's still wet, I need to braid it."

He pulls up the bamboo bench. "Sit down."

I scoff. "This ought to be good, cowboy."

By the time he's done, it's well after midnight, my braid is uneven—yet comfortable—and we're both exhausted.

I'm lying in his arms, eyes closed.

"Willow . . ."

I hum.

"That thing between you and your mother that . . . doesn't matter?"

I frown, suddenly not so stiffened by it. "Yes?"

"Forget I brought it up. I just don't like how upset you get every time you're alone with her. When I can't protect someone I care about—I get a little angry."

I smirk and curl up against him. "Don't worry. I'm taking care of it tomorrow."

The last thing I remember is him kissing the top of my head before I fall asleep and saying, "Me too."

Dallas was up early this morning, but not to go to work on the ranch—he was up early with Ellie. By the time I stepped out of the bedroom, they were downstairs, dressed and halfway through breakfast.

My hands feel normal again, but still a bit raw.

"Morning," I say.

Ellie beams at me. "Willow." She jumps off the bar stool and hugs me. "How are you feeling?"

"Hmm?"

I look over at Dallas, sipping his coffee innocently. Like the man didn't shut off my alarm on purpose today.

"Daddy said you weren't feeling good and to let you rest when I couldn't find my slippers."

I gasp and look accusingly at Dallas. "Always wake me up for a slipper emergency."

He chuckles. "Knew you two would gang up on me someday." He turns and pours a cup for me. I take it and stand beside him at the island, sipping slowly.

"All done," Ellie chirps, lifting her cereal bowl and placing it in the sink.

"I'll take her today." Dallas clears his throat and lifts Ellie's backpack.

I round the counter. "Coming back to take care of me some more?" I glance at Ellie. "Like with chicken soup?"

He chuckles and leans in for a kiss. "No. I need to go take care of something. I'll be back this afternoon. She's got art class with Rose later, so you've got the day to yourself."

I pout and he growls, biting my bottom lip. "I'll be home soon."

Home.

My eyes dance around the kitchen as they head out.

Dallas and I declared our love for each other less than twelve hours ago and I've never felt more at home.

More loved.

More cherished.

And when we switch to the banter and bickering? That's fine too. I'll take all of our versions.

Because I know he would too.

It's late afternoon when I call my mother.

"Willow, not this again."

"Mom, I'm serious. I've changed my mind. Don't call the lawyer."

"Sweetheart. What is the issue? You say you love the man, so this is the real thing. You're not compromising your integrity or whatever."

"I know. But I still want to wait. It just feels too soon. Plus, I don't need it right now. Let me just bring this up to Dallas first. I don't want him thinking—" I sigh. "Just, don't do anything yet."

There's silence on the other end of the line.

"Mom."

"Tell me what happens when he leaves you."

"What?"

"Tell me what happens when this one hurts you—blindsides you—just like the others."

I swallow. "He's different."

She sucks her teeth. "Of course he is. At least this one is giving you a way to get your inheritance, Willow. Don't miss this opportunity. Take your money. Buy that property you had your eye on."

"Mom."

"And do it yourself—like an adult, Willow."

"What is wrong with you?"

"I lost everything to your deadbeat father, Willow. He spent all the money your grandmother left me. I had to start over. Make a name for myself. I was mopping floors when I wrote my first book, did you know that?"

"You said you were a waitress."

"Yes. On the closing shift. Every night. Spending half of what I was making on your babysitter. Because I trusted and counted on a man who promised me everything and left me with nothing." She sighs. "Well, left me with something more important than any money could buy."

"Mom."

She sniffles. "I hate watching you struggle with late-night gigs for lousy tips, living with roommates who smoke pot or exes who toss you out like leftovers."

"Mom . . ."

"What?" she snaps.

"Thank you. I know you're looking out for me. But . . . I need to *tell* him about the money first."

"Fine. Tell him. Not like it matters at this point," she sighs, "since you're making me put it back."

This is the first honest conversation my mother and I have had over this money—over anything. I don't want to ruin it with another fight. I'll give her this much.

"Thank you, and I will think about withdrawing it for good and what we'll do with it, but he needs to be part of that conversation."

She grunts as if she doesn't agree or understand this part of a marriage.

I feel sad and angry that she got cheated out of something real and forever. But I'm not about to risk mine with a lie.

"So . . . tell me more about this book you're working on."

"Oh, it's just like all my others, what *I* want to know is where you're going on your honeymoon. You are taking one, aren't you? I heard you and Dallas tell your guests the other night that *timing* isn't ideal? You just got *married*."

"Mom, we can't think about that right now. Maybe when all this custody drama is worked out, we could, but neither one of us has *vacation* on the mind. Not to mention Dallas is hesitant to leave her for any number of days now and I don't blame him. Heck I wouldn't mind bringing her along."

I hear her sigh. "All the perks of getting married—and you want none of it."

"Oh I wouldn't say *none* of it," I say through a smile and just picture her rolling her eyes.

31

Willow

Wes swings by the house on Wednesday afternoon. He says the ranch gets a little lonely in the cooler months with fewer events and staff, so he stopped in with today's lunch special for me.

We sit out on the porch drinking iced lattes.

"I'm glad you're here, Willow. Rose really missed you."

"I missed her too—the city's a lonely place without your best friend."

"So you're here for good then?"

"Unless they kick me out." I shrug like it's a joke but it hits a little too close to my insecurities.

He scoffs. "Then you're a lifer." He looks around. "Hard to leave this place once you fall in love with it. Believe me, I've tried."

"Not very hard," Dallas says with a wink, walking up the steps, surprising me.

"You're home early." I smile up at him and he bends to kiss me.

"Hmm. Lips are cold."

I hold up the iced latte and take a sip. "Worth it."

"Well, I should get back to The Shack," Wes says, looking between us, a smirk forming. "Dal, brought you a roast beef in the fridge," he continues.

"Thanks for feedin' my girl, Wes. And again, the reception catering was incredible. Folks are still talking about the food."

"Oh, and if there's leftover cake, bring it on back," I add.

He laughs. "I'll check. Hey, any news on Ellie yet?"

Dallas sighs, glancing at me. "That's why I'm here. I went to see Noah this morning, he said he's got a date for us."

"When?"

"Friday."

I sit up. "This Friday?"

"Yep. He's prepping some questions for us and will call to go through them."

My stomach churns.

"Keep me posted," Wes says before heading back to work.

"You went to Hideaway Springs today?" I ask when we're alone.

"Yeah." He removes an envelope from his jacket pocket. "I went to get something for you."

I shift in my seat. Feeling cold, I pull my legs to my chest and fix the blanket.

"What is it?" I take the envelope from him and open it with caution, confused as I pull out several ripped pieces of paper. "Wha—what is this?"

"It's our prenup. I never wanted it to begin with, and now it doesn't exist."

"Dallas, let it go."

"No. I don't want anything that says I don't trust you or this marriage. I love you, Sunset." He bends down on one knee. "And I want to show you how much every day." He reaches into his shirt pocket this time and lifts a ring. A beautiful, yellow-gold band and teardrop diamond. "I know I already gave you a simple wedding band." He lifts my hand. "And you've got your grandmother's ring close to your heart. But I want you to have this. It was my mother's. You can wear it on your other hand, change it up, keep it safe somewhere. I don't care, but it's yours."

"Dallas," I breathe. "It's beautiful. But I can't take—"

"I want you to have it, Willow. Dad gave it to me when I was—well, I'd already gotten her something she had her eye on. So . . ." He holds it up. "Will you accept this ring and spend the rest of your life with me?"

"Yes," I breathe happily. "I love it." I take my grandmother's ring off and move it to my other hand. Then give him my left one. Noticing as it trembles.

I shake off the memory of Eric breaking into my apartment and rummaging through my things to take his ring back.

This isn't the same thing.

This is the real deal.

One day—there won't be a single part of me that doubts it.

"I love you," I whisper.

He watches me with those blue eyes of his, the kind of look that tells me he doesn't know how he got here. But he's happy he did. "I love you, too."

32

Dallas

"I need to talk to you," Noah mutters when we arrive at the courthouse on Friday morning. His eyes pass over Willow, sharp and unreadable.

If he wasn't the best damn lawyer in the state, I'd fire him just for that.

I slip my hand out of hers, leaving her with Dad and Silas by the benches in the hall. They both made it a point to be here today for support. Wilder and Rose are at the house with Ellie.

We kept her home from school today. Ginger's there too. This dumb hearing's putting everyone at the ranch on edge.

I hate this. It feels like some kind of cruel joke, to give a man a child and then threaten to take her away again three months later.

I shake my head, jaw tight as I follow Noah further down the hall. "I don't need another rundown of how this is gonna go. Heard you the first time."

"You know it'd do you some good to take this more seriously," he tells me, stopping near a water cooler, a healthy distance away from the people I arrived with.

I look over at Cole, sitting by himself on the wooden bench, fighting the urge to check on him, see how he's been holding up.

"Noah, the man's hurting. Last thing I want to do is go into battle with him."

"Glenda's the one going into battle." He looks to the side, jaw tightening. "Look, there's something I came across I think you should know about."

I narrow my eyes at him suspiciously. "Came across?"

He barely flinches at my glare, then glances back at Willow. "I know you think this is the real thing with her."

"Excuse me?"

"Just hear me out." He slips his hands in his pockets. "Dallas, I don't think she intends to stay."

My lips press into a thin line and I glance away. "Son of a bitch, you looked into her."

"You ripped up the prenup," he hisses. "I needed something to make sure your assets are protected."

My jaw clenches. "I told you she was off the table."

"Look, we're running out of time. This is important."

"If it was important, she'd have told me." I walk away from him just as Glenda walks in. Her eyes sweep over me briefly, then she greets Cole and sits beside him, leaning in, voice low and measured.

I move to stand next to my family.

"Everything all right?" Willow asks.

I meet her eyes for a moment. They're etched with concern and tenderness.

It's a few seconds before I respond, pulling her to my side and kissing her temple. "It will be. Soon as this is over."

"That woman looks wretched," she murmurs, resting her head on my chest.

Silas nods, sizing up the tall middle-aged blonde. "Agree. And don't take this the wrong way, but how is he affording her?"

Dad glares at them. "Either that woman offered free services to add a win to her books against the Thornes. Or he's got no idea what her billable hours look like."

I eye Cole's well-pressed but worn suit, his scuffed boots, his sad eyes. "I can't worry about that right now." My eyes flick to the guard motioning to us. "Looks like they're ready for us." I nod toward Noah who gives me the signal before heading toward the open double doors.

Willow squeezes my hand. "I'll be right behind you."

We're ushered in and take our seats before the judge enters.

"Thought you said this was a hearing. Why's it so formal?"

"It's just a courtroom," Noah says in a bored tone. "Not like there's a jury or anything. Odds are nothing will be decided today. They'll have you, Cole, and—" He glances behind him as a few familiar faces enter. "Maybe a few character witnesses."

I'm getting nervous and I don't know why. For the past month I've been more than confident that any judge looking at this case would grant full custody to me, the only living parent, more than ready, willing, and able to provide. End of story.

Now I have doubts.

Rachel, our social worker, is the first one on the stand. She answers a few questions from Glenda, then a few from Noah. Her responses are pure facts, giving background on the mutually agreed custody arrangement. That guardianship of Ellie would be transferred to me—her biological father. And the request she received a few weeks ago to cease the transfer until the hearing.

I'm next on the stand with Noah asking the questions he'd prepped me for.

"Mr. Thorne, would you remind the court when you found out about Ellie?"

I clench my teeth. No matter how many times I answer this question, it always boils my chest the same. "This past summer."

"How old was she?"

I glance at Cole. "Six."

"And what town has she been living in all these years?"

"Same as me. Right here in Blue River Springs."

"Fascinating. What do you do for a living?"

I sigh, growing tired of this and we've barely begun. "My brother Wilder and I own Blue River Ranch.

Everyone knows it. Everyone knows where and how to find me." I look over at Cole's side of the room.

"Objection. That wasn't the question and Mr. Thorne can't speak for *everyone*," Glenda interjects, dryly.

"Thank you." Noah turns to me. "And I apologize in advance for this, but could you remind us of your state of mind earlier this year? Before you found out you had a child who lived right here in town."

I take a breath. He told me he'd ask about Millie. And my . . . state of mind, the bar fights, neglecting my ranch. Because Glenda *will* point it out. And it's better to beat her to the punch.

"I lost my fiancée in the spring. She died in a fire." I swallow. "I was grieving." I look at Willow, her eyes misting, watching me relive it all. "Pretty hard. I lost myself." My eyes flick to Cole. "At the time, I thought she was all I had. But there were people—on the other side of my bedroom door—waiting for me. There for me."

"And how would you describe yourself after you found out you had a six-year-old daughter you never knew about?"

"I wanted to meet her. And the second I did, I knew she was mine." I grin.

"And can you confirm for the court if you immediately wanted her in your life?"

"More than my next breath. Still do."

Noah nods. "Thank you. So fast forward, as the court already heard, Ellie has been living with you ever since. And you're now married, is that right?"

I look at my wife, my heart easing instantly. "Yes."

Noah pulls out a few colorful papers from his folder and hands them to the judge. "And based on these drawings your daughter let me borrow, she seems to adore Willow. If you're wondering, Willow's the larger stick figure with the red-crayon curly hair—not the smaller one, who also ironically has curly reddish hair."

The judge flips through the pages and hands them back to Noah, who takes them and sits back down.

Glenda stands, approaching me. "How did your wife die? I didn't quite catch that part."

My jaw clenches because she does know. "Millie was my *fiancée*. In a fire."

"That's tragic. Where?"

I swallow, my gut twisting. "On my ranch."

She nods. "Where you've now brought your daughter to live."

"Objection," Noah calls.

"Strike the comment," the judge orders the stenographer.

Glenda continues unfazed. "Tell us more about Ellie's mother. How long were you two together?"

Another one Noah knew was coming. "Our relationship was casual."

"In other words, a one-and-done kind of thing?"

"Objection," Noah says. And he doesn't need to say more.

"Strike it. Counsel, get to your point," the judge orders.

"I'll move on. Last question." She steps toward me. "Mr. Hartly ceased the custody transfer to you after his wife's death, claiming you're unfit to raise a little girl by yourself. What day was that?"

"It was a Sunday. October fourteenth."

"And what day did you—out of nowhere—announce your engagement to Willow Brooks?"

I inhale through my nose.

She moves to her desk and picks up a photocopy of the Blue River Ranch newsletter. "I'll refresh your memory. It was Wednesday, October seventeenth. *Three* days later."

I look at Noah but he doesn't seem concerned.

The silence seems to irritate her. "Do you really expect this court—and your town—to believe this is anything but a performance?"

"Objection," Noah shouts. "We've already given the court proof of the legal marriage."

Glenda stretches her arms wide. "I'll rephrase . . . anything but a marriage of convenience."

"I don't expect anything," I answer. "I married the woman I love. End of story."

Glenda smirks like my response means nothing to her. "No further questions."

Noah stands, approaching me. "Mr. Thorne. In my experience, when a marriage was, say . . . temporary, for whatever reason, I'd highly recommend *and insist on* a prenuptial agreement. Did Ms. Brooks sign one?"

"We do not have a prenuptial agreement in place."

Noah grins. "Thank you."

There's a short recess where I call Wilder to check on Ellie, then return to the courtroom, taking my seat next to Noah.

Despite the tightness in his jaw, I toss him a smirk as I lean in. "Bet you're happy that I destroyed the damn thing."

"She doesn't want your money," he mutters back.

"Then why are you being a jackass?"

His head snaps to me. "She's *leaving* you, Dallas. My job as your attorney is to protect your assets. My job as your friend—is to protect your heart."

My brows shoot up at his sincerity. "Well, I appreciate that." Willow takes a seat behind me and winks. I flick my gaze back to Noah and lean in, my voice low but firm. "But you're wrong."

The doors shut and Judge Walker is re-announced. We stand briefly.

Cole is called to the stand and Glenda goes through her questioning. Poor guy looks nervous even as his own attorney questions him. To my surprise he downplays the state of mind I was in when he came to me. And my abrupt dismissal of him. But he doesn't hesitate to throw accusations that Willow and I are a sham and he knew it from day one.

She grips my shoulder from behind, squeezing gently.

I catch Noah's arm when he stands to question Cole. "Take it easy on him," I warn.

He rolls his eyes and moves forward.

"Mr. Hartly, why did your daughter—Tammy—choose to keep Ellie from her biological father?"

"She only said that the father wouldn't be interested. It wasn't until her last few days that she told us who he was."

"And when was that?"

He looks down at his lap and I swallow hard. "Three years ago."

"I'm very sorry. But it was only this summer—four months ago—that you came to the ranch looking for Mr. Thorne."

"I didn't know him. If he even wanted her. If he had a family of his own. My wife and I were scared to lose Ellie—she was all that was left of . . ."

Noah glances at me, letting me know he could rip him apart right now. But I shake my head.

"One more question. For whatever your reasons, you decided your granddaughter was better off an *orphan* than to let her meet her father, who you must have learned is a reasonably wealthy, well-respected ranch owner from a good family. Only after your wife got sick and you needed to travel for treatment, did you decide, *now's the time*. But here you are, questioning Mr. Thorne for doing something purely for convenience?" Noah holds up his hand. "This is a yes or no question."

Cole waits a beat, glancing at Glenda, then at me. "Yes."

"And now that you see Ellie's father has built a home, married a woman who the little girl adores, you still think he's unfit to be her full-time legal guardian."

Cole meets my eyes. "It's not real. It's a lie to cheat me out of all I have left," he shouts, his hands trembling.

"Noah," I mutter low, but loud enough for him to hear.

He glances back at me then sighs like his hands are tied. "No further questions."

I inhale deeply, conflicted with victory and compassion. The court *has* to grant me custody. This man is clearly still grieving.

My eyes linger on the other side of the room as Cole returns to his seat. Glenda doesn't seem frazzled one bit. She stands, tightening the fit of her blazer.

"I'd like to call Willow Brooks to the stand."

"Character witness?" I murmur.

Noah's jaw works. "Doesn't matter now, does it?" It's a blow-off and I get it. He's mad. He flips his papers upside down and sits back like it's out of his hands.

"Please state your name."

"Willow *Thorne*." My wife smiles brightly.

Glenda's clenches her jaw. "Officially changed, then?"

"Not officially yet." She winks at Glenda. "We've been busy."

The tightness in my chest eases with the grin she tosses me.

Not finding the humor, Glenda's heels click as she draws closer. "When did you first meet Dallas Thorne?"

Willow grins. "It was in New York. At the Lock Bar, where I play piano and sing."

"Oh, how fancy. Let me guess—love at first sight?"

Willow's eyes are fierce but her smile sharp. "Good guess."

Glenda gives a tight grin. "So the job sounds fancy, the Lock Bar—what'd you make there?"

"Objection, irrelevant," Noah calls out, tiredly.

Glenda smiles at the judge. "It is, I promise."

"Overruled. Proceed."

Willow blinks. "Um . . . enough to pay rent, not much more."

"Ah yes." She grabs her papers. "And who did that rental apartment belong to?"

"It was a *rental*, so the landlord." She grins tightly.

"Of course. Was the lease under your name?"

Willow takes a breath, unrattled. "No. It was my ex-boyfriend's."

Glenda nods, pacing in front of the stand. "The ex-boyfriend who terminated the lease a few days after you arrived at Blue River Springs, is that right?"

There's a beat before Willow answers, her expression even. "I wouldn't know, I don't talk to him."

Noah nods his approval.

"What kind of questioning is this?" I lean in and whisper. "What does this have to do with me or Ellie?"

"Give her a minute," Noah mutters, staring ahead.

"I see," Glenda continues, like she's trying to work out a thought in her head. "So you don't make that much money, but submitted a homebuyer interest form for . . ." she checks her notes, "the Lakeview Estates."

What? Where the hell is that?

Willow blinks a few times, shoulders stiff. My eyes drop to her throat, working with a swallow.

"It's a yes or no question, Ms. Brooks."

She takes a breath, eyes sweeping over mine briefly. "Yes."

"Can we ask why?"

"Objection, irrelevant," Noah calls out, *finally*.

"Sustained. Please limit your questioning to the case."

"I'll just get to my point," Glenda confirms.

The judge rolls her eyes.

"The Lakeview Estates." Glenda spins to face the court. "Which, by the way, is a beautiful new community out in the suburbs of Long Island, New York—starts at *half a million* dollars. How does someone who makes *just* enough for rent, afford that?"

Willow glares at her. Face pale.

I snap, turning to Noah. "Shouldn't you be saying something here?"

He ignores me.

Glenda gives up on an answer and moves on. "I'll rephrase as a yes or no question since you seem confused."

Heat floods my chest.

"Is it true that your grandmother left you an inheritance of five hundred thousand dollars?"

"Yes."

"How nice. And were there conditions?"

Willow's chest rises and falls. Face pale, barely breathing. "Yes."

"Will you tell the court what they are?"

I tear my eyes off my wife to look at my attorney. "What the hell is going on?"

Willow's voice trembles. "I would get the money when I turned twenty-eight."

"Well, says here you're twenty-four. Is that the *only* condition?" Glenda presses and I'm just about tired of her voice.

Willow looks at me with a hard swallow. "No. When I turn twenty-eight or . . . when there is a legal marriage."

"Which you did last week, so *that's* convenient for you too, isn't it? Now you can buy that lovely-looking house on the East Coast."

Willow shakes her head at the woman in front of her. "How did you . . ."

Glenda holds up her papers. "It becomes public when the money is distributed. Which it was—" she looks down, "—three days ago."

"No, I didn't—" Willow cries.

"Are you saying it wasn't withdrawn?"

Willow's lips tremble, eyes pooling. "Well, yes, but—"

"No further questions."

Willow's eyes meet mine and for the first time in weeks, I can't read her. I can barely read the look I'm giving her because I'm shaking with the urge to whisk her off the stand—and the urge to walk out of here for some air.

I lower my eyes. "This what you were trying to tell me?"

"Counsel?" The judge calls Noah.

He stands. "No questions, your honor."

Judge Walker turns to Willow. "You may step down."

Willow mouths an apology to me then takes a seat in the back.

Minutes later, I lose custody of Ellie after the authenticity of my marriage, my character, and, somehow, Ellie's safety on my ranch is questioned.

Noah packs up his briefcase. "This isn't over. I'll get it appealed. Evidence of Willow's intentions were held back."

I stand, buttoning my jacket. "Get it appealed. *Do not* bring Willow into it."

"Dallas, you lost custody because of her—"

"I lost because of *you*. If you knew, you should have done something. Instead of letting my wife get eaten alive up there."

He turns to me, stunned. "Were you in the room?"

I stalk away to the back of the courtroom to catch Glenda and Cole before they leave. I see them making their way out the courtroom doors.

Willow catches my wrist. "Dallas," her breath stutters, barely audible over the noise. "I'm so sorry, I—"

Gently, I push her hand down. "Not now, Willow." I make my way through the crowd, catching Cole and Glenda muttering low just outside the door.

Pulse pounding, eyes locked, I storm over. "This was between you and me, Hartly," I roar inches from his face. "*Not* her. Mark my words, I will get my daughter back. But you *ever* attack my wife again, I'll make sure you're so far off the page, you don't *exist*."

Cole's lips part, eyes narrowing in confusion. "But she's not—"

I hear the courtroom doors fly open behind me, then a sniffle as Willow's familiar scent breezes behind me. Snapping my attention, I catch her racing down the hall toward the exit.

"Willow," I call over the crowd.

She doesn't stop, pushing past the double doors and down the steps.

"Willow, wait." My tone isn't anxious or pleading. It's sharp and demanding. Like I can't sort the variations of my anger between Noah, Cole, Glenda . . . and her.

I reach the front doors, pushing them open and finding Willow at the bottom of the landing with Silas. He's holding her shoulders as she sobs. She says something and he nods, opening the passenger door for her.

He catches my eye and I nod my OK.

Pinching the bridge of my nose, I turn, finding Cole behind me, alone. His expression etched with concern as he watches Willow drive away.

I mutter a curse, ready to storm past him to find my lawyer when *his* steps out of the courthouse. She finds Cole, taking him to one side. "Well, I'm sure you'll find this fair, considering you won at the very first hearing." She hands him a piece of paper I can only assume is her invoice.

Cole grabs it, eyeing it closely. "This . . . is fair, huh?"

I shake my head, turning away. "You can call my office and work out a plan. Chat soon about the plan for pick-up." She heads down the steps, leaving us alone.

I yank the paper from his hands, not bothering to look at the damage. "I'll take care of this," I mutter, folding it up and tucking it into my jacket.

"W-why would you do that?"

I exhale a sharp breath. "Because we're family, Cole. That's what family does. You don't have to like everything they do, but you don't leave them high and dry." I eye him up and down. "No matter how old and mature they're supposed to be."

"Is she . . . is Willow going to be all right?"

I glare at him. "You better hope so."

I grab Dad and we head back in my car—since his ride just took off with my wife.

"You in a rush to get home?" Dad asks, voice calm like he lives in some world where everything is going to be all right.

My heart aches when I answer, "No."

"Didn't think so. Grab a few drinks at The Shack?"

I nod. "Yeah."

33

Willow

I wash my face for the third time since getting home—if this even is my home anymore.

Who can ever be sure?

It's been hours and Dallas isn't back yet. Silas left a little while ago after graciously giving me a ride.

He had stepped out of the room for a call when the judge ruled, so I sobbed through what happened and asked him to get me out of there.

Rose is leaning along the wall outside Ellie's room when I step out of the guest bathroom. "You *need* to calm down. It wasn't your fault," she repeats.

I shove the towel at her and step into my bedroom. "You weren't there. He had it. It was looking really good for him and then I got on the stand and blew it all."

"Not you. *Your mother.*"

My eyes sting again. "No one would blame me for taking my money now that I'm married. But the house—Rose. The house was all me. I can't put that on anyone."

"Couldn't you explain timing or something? Your plans pre-Dallas?"

I shake my head. "That woman was twisting words and stories so much—I don't even know how she's still able to practice law."

"Wilder tells me she's been fined by judges more often than they issue speeding tickets in town."

I sigh. "That doesn't help Dallas keep Ellie."

She picks at the fringes of my pillow. "When is Cole picking her up?"

"Sunday." I pout.

"Have you called your mother?"

"I don't want to talk to anyone."

Rose looks out my window, which faces the front driveway. "Well, you're going to have to, because Dallas just got home."

"It's fine. He'll want to sit with Ellie for a bit. Even if she is sleeping. Maybe you can nudge her awake?"

She nods thoughtfully. "She'll probably ask for you too, since you fell asleep holding her tonight."

I shake my head. "They need some time alone."

She looks around my room. "You can't hide in here all night."

"Good night, Rose. And thank you for today. I don't know what I'd do without you."

She gives me a long hug. "I love you. I'm sorry about what happened. Noah's going to fix it."

"I hope so. Because I'll never forgive myself if he loses her."

I didn't leave my room after Rose left. Heard the faint mumbling downstairs before he walked her out. Then he was upstairs, moving around, checking on Ellie—I could hear them talking for a bit and then it sounded like he might've read her another bedtime story.

After that, her lights went out, and a moment later he knocked on my door.

I didn't answer the first time. My heart was pounding too hard to speak. He didn't push. Left me alone.

But a short while later, there's another knock on my door, pulling me out of the daze I'm in.

"Willow, open the door."

I move toward it but don't unlock it, drawing in a shaky breath.

He sighs, his voice dropping to a whisper. "I'm not mad at you."

I hesitate on the opposite side. "You should be," I whisper harshly.

"Willow, I'm mad at a lot of people right now. You're not one of them. Open up."

I unlock the door and move back to the bed to sit down, tossing a pillow over my lap like a teenager in trouble. He enters after a moment, scanning the dim room.

"You get lost on the way to our bedroom?" he asks quietly.

I shake my head. "You know why I'm in here."

He closes the distance, standing in front of me. Gently, he brushes the hair from my face and lifts my chin. His shoulders fall, exhaling as he takes in my flushed face and swollen eyes. "Oh, Sunset."

The tears pooled in my eyes fall. "I'm so sorry." My hands start to shake and I break free to cross the room. "I ruined everything for you."

"Willow, stop."

"I swear, I wasn't going to take the money now—that's what I was arguing with my mother about. And the house—that was just ... I swear it's not what it looks like, Dallas. I can explain *everything*."

He catches my face, swiping away my tears, shushing me. "I know, honey." I fall onto his chest and he holds me close, his heart thudding fast and hard. He murmurs against my head, "I know you can, and I'll let you—just not tonight."

Between my fear of losing Ellie and the residual shock of my questioning, I tremble in his arms. He swears, kissing the top of my head, then my temple, my tear-streaked face. "I'm sorry I couldn't control it, Sunset." Then finally, my lips. "I'm so sorry I let this happen." He lifts me off my feet and carries me to his bedroom.

Our bedroom. Where he lays me on the bed and strips me of everything but my undergarments. Then helps me into one of his T-shirts. His scent wraps around me, instantly calming me, like he knew it would.

Stripping himself, he slides under the covers with me. "You're safe here," he assures me. "You're home. So why don't you close your eyes for me and get some rest."

I fall asleep like that. In his arms. His warmth.

When I wake up, it's still pitch-black outside, but I'm too restless. Feeling like I might burst out of my skin, I sit up.

Dallas groans beside me, eyes fluttering open and finding mine. "What is it?"

"I can't sleep."

He grunts, twisting. "*Tomorrow*. No more questioning today."

I nod. "Can you do me a favor?"

He groans. "Now?"

Five minutes later, he's carrying Ellie in from her bedroom, setting her between us.

I smile for the first time all day. "Thank you."

"We'll get her back, Sunset, I promise."

"How can you be sure?"

He slides back in. "Because I've been where he is. Nothing makes sense and every decision you make is destructive. He'll realize his mistakes. He'll right his wrongs."

"You really think so?"

"Honey, I hope so." He leans over and kisses my forehead. "Now, let's hit the hay," he winks, flashing me a grin that could melt steel.

The next morning, I explain everything to my husband over coffee on the back porch. The dream house. The pressure from my mother. The OK *I* gave her after signing the prenup—my moment of weakness—and when I called changing my mind.

He listens, reacting only slightly to everything I tell him. Muscles tightening, in a way that shields me, not blames me.

"I looked up the Lakeview Estates last night." He winks at me, moving his eyes to the view in front of us. "Think I got them beat."

I laugh. "No comparison."

He takes my hand, bringing it to his lips.

I breathe in the air. "In fact, the minute I stepped foot in this house, I knew nothing could ever compare." I watch Ellie out in the yard. Guilt mists my eyes again. "I'm sorry I didn't tell you."

"Why didn't you?"

"I wasn't going to take the money based on a fake marriage. It wouldn't be fair to Grandma. It felt like cheating her. That, and . . . I wanted this to only be about you and Ellie. Helping you was enough for me." I swallow, feeling ashamed about my insecurities. "After I signed the prenup, it triggered something I've been fighting for a while. That I'll always be alone. I'll never have that partner in life to be my equal." I bite my lip. "And something I tried to prove after Eric attacked me. That I can take care of myself."

He searches my face. "Willow, I'll always be on your side. Your partner, your equal. In everything. But I'll never stop protecting you. Taking care of you. That's . . . non-negotiable."

I smile. "I can live with that."

He turns to me, raking his arms around my waist. "But I will be teaching you how to high kick without making a fool of yourself."

"Deal."

My stomach twists when he kisses me. Because I think of how perfect this moment is.

And how it will be ruined tomorrow when Cole arrives.

34

Dallas

It's the first time since moving in that we're using the dining-room table. Aside from the engagement party and wedding—where food and drinks were everywhere—we haven't hosted a dinner.

But it's Sunday evening, the night Cole is scheduled to pick up Ellie, and everyone wanted to be here. To make Ellie feel like our family is expanding. Not falling apart.

To make her feel loved—not abandoned.

The way Willow phrased it with her last night before bed somehow managed to make her excited.

We didn't mention anything about it being permanent.

One thing at a time.

Besides, Noah's already working on the appeal. And he's determined to win this time.

No surprises.

No tactics.

Just facts.

Ellie belongs with us. In the home we built for her.

Willow tugs at my shirt as everyone gathers at the table.

My hand wraps around her waist naturally. My heart still skipping with how well she fits.

"Come upstairs with me," she whispers.

I grin. "Can it wait three hours—say, long enough to eat dinner and kick everyone out?" I wink.

She shakes her head. "Please? It's important."

I toss the oven mitt down and follow her out of the kitchen and up the stairs.

She drags me by the hand into her bedroom—her old bedroom.

"Good thinking, no one will look for us here." I tug on her dress and she giggles, pulling away.

"No. This room. It's empty. Invite Cole to live with us."

"What?"

She takes my hands. "Think about it. It's like we told Ellie, he's lonely. He needs a family. A reason to live. Ellie can only do that for so long before he starts feeling guilty. Let's give him all of it."

My heart swells at her selflessness. "Baby, are you sure about this?"

She nods enthusiastically. "Dallas, I don't want to wait to see if we can win her back. She's our daughter. He's her family, which means he's *our* family."

I exhale, glancing at the room. "We'll need to do something about those pink fringy pillows."

Cole arrives on time, as expected. He's always on time. If not a few minutes early.

Ellie's packed a backpack only. I'll have to explain that the rest needs to come slowly, not all at once, so she doesn't feel like we're giving her away.

He lifts his granddaughter with a bit of a struggle when she races up to him. "You've got to stop growing, El," he grunts.

She giggles as he sets her down.

Cole squints at me in the middle of the living room, rubbing his hip. "It was probably the backpack."

I chuckle. "Probably." Then nod him toward the kitchen. "Come on in. We're just cleaning up dessert, but there's still plenty. Everyone just left."

He follows me with hesitation but I don't call attention to it. Willow puts on a fresh pot of tea, shooting Cole a warm smile. "Green tea OK?"

Cole watches her as she moves about behind the island, and as harmless as I know the man is, I'm instantly alarmed.

I remind Ellie to sweep her room again to see if there's anything she forgot.

Cole removes his hat. "Willow, I . . . I'm sorry. I swear, I had no idea what Glenda was going to do to you. That wasn't—well, she didn't—" He sighs heavily. "I apologize."

And as they have the last two days, her eyes start to well. "I know, Cole. Thank you. And it wasn't your fault." Willow glances at me—equally nervous about the question we have to ask him.

He might take it the wrong way. Or think we're pulling one over on him. We haven't exactly had much time to think it through, since we had to get back to the dinner we were hosting.

Cole takes a breath like he's not quite done. "I, uh . . . I don't think I was wrong about you two making up this engagement to help your case. But I was wrong about you doing it to keep her away from me."

Willow freezes and I move to stand next to her.

Cole glances at me. "This man loves you very much. Knew it the minute he threatened me in front of six police officers," he scoffs, then swallows painfully, looking down at the tile floor. "I'd have done the same for Maya."

I circle the island. "Cole, why don't we go sit in the living room?"

Willow prepares a tray of tea, berries, and pumpkin pie and meets us in the living room. Ellie prances down with Buttons in her hands.

"I'm ready," she gasps. "Can I have more cake?"

"I'll allow it. Come here, Slippers." Willow lifts her onto her lap and I swear they could be mother and daughter, with their red curls and killer smiles.

We sip tea quietly, awkwardly, attention on Ellie and her devouring a second piece of cake.

"Go grab some milk," Willow urges. "And don't forget your blanket."

Ellie nods, skipping away.

"Pack light, pumpkin, I'm bringing you back tomorrow," Cole calls after her. Then he looks at me and Willow. "She belongs here."

My heart skips, relief and tension washing away so profoundly that I barely react.

But Willow does, exhaling with tears and reaching an arm over. "Cole—we don't know what to say. Thank you. But Ellie belongs with *all* of us. Not just . . . on certain days of the week."

"Yeah, well, doesn't need to be so formal, we are family, after all, right?" His gaze lands on mine in a way I haven't seen in weeks. With trust.

Willow's eyes flick to me and I give her a nod.

She clears her throat and swipes her eyes. "Dallas and I wanted to invite you to stay here with us. We have a spare bedroom. Lots of room."

Cole nods. "Yeah, and cake."

"And a family," I add.

He watches us for a moment then chuckles softly, shaking his head. "I appreciate the offer—more than you know. But that's a lot of stairs for an old man like me."

"I'll build you a room down here," I offer without a second thought. It's not just for Ellie. We could take care of him.

"Thank you, Dallas." He stands. "But y'all are newlyweds. Probably thinkin' about growing your family soon. Getting a puppy or whatnot. That's a lot of excitement for someone who turns in around seven p.m."

I stand and squeeze his shoulders. "Our door is always open to you. And the offer will still stand if you change your mind." I clear my throat. "With everything that's happened, Cole . . . Your message didn't go unheard. Maya and Ellie were all you had. And I never want you feeling like you've lost your granddaughter. Not after you brought her into my life." I swallow, thinking how much my life's changed since he came looking for me during my darkest days. "Not when I owe you everything."

He gives me a small smile. Then reaches for Ellie's hand. "Suppose I need to call Glenda tomorrow. Make this all official."

I shake my head. "Please don't call that woman. Noah will take care of it."

Ellie squeezes my leg. "See you tomorrow, Daddy."

I bend down to give her a tight hug. "Love you, baby. Now you make sure Grandpa gets to bed on time. It's about an hour before your bedtime." I wink up at him and he chuckles.

"See you tomorrow," Cole calls back as we walk them out.

Willow and I watch as they drive away. My heart is still in my throat, fearing I might wake up any second and tonight—Ellie's pick-up—would be playing out entirely differently. And when I wake up—he'd be taking her for good.

Life can't be that cruel.

Willow leans into me, trembling. "Did that just really happen?"

I wrap my arm around her, feeling her heartbeat against my chest. "Think it did."

She nods, a sob escaping. "And she's coming back tomorrow."

I turn her fully to me, brushing her hair out of her face. "Told you he just needed time."

She shakes her head. "What did you say to him?"

I roll my eyes sideways. "Hell if I can remember. I walked out of that courtroom seeing red. Found him and got in his face for attacking you. I could sit there and take all the shit they want to throw at me. The fire, my heartbreak, the bar fights—but dragging *you* through the dirt? That's crossing a line."

She slips her arms around my waist, shivering. "Come on, let's go inside."

Willow and I finish cleaning the kitchen together—after deciding to wait to tell the others about Cole and Ellie. Still needing time to sit with it ourselves. I could say it out loud all I want, that I knew Cole would come around. That it was the grief talking and, deep inside, he knows what's best for Ellie.

But it still feels unreal.

"We should call Noah," Willow suggests.

"I'll give him a ring tomorrow. The guy lost my case, think it'd do him good to let him simmer for a bit."

She rolls her eyes, running the towel over the last crumb on the counter, leaving it spotless. I can tell she's still tense, and all I want is to quiet every storm brewing in her.

Because as hard as it might be to believe, we won. We all won.

I lean into her from behind, swiping my fingers up her bare thigh. Her head falls back with a moan.

"Sunset. You see that?"

"What?"

"That counter's looking like the perfect spot to find out just how loud my wife can scream my name." I give her a sharp spank under her skirt and she shrieks, flipping to face me, cheeks flushed, brown eyes filled with a little misbelief and a lot of desire.

"Lie back."

There's a beat before she does. Like she wants to hold on to this moment with me. I step between her thighs, holding her face as she lies flat. "Thank you for staying. For saving me. For your stubbornness, for the rest of my life."

She looks at me like she's ready to say the same. But tonight isn't about what we've overcome, our battles or our scars, or even our losses. It's about what we've found. A new home, a new family. And a forever neither one of us thought we'd get.

35

Dallas

Six weeks later

I kiss my baby girl on the forehead, keeping her quilt tucked under her chin, and turn off her light. It's going to be a cold night and Ellie keeps hoping for a white Christmas.

I walk quietly to the door.

"Daddy?"

I turn back with a smile, my heart still warming every time I hear the word.

"What if Santa goes to look for me at Grandma and Grandpa's house?"

My chest tightens, reminding me this is her first Christmas with me, the pressure to make it a memorable one. A special one.

"You don't have to worry, cupcake." I wink. "Santa always finds the good ones. And if he happens to drop a present off for you there, Grandpa will bring it when he comes for breakfast."

She grins, satisfied, eyes already drifting shut.

I watch her for a moment until her breath evens before stepping out.

I make my way down the stairs slowly, tracing the handrail for the first time since I built it. Remembering the sadness. That hollowness that eventually turned into conviction and purpose, a new start. A new beginning for Ellie and me. A profound resolve that came from wanting to give her the world.

But there was still that emptiness. Tangled up with fear and doubt.

It occurs to me that *she's* been here since day one. Fallen from some cloud to help me through it all. To fill the hole in my heart.

No matter how much I give in return, it will never measure up to my gratitude for her.

Tomorrow is Christmas Eve and the house shows it. Presents are piled up around the tree that nearly reaches the ceiling. Stockings lined up along the fireplace. Lights *everywhere*.

With the kitchen clean and empty, I know where to find my wife.

Shortly after our wedding, I started a new project in the house. One I had kept quiet about until the day Silas and I started breaking down walls.

At first, Willow thought it was that extra room for Cole in case he decides to move in. But when the gold sound-absorbing panels and special lighting started going up, that was a dead giveaway.

She realized I was building her dream studio.

Together, we furnished the room to perfection; leather loveseat, digital keyboard, speakers, microphones and fully equipped recording workstation.

Willow insisted on using some of the funds her grandmother left her to buy the equipment and hire professional producers in Denver to help record her first album.

Now that the room's done, the boys are in here at least once a week helping her learn to use half this stuff and get her sound just right.

But it's the practicing and singing her and Ellie started almost every night after dinner that has my heart twisted in the best damn way.

I couldn't be happier. Couldn't be prouder of both my girls.

The guilt still comes and goes, but it's less stabbing now. It's just a way I deal with Millie's memory and I've got the most patient woman in the world by my side.

Epilogue

Willow

Four months later

As I sip my foam-rich coffee, the morning sun stretches across the kitchen windows and skylight. It warms me more than the steaming cup ever could. I watch the water shimmer against the new light, sweep my gaze over the wildflowers growing along the riverbend.

If you'd told me a year ago I'd be waking up at the crack of dawn and still feel as content as I do right now, I'd laugh and blame it on bad mushrooms in my ravioli.

It's no mushroom, I muse as I rest my hand over my swollen belly. It's restless leg syndrome, frequent potty breaks, and my mind swirling a mile a minute with my due date looming.

That and . . . today.

It's the one-year anniversary of Millie's accident. The day Dallas lost the woman he loved. The day he wanted to be buried alongside her.

After our wedding night—the night we conceived this baby over by the oak tree—I've never doubted his love for me. Or what he's proven every day since—that we were meant to be.

Despite that, there's no doubt he's hurting today. I just worry how badly.

Seeing movement from the side of the house, I catch sight of him riding up on Trouble.

A grin tugs at my lips as I grab my sunhat and coffee and step out onto the back porch.

He catches me watching, a guilt-ridden expression on his face until he sees my smile. Tension easing instantly, he hops off and comes to me, looking up from the bottom steps.

"Morning, beautiful."

I lean against the rail, my eyes shifting to his dark horse. "When you going to teach me to ride?"

His eyes dip to my belly and he pulls off his leather gloves, shoving them in his back pocket as he slowly climbs up the steps.

"When I'm OK with you riding without me pressed against your back."

I perk a brow. "When will that be?"

He leans down with a soft kiss to my cheek. "Wouldn't hold my breath."

A shiver runs down my spine as he presses a kiss beneath my jaw.

He pulls back, hand still warm against my neck. That guilt back in his eyes as they meet mine. "Hopin' to be back before you got up." His thumb brushes over the curve of my stomach. "Restless again?"

I cock my head at him, reminding him that today isn't about me. "Dallas."

He shakes his head lightly, his voice hoarse. "I'm all right." Then kisses my forehead. "I promise." He steps around me and leans against the porch fence, looking out along the horizon.

I shift to stand beside him, pressing my shoulder against his and following his gaze.

"Haven't been to her grave in . . . I don't know, months. Brought her some roses. White. She was no simple woman, I'll tell you that. But she liked white."

"You could've stayed longer, you know?"

His eyes meet mine, stormy and conflicted.

I shrug, feeling helpless to offer him much comfort other than letting him know I'm here for him. "Didn't have to slip out so early, either."

"I know." He slips an arm around me and I lean into him, that woodsy smell wrapping around me. "Stood there . . . looking down at the grave I once wished I was buried in . . . and could only think of you."

My brows furrow but I twist my chin up.

He lets out a breath, almost a laugh, running a thumb against my jaw. "Pictured you pullin' me out. Bringing me back to life. Just like you did the day I found you here."

My heart melts and breaks at the same time. He swipes a tear I didn't realize had fallen down my cheek. "She would have loved it here, Dallas."

He brushes strands of hair from my face. "Maybe for a while."

"Well, I'm happy here." I wink. "The cowboy was just a bonus."

Trouble snorts from a few feet away, feeling abandoned or uncomfortable with all this sappy stuff.

I laugh in his direction. "You'll get your turn," I call out.

Dallas lifts my hat, kissing the top of my head. "Not today. I'm going to put him back in the barn and make my girls breakfast."

I put my hands flat on my belly. "And boy."

He chuckles. "Fine. Extra bacon for you."

The back door swings open, Ellie stepping out with her wild bedhead and squinting eyes.

"Hey, Slippers." I smile as Dallas lifts her up off the cold stone floor—since she's barefoot again.

I move to the bench and lift one of the pillows, where I keep an extra pair of knitted booties for her, and slip them on her cold feet.

"Why do you look sad?" She rubs the stubble along her father's jaw.

"I'm not sad, sunshine. Just remembering a sad time." He swallows. "But you and Mommy made it better. And you keep making it better every day."

Ellie smiles warmly at me, like it's been our plan all along. A breeze blows her hair over her face and I brush it back, a smile tugging as I take in my favorite scents.

I breathe it all in. The sweet hay lingering off his vest, the fresh flowers growing along the land, the fruity shampoo off my little girl's head.

It all seems surreal and unfair at the same time. That I get to have them. Live the dream I always wanted. And the one I never thought I'd get.

I lean against him, content in the quiet. He must catch me staring at the oak tree because he leans down, lips grazing my ear as he asks, "Ready to do it all over again in a few months?"

I put my hand on my belly with a smile. "Which part?"

"The vows." He chuckles then dips his eyes. "Then, who knows?"

Since our wedding day, Dallas has been dropping hints at a do-over. With Cole in the crowd, without doubt or questions or prenups or lies. Just a true celebration of two people who vow to love each other. After the new year, we set a date for September.

And as with any news in Blue River Springs, it traveled fast. So our plans for a private, intimate ceremony went out the window. It's now the event of the year.

I smile at the oak tree. "Same place, right?"

He follows my gaze. "Same place. No matter how many more people we need to invite." His fingers trail behind my neck, sweeping my hair aside then pressing a kiss to my temple. "I'm marrying you again under that tree this fall. At sunset."

Acknowledgements

Willow and Dallas had my heart from book one and I knew that when it was time for their story—they'd break me a little. But quickly put me back together in the most beautiful way. Writing them was equal parts maddening as it was rewarding. I love a good loath-to-love storyline and this one got more addictive with every page.

Of course their story might never have found your hearts if it weren't for the people I want to take the time to thank and acknowledge.

First and always a huge thank you to my family who pretend not to notice when I slip out my laptop in the middle of movie night because an idea struck.

Thank you to my fantastic team of bloggers, and early readers and virtual cheer squad. You guys are all truly amazing and make all of this worthwhile.

My assistant, Zsuzsanna at Midnight Readers PR, for everything you do everyday to keep what I do organized and stress-free. I'll always be grateful for the day we met.

To Betty, Emma, Kerri, Liz, and Steph for your support, inspiration, and being behind me no matter what I'm writing next. You're stuck with me forever.

My agent, Sarah Hornsley. Thank you for taking a chance on my stories so that more people can. Sincere and lasting gratitude for your guidance and our partnership.

To Bea, Emma, Jill, Vishani, Katie, and the entire team at Embla Books for all the behind-the-scenes magic they make happen. I'm forever grateful that *Blue River Springs* has captured your hearts the way I've meant it to. Thank you believing in this series—and in me.

About the Author

Roxanne grew up in New York City, where she studied theater and screen writing. Her passion for storytelling started very young—even if it never made it on paper.

She now writes contemporary small-town romance with strong realistic heroines, steam, banter, and a healthy dose of angst.

A mom of two, when she's not writing, Roxanne enjoys baking, jogging with her golden-doodle, and practicing flirty banter with her real-life male hero.

Website: https://www.roxannetully.com
Newsletter: https://geni.us/rtnewsletter
Instagram: https://www.instagram.com/roxtully.author/
TikTok: https://www.tiktok.com/@roxtully

About Embla Books

Embla Books is a digital-first publisher of standout commercial adult fiction. Passionate about storytelling, the team at Embla believe our lives are built on stories – and publish books that will make you 'laugh, love, look over your shoulder and lose sleep'. Launched by Bonnier Books UK in 2021, the imprint is named after the first woman from the creation myth in Norse mythology. Embla was carved by the gods from a tree trunk found on the seashore; an image of the kind of creative work and crafting that writers do, and a symbol of how stories shape our lives.

Find out about some of our other books and stay in touch:

X, Facebook, Instagram: @emblabooks
Newsletter: https://bit.ly/emblanewsletter